# BELMOPAN

## B J FRENCH

Available at amazon.com
www.pillarsofthemoon-belmopan.com
www.facebook.com/brianfrenchauthor

Cover design by Melissa Roshini
Book design by Xuanyun Malcho

ISBN: 1482771578
ISBN-13: 978-1482771572

## ACKNOWLEDGMENTS

To my wife Susana, for the ongoing support and encouragement. Family and friends that have helped me through the tough, then picked me up when I was down, and threw me back in.

## DISCLAIMER

'Belmopan' is a work of fiction. Names, characters, places and incidents are either products of the author's imagination and/or are used fictitiously. Any resemblance to actual events or locals, or persons, living or dead, is purely coincidental.

# CONTENTS

# INTRODUCTION

One has to consider how such a wonderful creature such as man, with grace and intellect, can soar to unparalleled heights, and yet when provoked and instigated, can slide to depths of perversity and degradation.

Throughout our prolonged history, there have been discovered unchangeable truths: inflicted pain is unpleasant and a gentle caress incites pleasure and serenity. Hunger pangs are discomforting, while eating is satisfying. Making love feels delightful, while receiving a punch in the nose, hurts. We as sentient beings are drawn to pleasurable experience and should shun painful experience. You may say, "ah, how profound" but it is truly one of the basis of our existence and all other behavior; to suggest otherwise is unnatural, copied or learned behavior.

I have often wondered why a human being can be incited to kill another and yet ignore the inevitable pangs of guilt and remorse, at least for the time required to fulfill the deed. With the aid of our own physiology, a concoction of hormones, we can be incited to rape, murder and engage in a few less-obtrusive acts against our friends and neighbors; and yet, if we refrain for a time from stimulant exposure and are not subjected to reconditioning from outside sources, we can revert back to a tolerable level of moral conduct, should we desire to do so. The key phrase here is "desire to do so". We must believe that people truly would like to help one-another and co-exist more closely than we do today. Through isolation, whether through self-infliction, media stimulation or geographic necessity, we grow apart and fearful of close relationship. We watch in fear while regimes and groups of people struggle to be heard and are driven or swallowed up by waves of misrepresented truth and seductive lies.

We have seen a tide of destruction weaved throughout the fabric of our history since its first recording. Is there a force that has propelled this abhorrent, learned behavior throughout our midst, unrecognizable and therefore unable to harness. Has there been a small group of individuals or individual that has been at the center of this storm of violence, and if so why have they, or he, been unimpeded from their actions and allowed to perpetuate this dominion. But, there has also been a resounding, positive influence lurking almost un-noticed, a light, seemingly more powerful than existence itself, in the background, as if waiting for mankind to reach a certain level of maturity, or enlightenment.

Throughout our recorded history, there are clues to this great mystery that has intrigued us all. The solution to the unbroken chain of destruction is simpler and easier than you think; it could it be as simple as an insignificant little jade bowl, engraved with the hieroglyph of the Maya.

There are several 'pillars of truth' that stand firm for us, all we have to do is remain steadfast in our belief that we are more than just mere mortals driven by our uncontrollable passions, and rise to the heights we were originally intended.

# ONE

*Dia uno (day one)*

The small, clay figurine that emerged from the earth was a prize. Its small, extended belly and protruding breasts denoted a female ready to give birth. Approximately three-inches in height, she was stylized with a pointed head and enlarged hands that clasped her belly; her feet were tucked beneath her thighs and were slightly spread to expose enlarged genitalia. This was the first time in twelve-hundred plus years that this little lady had looked to the sun, and what a glorious sun it was. Buried beneath, where she had slept, were a little, clay dish and a bag filled with cutting utensils, flattened to look more like the rotting mulch that surrounded it than its original leather.

The dig assistant waved over the site supervisor, who in turn radioed the project director. Within a short period of time, they were all scrutinizing the little figurine and taking photos of the immediate area of excavation. A crowd of onlookers and associate workers began to mill about just beyond the grid pattern anticipating what the ground had released into their custody.

The heat of the day had reached its apex and with the excitement of the find, a call to break would be in the offering. Carefully collecting up the valuable pieces the director had released in a wooden box, Shawna walked gingerly from the grid; a small entourage of curious companions followed closely down the wooded path to the tented compound that housed the temporary lab and living quarters.

"Great find Shawna!" came the cries of her colleagues as they gathered around the tables to eat and drink their refreshments.

A little overwhelmed by the heat and the exhilaration of the discovery, she felt the need to be alone. Slipping inconspicuously from the crowd after returning her food tray, she left the small compound to find shade and cool in one of the numerous alcoves created by time's assault on the limestone ruins. Close to the jungle, Shawna sat secluded, hidden in the base of one of the many temples that made up the unique core of the Mayan metropolis. She listened to the wind in the trees and the din of life that harbored itself within the dense, jungle wall of vines and foliage. The loud clicking of beetle's wings attended her to the aerial barrage of assorted insects that she had become aware of and now accustomed to. The curt cry of an allusive, large-billed, Toucan bird reminded her of the fact that, as she did today, a thousand years ago, a Toucan would have cried to another as they sat and looked to the jungle just beyond the metropolis that this once was. The mystery of these ruins and their vacation that had happened all so suddenly, gave rise to much speculation but little in true substance. She rubbed the thighs of her up-bent legs in a pensive gesture and closed her eyes to absorb the force of life that surrounded her.

Shawna's mind drifted to a place in the north; a different land that had a history and culture far more immature than this, and yet whose roots began in this very place not so far distant. Her family had its early lineage in the pueblo district of the mid-west. Through rough times of invasion and famine, they chose to migrate along the Columbia River basin to finally settle on the Pacific Coast. She remembered her Aunt and Uncle who raised her and now reside near Neah Bay, at the tip of the Olympic Peninsula; she missed them. Her work over the last year had been very stressful and physically draining. Moving residence and changing jobs several times to position herself in such a way as to be useful in the acquisition and transportation of the infamous 'Pillars of the Moon', jade bowl, were culprit. There was the passionate, short relationship with a Canadian photographer she had regretted to leave behind, whose help in procuring that same relic had been invaluable; it left an emotional bruise. She recounted the reasons for her speedy disappearance from the North. Initially, before her birth, was the loss of an Uncle Daniel, in the thirties, while he was in pursuit of this very sacred Jade Bowl; then more recently, the beatings of several colleagues who had made clandestine inquiries as to its local; and now, just months ago with the near death of her dear friend Peter by being shot in the alley behind the Royal Museum in Victoria, British Columbia. She could lose no others. There were only a select few who knew the whereabouts of the bowl now, and Shawna's invaluable role in its repatriation; this circumstance was to remain unchanged.

"Shawna," echoed in her ears. "Are you OK?"

She looked up to see a handsomely dark, young man with a boyish face, of Mayan decent looking down to her, his lean frame silhouetted against the brightness beyond the alcove.

"Yeah," she replied, shaking the sleep from her head. "I must have dozed off."

"It's very beautiful here isn't it," Edmundo sighed turning back toward the jungle beyond the perimeter? "When you did not return after lunch, some of the people got a little concerned. The Mayan gods have not had their appetites satisfied for a number of years now, you know."

Shawna gave a chuckle. "And how many young maidens have you personally saved from the clutches of these gods?"

"Not near enough," he responded with a hearty laugh. "Come, we have to get back to the dig before the vultures descend and make a mess of things."

"Ok!" Shawna chimed, reaching for his outstretched hand. "I've grown weary of waiting upon the gods for the few, measly morsels they cast our way."

"Patience Shawna, they have waited over a thousand years for appeasement, let's not tempt them any further."

Edmundo was an assistant to the site supervisor. His knowledge of local history, as well as being able to speak Mayan, was an asset to the operation in many ways. His youth and vitality were thankful in comparison to the often austerity and sobriety of the other residents at hand. Not only was he in a position to learn but often teach as well. He took pleasure in being able to hone his English, language skills as a dig assistant during the summers, and in the cooler season as a tour guide for the Belize Tourist Board. He would often unleash his flamboyant orations describing sacrificial mutilations with glee on the unsuspecting tourists that came to visit the many Mayan ruins.

As they returned through the open plaza, the surroundings were deafly quiet as if a switch had been flicked. They stopped for a moment to search and listen to the adjacent jungle - total silence. Looking toward each other in quandary, they continued to walk toward the distant compound. A gust of wind shook the treetops while a Howler monkey began to expound his distress for infringement of its territory. Weary of the experience, they both grimaced, acknowledging the monkey's concern and burst into a run. Clearing the plaza through the ball court, they followed along the path through the center passed the spectator compound; the resonance of the jungle began to increase and the silences dwindle.

It was two in the afternoon and time enough to put several more hours in at the temple's upper court. Great mounds of rubble lay either side of the cleared pathway leading to the excavation area sheltering the clearing from the encroaching jungle. A large, water reservoir lay off to the right nearly hidden by trees and vines that bathed in the open, sun light close to the ravine's edge. Black ABS pipes ran along the length of the walkway, to and fro from the compound and the excavation area, delivering the much-needed water for the washing of soil and bodies alike. It was only a short distance between the two, but very secluded with the density of the jungle between. Radios were supplied to team leaders in case of emergency, but to date there had never been any call to use them apart from the usual chatter of 'break time', 'more water please', and 'what's for supper?'

Shawna and Edmundo had become good friends over the last weeks. Her arrival from Belmopan with the Director of Antiquities for all of Belize, had left an impression with the other co-workers that had set her apart from the rest of them. Edmundo was impressed with no thing and found Shawna's cool and mature demeanor a catalyst to his pranks and practicality. Frequently, they would banter back and forth in one-upmanship leaving the rest of the work team in flux as to their comrade status. Wherever Shawna was working, Edmundo was always a short distance away and helping her out whenever he could. Their warm friendship had developed with no contrivance, but Shawna had always remained slightly distant. He felt slighted by the chasm but understood, like the gods, that the best things usually come around of their own doing in the end.

There were only a few others working closely beside them in the grid area. It was rewarding work but for the most part painstakingly slow; every spoonful of soil being scraped away from the carved, stone floors and walls was then immediately scrutinized should any abnormality be found in its consistency.

An hour had passed with little success to crown the earlier achievement when the skies began to darken with rain clouds that crept along the mountain range, unimpeded from the sea. Within minutes, the wind began to pick up and surrounded the site as if a force of its own identity was making claim to the majesty and grandeur beneath the rubble.

"Come on Shawna," Edmundo cried. "We had better head back."

"I'll be right with you. I have several more inches to clear. Don't worry," she said with a wave, "two minutes!"

A phone call from his sister at the ministry a half hour earlier, concerned Edmundo; he wanted to return it before the reception completely collapsed with the approaching storm. A doctor, who said he had come all the way from Canada to find a Ms. Shawna Brook, working one of the sites, asked for information. Edmundo had told her to find out more information on this fellow and he would get back to her.

Edmundo waved an 'I give up' at the sky and slowly descended down to the foot of the wide, stone stairway with the others. With an armful of picks, garden spades and brushes, he slowly followed down the path when all of a sudden, 'Crackkk!' He turned just in time to see a continuous bolt of lightning hit the pinnacle of the temple and what he thought to be the outline of a man just below the bold petroglyphs on the next tier.

"What in the heck?" he objected out-loud. "What is he doing up there? All staff apart from…," he stopped in mid thought.

Fear gripped him. All he could think of was Shawna. Dropping the tools there on the path, he bolted back to the base of the stairs and started to scream after Shawna. With no reply through the increasing droplets of rain, he raced up the stairs to the plateau and the work area. Shawna was nowhere to be seen.

"Shawna!" he screamed again and again, but no

answer.

Walking over to where she had last been, her tools lay scattered as if dropped, a Macaw feather lay floating in the water that had accumulated in the hollowed area. Down the slope away from the temple, the strings of the grid pattern stretched toward the jungle. In the increasing wash of the rain, the footprints and the scrapes in the loose soil by the edge of the dig began to melt away. Racing down the side of the elevated tell in the slippery mud, Edmundo slid feet first into the foliage and denseness that lay beyond. Stunned, he lay on his back, buried to his waist in tangled underbrush, looking up to the droplets that danced and eddied before his eyes, he began to lament. Defeated, he lay in terror, someone had taken Shawna.

It seemed to take hours before the police came. With the cloud-cover of the ensuing storm and the quick setting of the sun, by six, it had been almost impossible to start a search. Several, small groups, headed by Edmundo and a few radioed lead men, made short forays into the jungle but were turned back by the swarms of mosquitoes in the newly damp undergrowth. Discouraged and distraught, they returned with only trace evidence of the escape route. By seven o'clock, several Gazelle helicopters from the British contingency doing maneuvers at the Corozal Training Area, aided in the search, but by eleven o'clock, ground operations were called off until the morning. The spotters in the Gazelles would continue with their night vision goggles. It would be doubtful, after the slow drizzle through the night, that there would be any trace left by Shawna's abductors. The British were able to set up a ten-mile perimeter around the site, with the 'Jungle Jedi' heading up the reconnaissance, but gave few guarantees of success. A small group of men, traveling light would be fast and almost impossible to trace along the ravines and dense foliage of this mountainous area. There was always a possibility of a chance sighting, and with that, hope.

"But why would anyone wish to kidnap Shawna?" came the question at the meeting in the tented cafeteria.

"At this time we can only guess and hope for the best," replied the director of the camp, half sitting on the lead table at the front. "I have made a call to the Ministry in Belmopan, for direction and have had the Belize Defense Force called up. I have decided to suspend operations till we have some idea of what has happened.

"When is the full moon?" questioned Edmundo, straining to look at the large display board outlining the daily proceedings.

"Why do you ask?" petitioned an assistant sitting close by. The room became silent.

"There was a feather at the abduction site; the same kind that adorned the ceremonial headdresses of the priests long ago."

"Are you insinuating she was abducted for some ritual to be held at the full moon?"

"I certainly hope not. But the feather was placed there for a reason, a calling card."

"Thank you for your insight Edmund," came the call from the director, "but I think we shall wait until we hear from the Ministry."

With that, the director left the for-front and went to sit with several of the British officers to one side.

"By the time he gets answers to the questions that may or may not help, Shawna could be dead," Edmundo whispered to several of his colleagues close by. "I'm outta here."

Grabbing his field radio and a few belongings from his quarters, he loaded his small, blue pickup truck and headed away from the compound. The question foremost on his mind, 'who was this fellow from Canada and what did he want with Shawna'?

**Abducted**

Miles away, along a jungle path lit only by small, hand-held lamps, five men traveled at lightning speed. Bundled and slung from a long pole straddling between two men running tandem, was a body almost unrecognizable but for locks of black hair that fell from the loosened wrap around her head. Shawna was exhausted from the continual pounding and swaying of the pole being jostled around. Every half hour, a change of couriers was in order and a quick moment of relief from the bindings at her wrists and ankles that lashed her to the pole. Her kidneys ached from the wide swath of cloth that had suspended initially from the center of the pole, covering her hips but had now worked its way to her waistline. She desperately needed to relieve herself but that seemed to be of no concern for her captors. Unable to control the urge any longer, her insides let go and the warm fluid filled her dangling posterior and the wrappings that bound her. Taking no notice of her mumblings of discomfort and the smell, the journeymen continued as if there was no purpose but to run, and run, and run.

With the sun beginning to rise, and after a severe pounding in which she rose and sank from consciousness, Shawna began to hear the mumblings of a man speaking in a mixture of Spanish and another language. She was able to recognize a number of words and piece together that there was a helicopter buzzing around. Shawna was not certain but got the impression they were to change direction. She barely understood the meaning but recognized the word 'auto'. Throwing her recklessly down to the ground, they began to unleash her bindings, careful not to expose her face. Ripping the short pants from her body, not bothering with her now torn undergarments, one of the men dowsed her with cold water in an attempt to wash the lingering stench. Unsure of their intentions, in fear she fought to keep her legs together as not to expose her nakedness. With brute strength they pulled her thighs apart and dowsed her once again, washing the urine from her body. To her astonishment they wrapped her tight with new linen and threw her into the back of a waiting vehicle; she could only presume it was a van. Her body fell asleep but her mind, though exhausted, raced at the probabilities of her abduction. It all came back to one thing, she knew something that they needed to know; it all added up to the Jade Bowl.

"What do you want with me?" she screamed, frustrated and sore from bouncing on the metal floor of the truck. "You cowards, do you not have the guts to show your faces?"

It was best she saw none of the faces, for if she had, they could have killed her. Their mandate was obviously of pickup and delivery, for if it had not been, with her beauty, she would have experienced greater humility and indignity.

A crashing blow to the side of her head brought numbness and darkness. The next moment she regained consciousness, she was lying on a grass woven cot, still wrapped in the linens she had been incarcerated; her face was exposed and bloody. She could barely move and could only stare at the network of timbers supporting the grass-thatch roof; she guessed it was mid morning. What seemed like an hour passed and she heard little apart from the rustlings of mice intent on procuring residence, or food in these fine dry quarters. She gently tugged at the bindings at her wrists trying to loosen them; the shuffle of feet on the threshold of the door warned her of a coming visitor. Bracing herself for what was to appear in the doorway, she covered her face as best she could. The wooden, plank door swung open and a small, brown woman, carrying a washbasin and a towel, strode to the side of the bed. Placing the furnishings down on the side table, a tree stump, the slight woman looked toward a plastic bucket in the corner. Shawna wondered at the response in light of the state of her incarceration and how she was to use the facility in her bound condition. Meek and very gentle, the woman began to wash the residue from Shawna's face. It became obvious that she was a true Mayan native and could communicate no English with Shawna. Rather forlorn, the native woman continued the task of wiping her body and unraveling the linens that restricted Shawna's movement. At last, the remains of the traveling ordeal lay in the bottom of the clay basin along with a soiled pile of linen by the door. The little woman placed her hands on either side of Shawna's face in tender embrace and smiled a girlish, toothless grin. Retreating back through the doorway, she left Shawna sitting on the side of the cot, near naked with only her torn undergarments covering her lap. With the clanging of the bolt on the exterior of the door, Shawna got to her feet and peered after the little woman through the spaces between the bamboo poles that made up the walls of the hut. It was no surprise to see a guard, sitting in a green, plastic lawn-chair not ten feet away, intent on following the servant lady with his eyes. She disappeared into a distant hut while he returned to puffing on his cigarette and cleaning the rifle that lay across his lap. Barely able to run her abraded fingers through her fine, black hair, Shawna resigned herself back to the cot to rest her disfigured, swollen ankles and sore wrists. Retrieving the linens piled by the door, she lay back down and began to empty the pent-up emotion she held inside. She slid into fitful sleep.

She did not move or wake until dusk when the door opened and the little lady scurried in closely followed by the guard who had been sitting across the path. Without taking his eyes from Shawna, he sauntered over to the corner and sat on a make-shift chair of logs and grass. The smell of his stale sweat permeated the room and made Shawna feel sick to her stomach. Trying to cover herself from his gaze, she pulled the torn linens up tight under her chin. The Mayan woman carried a tray of tortillas, fresh tomatoes and a small bottle of drinking water. Overcome with hunger, Shawna began to gorge herself on the food till every crumb and seed was gone. Briskly wiping her chin with her forearm, she placed the tray on the small stump and watched as the guard's eyes darted over the naked areas of her body. A toothless grin came to his face. He started to laugh and got up to approach her. Shawna braced herself for his advance by positioning herself to kick. The little lady jumped to her feet and rushed to put herself between Shawna and the belligerent man. Angrily, he pushed her away to the corner and advanced to Shawna, but once again the

Mayan woman intervened to Shawna's' safety. Perturbed, the man twice her size, tried to push the little woman aside when all of a sudden she let her shawl fall away to expose herself to him. He grabbed her by the throat and followed as he threw her out of the wooden door before him. The door slammed shut and bounced several times under the force. The latch popped up and had not secured itself. Realizing the circumstance, Shawna eased herself from the bed and crept over to the door to ease it open. The guard had chosen to remain close to the hut and forced the Mayan to the ground. He grunted as he groped and tried to enter her. She sobbed and stifled her screams as his weight came down on her. Shawna, gripped with fear and anger, dare not scream but slipped from the door and finding a piece of log crept up behind his prone frame and struck as hard as she could. The log gave a hollow thunk as it hit his head. He gave a sigh and toppled to the side. The little lady gathered herself as best she could and staggered toward the jungle motioning Shawna to follow. As Shawna looked back toward the small compound, she could see several men sitting by a fire unaware of what had taken place.

Shawna's feet ached as she dashed behind the women, trying to keep up. The linen that wrapped her body was little protection against the branches that lashed and tore at her as she fled into the dark. There was very little light left from the day, and beneath the canopy of the forest, it was darker still. After a while, the Mayan began to slow and Shawna was able to keep up. They scurried through the underbrush as best they could until the little women stopped and turned to find shelter in the tall foliage near a tree. Signing Shawna over to her side, they both cuddled close under the palms and the dampness of a Mayan shawl. With their backs to a tree and clutching each other in their arms, they fell asleep.

The cry of a Toucan woke Shawna from a sound sleep. The little lady was not awake yet and was cold to the touch. Her eyes fell to the pale, yellow skin of the hands of her savior and the blood soaked shawl that had kept her warm through the night. Her little angel had hemorrhaged and had bled as they raced through the night to find shelter and safety. Shawna sat motionless, cradling the near lifeless body as if to subdue the call of death and nurture this frail body to strength. Panicking from the circumstance, the only response she could muster was to sing childhood native songs she remembered from long ago and stroke the short, bobbed hair of the little lady. The hum of the jungle slowly became louder and louder till she could bare it no longer. She began to sob uncontrollably.

She sat unmoving for what seemed an eternity till she heard the low voices of men through the din of her surroundings. A bolt of fear ran through her. Controlling the urge to run, she sat motionless, peering between the leaves of the hovel in the underbrush. A Howler monkey gave a loud cry from the tree above and the men turned to gaze into the treetops. A short Mayan looking man at the rear of the troop gazed up and then down to the base of the tree. Breathless, Shawna stared back at him and tried to reassure herself that she was not visible. The men, satisfied that the Howler was alarmed at their intrusion and nothing else, continued along the cluttered trail out of sight through its density.

Shawna remained cradling the woman for a short while to assure the men would not return. Slowly, placing her on the ground, she wrapped the shawl around the woman's body leaving her child like face exposed to the early morning sun. She eased herself from the hiding place. High up in the tree, the monkey began to stir. Not wanting to disturb the belligerent pongid, she stopped to peer in the direction of the patrol.

'Thunk!'

Shawna felt a sharp pain in her arm. She looked at a small, feather endowed thorn protruding from her skin. Glancing up to the monkey, she wondered what he had thrown to violate her in this way. Feeling dizzy from her upward gaze, she sat down on the ground to catch her balance. Before her, in the underbrush not too far distant, a slight, scantily clad Mayan stood with a long, thin pole resting on his foot. Beside him, the Mayan, she had seen at the rear of the patrol, looked on in quiet.

Shawna never completely lost consciousness, but slowly lost control of her body. Drifting in and out of a daze, she listened as the two men crawled in the underbrush to inspect the little woman. She then felt the grasping of their hands as they dragged her to the enclosure shared by the woman. They left; she slept.

By mid-afternoon, the men had returned, accompanied by several women. Lamenting when they saw the little lady, they cuddled her and cried. Persuading Shawna to rise with tea, they comforted her and gently stroked her face. The men lifted Shawna out of the enclosure and began to pour more of the same fluid into her mouth. Barely able to hold it in, she swallowed as best she could, spilling half of it down her chin. They seated her against the tree opposite to where the women prepared the little lady with wrappings and went back to give them a hand. Within twenty minutes, Shawna began to get feeling back in her legs; the men lifted the little Mayan woman in a large shawl and prepared to carry her from the site. The women helped Shawna to her feet and together they slowly trod their way up and out of the small ravine area where they had been hiding; the Howler monkey remained silent through the whole process.

It was almost dusk when they arrived at a small village by a river's edge. The dogs were the first to greet the small troop while the chickens and pigs were less inquisitive and disappeared from view. The elders of the village were quick to come forward and met the travelers with embrace. Children came to the doorways of the small grass huts but were kept from advancing to the procession. The men continued to carry the Mayan woman through the village to one of the far huts. Shawna could only speculate that this was the woman's village. An old woman, supposedly the mother, began to weep as she followed and closed the door behind. Shawna was taken to a different hut along with several other women who helped her to clean and dress. The rest of the men gathered in the center of the small, community clearing, and then disappeared into the forest.

# TWO

*Primero dia (day 1)*

It was like walking into an oven as Brian eased himself down the flight of portable stairs from the plane. A haze of humidity hung in the distance beyond the runway. The semi-air-conditioned small passenger-jet had been deliciously cool in comparison to the heat that waited outside. As Brian stepped onto the hot tarmac, he could feel the heat radiating up through the soles of his sneakers, his full-length jeans began to dampen and weight. Within seconds beads of sweat dripped down his temples and soaked the rim of the Canucks cap that sat askew atop his head. The walk across the steamy expanse towards the terminal, with his hand luggage pulling relentlessly at his arms, seemed to take forever; the small bags felt much heavier. The hot air was thick, and all the while he plodded along, it sluggishly squeezed in and out of his lungs.

Once inside, the atmosphere in the small immigration area was pungent with sweat, full of passengers waiting to leave on the continuing flight to Honduras. A large, black dog pulling a security guard, darted back and forth between the scattered baggage of the waiting patrons, sniffing for contraband making all but the righteous few nervous. By a group of elongated worktables, the uniformed Immigration Officers carefully leafed through the bags of the disembarked passengers, with not so much as a hint of a smile or goodwill.

"What is your business here Mr. Uhh?" the inspector asked, scrutinizing the passport for my name. He patiently leafed through the pages, oblivious to the sweat that perched itself on his brow.

"Alexander, Brian Alexander."

"Yes, Mr. Alexander. What brings you here?"

"Vacation, I am here for a couple of weeks for relaxation and sight-seeing the ruins."

"Yes," he replied. "We have many of those. I hope you brought plenty of film?"

Brian nodded in agreement.

"May I see your camera?"

Without hesitation, he reached into his bag and produced the small package.

"Small isn't it," the guard insisted.

"Yes, it is digital, not as cumbersome as they used to be. I can hook it right up to my computer and edit, copy, or do anything I wish with very little hassle." He reached for his phone, "This will be next, as soon as I can afford it."

"Yes, we could use a little bit of this technology these days," the officer replied handing Brian back his camera. He reread his name and looked closely at him and then to his passport. "Thank you. Have a nice stay."

Brian quickly gathered his things and followed the directional signs to the main hall of Arrivals. Forcing his way through the maze of bodies and luggage that cluttered the exit, Brian came to face a line of local taxi drivers. Perspective drivers greeted the few passengers before him, and within moments his hand was being shaken.

"Hi. Welcome to Belize," came the salutation from a middle-aged, well weathered, black man. Taking the luggage, he proceeded to the rear of the taxi." My name is Bart. Where would you like to go?"

"Ah, the Royal Reef Hotel."

"Ok! Hop in,' he replied, without the slightest concern.

After haggling a short while for twenty Belize, or ten dollars U.S., they headed out of the dusty, pothole laden lot.

Bart gave his passenger a little grin and chuckled at the response, Brian later found out the standard fare was indeed eighteen.

The ride from the airport was fast and bumpy. Brian had barely enough time for a few fleeting thoughts of Shawna. The roads looked and felt as if they had not been repaired for years. Considering the timeline of the British leaving after their occupation, it was obvious they took the road repair equipment with them.

Bart, with his gregarious, friendly personality, would not cease to turn his head and talk of his children, his wife and their life together here in Belize. Many times during the twenty-minute drive, Brian would close his eyes and brace for sudden impact. Needless to say, the hotel was eventually arrived at, but with the windows wide open and air blowing limitlessly through, it was quite an initiation.

"Any time you need a ride, you give me a call 'Mann'. I'll take you anywhere."

"Thanks, Bart. I appreciate that." He did not know how to take Bart's jocular nature, but learned there would be no better service than what Bart could offer. They shook hands and Bart delivered the luggage from the trunk and disappeared down the road in a cloud of dust. Brian headed for the foyer and check in desk.

The interior of the hotel was quite light and neat. The marble, tiled floor reflected the identical exit doors at the rear of the foyer. A small fountain, off to the left, adorned with a variety of native foliage, shadowed a small, sitting area overlooking the pool. Just to the right a young, attractive girl in a trim, white blouse and navy skirt, smiled at him and waited for Brian to approach the front desk.

"Hello," he said, returning the smile. "Brian Alexander. I have a reservation."

She punched at the keys of the computer terminal and after several seconds looked up. "Yes, Mr. Alexander, I have it right here. May I have your credit card please?"

"Sure," easing his wallet from his back pocket. "Could you also check for any messages?"

"Yes, of course."

Steve, his brother-in-law, would be coming down in the next day or so, but needed to leave his arrival times at the desk. Steve had been very patient over the few months previous; the construction business had been down sized temporarily to accommodate Brian's studies in Victoria. It had taken Brian more time to glean the necessary information from the clues left behind by Vincent daLima (Brian's somewhat mentor), before making the commitment to come down to Belize to look for Shawna and the jade bowl - the very reason for this journey. The late Vincent daLima had been able to point him in the right direction, but all the necessary details had to be extracted from endless books, memoirs and his personal files. It was only after a short trip to Albuquerque and meeting some of Shawna's associates that Brian was able to discover that she had indeed gone to Belize and to an archaeological dig not too far distant. Brian just had no idea how to find them or who he could hire to accompany him. Steve offered his services right off the bat, citing their escapades of a few years earlier as credentials. Brian had made it through customs but was not sure whether Steve would be as fortunate. There was one contact name that they had, but there would be no guarantees of help, or loyalties, from any of the nationals. He would be meeting their contact tomorrow evening at a little cantina in downtown Belize City. His name was Magnus, Dr. Magnus.

The 'doctor' had been a man they had met and had financial dealings with on a trip to the Yucatan Peninsula previous. Steve and Brian had engaged in a short vacation for two weeks sampling the local cuisine and diving the pristine waters that lay just off the coast of Cozumel. Unexpected, the opportunity to go inland and visit some of the cenotes (large water holes) in the area came along, but misfortune shadowed them and the excursion turned into an exasperating experience for the two. If it had not been for the doctor, they would have ended up deported, incarcerated or shipped back to Canada in cuffs. Still uncertain as to whether they had been set up or not, an opportunity for the doctor to take advantage of the two of them in their ignorance was a possibility yet to be determined. Either way, it had not been profitable for the parties involved. It was this kind doctor that staved off prosecution and who Brian was to meet the following night. He was looking forward to the conversation and discovering the incidental details of their last meeting of almost six years past.

The clanging of the keys hitting the countertop reverberated throughout the foyer. The desk attendant looked toward several bellhops' and summoned one to attention with the wave of her hand. Before Brian was able to bend to pick up a piece of luggage, the bellhop had come to his side.

"Hello, my name is Jose'," he announced with a smile.

He was young, barely twenty and had a smile that would warm the heart of any cantankerous old maid. Jose was dressed in a full-length, white shirt with long, dark pants and sandals. His manner was firm and insinuated a confidence beyond his years. He grabbed the keys from the desk, bent over to collect Brian's remaining luggage to place on a pushcart and forced his way through the glass double-doors at the rear of the foyer. Out into the air, the smell of the green foliage mixed with the chlorine in the pool teased his senses like a mild smelling salts. He awoke to the fact he had finally arrived. Brian, although emotionally subdued, was looking forward to the intrigue of the task ahead.

The hotel was next to the waterfront with little more than a grass strip and a wooden walkway holding back the tidal encroachment of the sea. Like most hotels in the tropics, the doorways to the rooms were entered from an open balcony that usually spanned the length of the complex; a little odd for northerners at first sight, but considering the need for a refreshing breeze to blow in off the ocean, it made considerable sense. The view from both sides of this complex was pleasant, with the door to Brian's room overlooking the pool area and palms, and the window looking east, toward the open ocean. Off to the right was a group of wooden buildings lining either side of a wharf jutting out several hundred yards into the bay. A dive flag atop a pole lazily flopped in the gentle, ocean breeze welcoming those who would venture to the ocean's visual bounty beneath the waves.

As he placed the luggage in the room, Jose' turned with a smile, "If there is anything 'jou' need or need to know, I am your man."

Catching a glint in his eye, Brian had an understanding of his intent and would likely rely on his good nature to help him in the future.

"Here Jose'," as he handed him a ten, "I'll come down and talk to you a little later. There are some things I will need as well as directions to some places. Perhaps you can help me?"

"Any time," he responded as he left and closed the door behind.

Leaning back on the bed headboard with pillows to support him, Brian closed his eyes and let his mind drift to the circumstances that lead him to this place. Vincent had encouraged him, in a way, to investigate the plight of the jade bowl and its courier, but it was Shawna's dark, mysterious eyes flashing before him along with the fear that constricted his aching heart, that pressed him on in the endeavor. The highlights of the last night they had spent together began to tease him and he found himself trying to block them from his mind as his body responded in like manner. The last few moments of her in his eyesight, along with her father as they stood just beyond the stone circle on the small plateau above Ossette, initiated a chill that ran down his spine. Brian began to recall the starry sky, and, as the herbal tea began to have its drugging effect on him, the humming of machinery as well as the crackling fire increased in intensity.

There had been a file in Vincent's office that had alluded to the correlation of time-periods and human sacrifice around the world. The information had been scattered and inconclusive, but compelling. Certain facts brought to light the eradication of the practice of this horrific act in one area of the globe, only to resurface in another far, distant corner, after a relatively short period of time. The thought began to play on his mind as he remembered the dreamtime, embodied as the young, native traveler, and the strange, extenuating circumstance of this traveler's bones being found deep in a well on the Hopi reserve, the jaguar finger-ring being the only remaining clue to his murder. He could rest no more.

Getting up from the bed, Brian looked toward the luggage that was piled on the floor and decided it was best to get things started. After unpacking a few things into the drawers, he had a quick shower and within a few short minutes was heading down to the lobby to try and find information on the Mayan ruins and the necessary guides to locate them. Unlike the Upper Peninsula, the jungle here in Belize, was denser and the roads somewhat treacherous and illusive; the need for a guide was a must.

Getting off the elevator, Brian engaged a housecoat-clad, middle-aged gentleman cutting across his path. With hair slicked back smooth and towel draped over his arm, this man gave the appearance of heading to the pool but instead walked alongside him to the glass doors of the lobby.

"After you," I said, opening the door wide and turning slightly to face the pool.

To Brian's surprise, staring back at him was a scantily clad, well-built brunette lounging on one of the deck chairs. She gently nudged the large sunglasses perched on her nose and returned to the book that rested on her knees. Sensing she was side-glancing him from behind the dark glasses, he gave her a smile and then continued after the gentlemen he had just let in. The man turned to the lounge just off to the right while Brian proceeded to the desk for an enquiry; a 'be back in several moments' sign was perched on the counter. Turning to search the almost empty lobby for help, he noticed a group of inactive of bellhops milling by the door. Jose was not among them.

The Royal Reef was not a big hotel but should have been busier at this time of the year. Built after the great hurricane of 1931, it was fairly modern having received several facelifts with each new owner that eluded to raise the fortunes of those (stockholders) who financially embraced her. Belize was not as well developed, in the Americanized sense of tourism, as it could have been; some patrons remained happy it remained so. Since the British had left all those decades ago, there had not been the influx of tourist dollars to invest in a much needed newer infrastructure, although, there was foreign investment. It was a chore to keep it in the nation's best interest and not let development run amuck. Support for the aging waterworks and road-systems, was a slow and seemingly unrewarding task that was aided only by the British, who still had a vested interest in Belize's prosperity. Initially, economists had sighted the drug smuggling difficulties and the amounts of laundered money sifting into the system that compromised the monetary policies needed to stabilize the economy, but recently the government had gone to great lengths to encourage trade with neighboring countries and loosened the laws on foreign ownership of land. Belize itself is relatively safe and has no more and no less of a drug problem than the other countries in the area, but still remains a geographically-good, stop-off point for producing drug-lords to refuel their planes at private airstrips in the secluded jungles, usually on their way to the wealthy Estados Unidos. Few have been the millionaire made by an early morning stroll along the beach, or jungle path, with the discovery of a washed up payload ditched from a federally, tailed courier plane. Another concern has been the lucrative, illegal trade of real and counterfeit, antique artifacts heading to foreign markets. With the government's slow progress in eradicating these ongoing infractions, for whatever reason, the International Banks, save one, were at a standoff with a wait and see attitude. Luckily, the Government had enough assets of their own to support the Belize dollar through the transition period.

Just off to bellhops' left was a large, colorful, announcement board. Astounded, as he strolled up, Brian found exactly what he was looking for. There was an empty chair behind a small table covered with flyers and timetables of the ongoing tours. As he leafed through and gathered some of the slips, a different, uniformed, young woman strolled up and slipped in behind the table.

"May I help you find something?" she asked, her strong, Spanish accent curling the words pleasantly.

"Thank you. Uhh, are the tours daily or do you have to book regarding availability?"

"Both," she replied with a smile. "There are scheduled tours within Belize to Xunantunich and Corazol, and outside to Tikal, Copan and Palenque. They are one, two and three day tours respectively. Within Belize, most are day tours that you can either arrange for yourself, or we can arrange travel and a guide for you."

"Oh! And you can set it up a day in advance?

"Usually," she replied, twisting her mouth into a smile.

"Thank you." Brian turned and exited the front doors.

Once outside, the heat hit him like a soft pillow; the sun was high in the sky. Dressed lightly in a cotton shirt, long pants and sandals, Brian knew within moments he would be sweating. There was a long stretch of open road to the south just right of the shoreline that seemed to go on forever and within five minutes of walking, a taxi pulled up alongside and offered its services. The driver smiled from ear to ear and with a "where to?" they headed off in a cloud of dust toward the heart of Belize City.

Crossing the motley, swing-bridge over Haulover Creek to the old part of the city and the market, Brian couldn't help but take notice of the smell. It was not all that repugnant, but it couldn't be escaped; the odor emanating from the waters below. The flotilla of open skiffs and speedboats lay huddled close to the docks waiting for the remainder of their cargos of colorful produce, boxes and people to be on-loaded and whisked away before the ebb tide had ceased. The majority of the motley flotilla was on its way to islands and cayes just an hour off the coast to the east. Children played precariously close to the traffic in the streets as the two drove past. Women in colorful dresses, sporting bags of goods in their hands and on their heads, gave them side-glances as they meandered through the maze of pedestrian traffic.

Brian had come down town to try and locate the little restaurant that he had agreed to meet the Doctor at. Although, somewhat wild at night, this was a quaint area with narrow streets and close buildings that towered two and three stories above. There was an odd blending of old and new architecture as a result of Hurricane Hattie that devastated the area some years back, killing hundreds of people. Like most port towns, it had a colorful and sordid blend of residents and drifters, and an underbelly that, for the most part, was better left unexposed.

Turning on to Regent Street, located on the map as a scratch, Brian finally came across the hanging sign above the door of 'el Hostal de Fraudulento Abogado' (the Inn of the Fraudulent Lawyer). It was a bright, quaint, adobe-style restaurant with a fenced-in open, eating court. Looking through the high, wrought- iron-fence, he could see the small, plaid, cloth-covered tables adorned with flowers and vases waiting for expectant patrons. The back wall was covered with flowering vines and small multi-colored lanterns that would light the courtyard at night. As he entered in through the front doorway of the kitchen area, he heard the familiar, "Buenos tardes senor."

"Buenos tardes."

"May I help you?" came a pleasant voice from behind the bar counter. The attendant put his cleaning cloth down to be more formal.

"Yes, I would like to make reservations for tomorrow night. There will be three of us."

"Si, senor," he replied without writing the request down.

"About eight-o'clock"

He nodded in return.

Brian smiled back at him and hesitatingly left assuming he would write something down. He waved, and Brian returned the gesture then retreated outside into the sun and the waiting cab.

"Thanks for your time," Brian saluted to the driver through the passenger's side window. "I will walk back to the hotel from here."

"Are you sure amigo?" he asked reaching for the bill in Brian's outstretched hand, "Gracias."

Brian watched as he slowly drove down the street and turned the corner out of sight. The narrow, side street had little auto traffic and the few pedestrians that graced the street were oblivious to his being there. It was nice to be in the warm climate, away from the cool, dampness of British Columbia. He had not presumed to take the time to do the tourist thing, but was intrigued by the colorful streets and the collage of people and ethnic races that crowded the main streets. He walked slowly through on his way back to the hotel; the diversion was appreciated.

The time was four-o'clock when Brian passed by a poster depicting a Mayan Figurine and clay, wash basin, attached to an iron wrought-fence. Deciding too drop in at the quaint, historic museum, he passed through the front gates and by the wooden enclosure that had been the original guard-station. It was a modest, two-story, stone building of colonial architecture, housing the historical archives of the city, and to my surprise, a small but wonderful collection of artifacts; a separate walkway led to the entrance to the historical prison. The entire complex had been newly renovated over the last twenty years, but still held its heir of British colonialism.

Once inside, he approached the reception area to the left just inside the front door and was greeted by the women behind the counter.

"Buenos tardes Senor," she chimed.

"Buenos tardes Senorita," Brian returned with a smile, and continued, "Mayan exhibit?"

She Pointed down the hall to a stairway as a lead to where he was going, but was given a curt 'uh hum' as she directed him to the cash register where he was to purchase a ticket. Passing the small, bookstore area just behind a set of glass doors, he knew full well he would have to venture upstairs to find the Mayan exhibit. Slightly overwhelmed by the caliber of the artwork along the stairwell, he took a deep breath and entered the upper, exhibit hall and was stunned by the small, but impressive, collection of photographs and clay figurines. To his delight, in the center of the main, exhibit room, beneath a glass cabinet, was a replica of the famed Jade Skull of Altun Ha. It was small; barely the size of a woman's fist; the original was of similar, crystalline formation as the Olmec, jade bowl. Brian stood for some time and gazed at its impressive style and formation, wondering as to the whereabouts of the original, older counterpart.

Continuing down the hall of white, stucco archways and murals, the sound of his flat sandals resounded on the marble, tile floor and echoed loudly through the corridors; it was impossible for subtlety. Brian walked to the rear of the final exhibit and read a sign on the wooden, mahogany door, 'Keep Shut'; a poster of butterflies and beetles adorned the upper-half, alluding to the exhibit within. From the outside, he could hear laughter and the shuffling of boxes. Grabbing some paper and an empty file folder that lay close by and placing them beneath his arm, he entered the room to find a couple, obviously employees of the museum, in passionate embrace.

Taken back by the sight, Brian bowed his head with an, "Excuse me."

"Oh!" came the cry of the women as she straightened her skirt and came directly in front of him. "Forgive me, may help you with something."

"Well, yes," Brian replied, with an embarrassed, half grin. "I am Dr. Alexander, from Canada, and your name would be?"

"Delacruz, Maria Delacruz." The name on her tag confirmed.

"Well, Ms. Delacruz, I was sent down to Belize to get in touch with a colleague who is working at one of the archaeological digs close by. I am actually looking for someone who may be able to help me in locating her, and perhaps take me to the site."

Saying nothing, she looked at Brian searching his

eyes and straightening her skirt further. "I may be able to help you," she replied, looking back sheepishly into the room and closing the door slightly.

"Her name is Ms. Brook, Shawna Brook. Would you happen to know where she is working?"

"Well, Doctor, it would depend on the project site she is at and the team she is working with, they do move around a little bit," she noted with a grin.

"Yes, I realize that, but I had to leave in such a hurry, I left my papers at home and my secretary has just left on holiday, so I can't get in touch. But I think she was either at Caracol, or Xunantunich."

Brian glanced back to the young man in a crisp, white, security-uniform shirt and blue trousers, just inside the door packing several boxes; he did not seem bothered by the intrusion. She looked uneasy at my scrutiny and raised an eyebrow.

"Perhaps, I can take her name and make a few phone calls for you. Can you be reached in the area?"

"Yes, that would be very kind of you. I am staying at the Royal Reef for now, and you can leave a message with the front desk and I will return the call, and perhaps the favor," he returned with a grin.

She blushed a, "thank you," and re-entered the room and closed the door.

The loud thudding of Brian's sandals did not matter as he raced out the rear entrance into the humid, late-afternoon air, "Yes!"

Once back at the hotel by the elevator doors, there was a line of people waiting to be seated in the dining room. The shapely woman he had seen by the pool earlier was now walking arm-in-arm with the fellow Brian had opened the door for and followed into the lobby. It was obvious then that she had been watching and following him, and Brian had just been in the way, 'a mechanical door-opener' as it were. The two took no notice as he approached the flights of stairs that lead to the walkway and his room. Brian glanced back to the elegant pool and the surrounding palm trees, and wondered whether he should take a dip or wait till later. With his hunger getting the better of him, Brian quickly changed into some fresh clothes and headed for the dining room.

The room was half-full with a variety of ethnic patronage. The majority were Americans that had obviously come to alleviate the early, spring blaws. Two tables of colorful food along the left wall, with a chef attending the hot meats at the far end, gave the room a banqueting appearance. The view to the outdoors exposed an open-air veranda lined with tables, while patrons sallied in and out of accommodating sliding, glass-doors. Walking through the maze of tables, the Canadian chose to seat himself outside and wait for the server to attend him. Looking through the menu, there was nothing that caught his attention and decided to take what was available at the buffet.

"Would you like something to drink?" came a feminine voice from behind him.

"Yes, thank you. Beleken, please?"

After several moments of day dreaming, the beer appeared before him as effortlessly as the ten dollars beside it, disappeared. Seagulls played and danced their determined watch in the azure, blue sky that slowly deepened into the horizon; it would only be a matter of an hour and the sun would begin to set behind the hotel in the west. The breeze had already started to shift from the land back out to the sea, and was delightful. The sheltered veranda was comfortable with the occasional puff of air that freshened the sun-bleached, deck area. The familiar couple had chosen to come out and sit not far distant, and drink their cocktails and smoke cigarettes. Within ten minutes, they had started to argue and Brian found himself heading back indoors to sit and enjoy the assorted delicacies of the buffet in the company of a group of German tourists; it was obvious they were there for a good time and within minutes he was welcomed. Introductions were long and languid, and, with comfort and familiarity pouring from the glasses, boldness incited stories of intrigue, embarrassments and embellishments. After a number of beers, an assortment of marine delicacies, cooked and raw, coffee and desert, it was time to move on. Thanking them all graciously, Brian balanced his way through the sliding glass-doors onto the balcony and the multicolored string of lights that adorned the walkway along the shoreline. Above the gentle crashing of the waves, he could faintly hear the booming, bass music of the bar off to the right along the dock. Thinking he might take a stroll down to take a look, Brian quickly glanced the area in the hopes that he was alone, and proceeded down the steps to the boardwalk by the waterfront. After a slow walk that helped to clear his head, he stood for a moment to look at the stars that appeared extra bright in the domed canopy that stretched from horizon to horizon. Trying to recall the last time he had taken the time to look up, Brian came to the conclusion that it had been at Ossette, the infamous night of native, herb tea, and dreams beyond comprehension. He had obviously not been himself that night but did remember the clarity of the stars, the humming in his ears, and the shooting star that was salutary to the passing of a great soul, that of Vincent daLima.

The bar was quite wide-open with a central counter where the bartender and maids did their exchange. The speakers above, blared out reggae while bodies entwined, swayed to the beat below. Brian found himself a seat at a table not far from an additional, food bar, but close enough to the dance floor as not to be excluded. A shapely, black girl came over to greet him with a smile and yelled above the music, "What you havin?"

"Ah, Beleken!"

Not too sure why he ordered another one, perhaps the worst beer he had ever tasted, he was perplexed, but the thought of ordering a coke at this place would be like ordering a glass of milk. Seated close to an aisle where people would come and go out the back of the building to the dock area below, was perhaps the best place for him to exit unnoticed, if he so desired. It was well lit and really quite romantic for those who were so inclined. It did not take long before Brian noticed the woman from the pool, dancing on the floor with a guy, not her companion of the morning. Looking around the entire bar, he did not catch glimpse of the earlier companion at all. Trying to stay inconspicuous, Brian tried not to look at her and draw attention to himself, but when the song had finished, they both came his way to go out to the back, wharf area. Sitting back as far as he could, with the Beleken at his lips, Brian tried to stay unnoticed. He was not sure at the time why he felt that way, she was a good-looking woman, tall with long legs and dark complexion; she must have been a mix of black and Hispanic with fine features and straight hair, quite a sight, and good modeling material. As they both walked by, Brian noticed her take a look at him and give a smile. The bottle dropped from his lips as the exact opposite to what he had hoped would happen, did. As the music started up again, the dance floor came alive and he forgot about the woman till she came back in with her companion close behind, but instead of going back to the floor, she slid herself in beside Brian at the table. Her companion stood and watched.

"Hi," she sighed.

It was not so much of a romantic gesture as it was a slurred greeting. Brian could tell by her eyes that she was not in the same frame of mind she had been when she had left those few minutes previous. The faint, pungent smell of ganja emanated from her hair and clothes, and knew she was quite stoned. She was wearing expensive jewelry and had a polluted air of dignity about her. Looking at the fellow she was with and considering the condition she was in, it was Brian's conclusion that something unpleasant was more than likely going to happen. All of this was none of his business of course, and he had not asked her to sit at his table as the fellow that intently stood over the top of them would contest, but she was there and she did not appear to be leaving.

The stoned fellow pulled up a chair directly in front of Brian and stared at him with red, bloodshot eyes. Putting his bottle to his lips again, Brian wondered at this predicament.

"Would you like a beer?" Brian asked. He didn't return an answer.

Within moments, the woman beside started to doze, slouched on the bench beside Brian. The goon started to look around. With the changing music, and a reggae beat, he got to his feet and grabbed her arm to pull her back to the dance floor. Waking up slightly, she gave me a grin and pulled herself to her feet and headed back to the dance floor, her arms flailing loosely by her side as she followed him over to the center to dance.

'Good,' Brian thought to himself as he took another sip, relieved of the tense moment. After several more minutes of watching the flow of traffic pass by him, Brian turned his attention back to the dance floor and watched as the couples swayed and jerked to the music. Feeling more in the mood with his meal moving down from his diaphragm, Brian noticed a girl's shiny, dark, naked thigh popping out between the couples as they danced. It did not take long to realize that it was his friend and her companion with his hand down the front of her panties exposing his rubbing motion and her response. They stayed locked in embrace till the end of the song and slowly swayed their way back toward Brian.

'God, please let them keep on going,' but no, she plunked herself down on the bench and crossed her legs. She began to nod out again, 'what am I going to do?' Most guys would probably applaud the crass show of infidelity, but Brian had one girl on his mind.

"Why don't you go and get some beers," Brian shouted at her companion and gave him twenty BZ dollars.

He looked back at Brian with distrust and then looked to his date, "OK!"

It took him several minutes and several glances back at the two of them sitting at the table till he disappeared behind the crowd of bar flies crowding the counter. Ceasing the occasion, Brian grabbed her under the arm and around the waist and lifted her from behind the table. Slipping out the back aisle, they were out of sight in seconds, half carrying, half dragging her along the boardwalk toward the hotel. Luckily, several employees were out on the patio doing prep work which allowed them to enter the normally closed dining room and through to the lobby. Once in the lobby, they approached the front desk only to find the attendant not there. Realizing, there would be no place to put her in this condition; Brian stood and waited with her draped over his arms till he could hold her no more. Seeing the waiting area beyond the tall, grass foliage, they staggered together to find a place for her to sit while Brian found someone with a key. Leaving her temporarily, to scout around, Brian finally found Jose just outside the front doors, talking to a cabbie.

"Jose, how you doin? Do you think I could see you for a minute?"

"Chure, what's up?"

"Could you give me a hand; I need to get one of the guests up to her room."

"Why, what has happened?"

Without saying a word, they quickly walked back in and over to the sitting area. Jose and Brian stood, momentarily shocked, to find her sitting on the floor naked trying to get her underpants unraveled from her one shoe that remained on her foot.

"What have you done amigo? You can't do that here," he screamed looking at me.

"I didn't do anything. I am trying to get her to her room, but I don't know where that is."

"Here, you get her dressed," Jose yelled, throwing Brian her dress. "I'll find the key.

"Who is she anyway?" Brian yelled after him.

"Her name is Amalia. She is the fiancée of an American who does business down here. Only you don't want to know him."

"Have no intention of it."

"Here, I have the key. Let's go!"

With Jose on one side and Brian on the other, they more or less carried her to the third floor and on to her suite. Slipping the key into the lock without knocking, Jose entered the room.

"You didn't knock!"

"Why?" Jose countered. "There is no-one here."

"How do you know?"

"I know," he whispered, "he has a girlfriend."

"This guy has another girlfriend as well as," Brian tilted his head in Amalia's direction.

"Si."

With an astonished look on his face, they walked her into the bedroom and eased her down on to the bed. Jose put her one loose shoe down by the bed along with a tiny, black purse she had managed to retain throughout the evening. She grabbed Brian's hand as he tried to cover her up with a sheet. Her satin, dark skin and black, sparkling pools for eyes were seducing him to stay, but he knew that discretion was the best part to play.

"Amigo, stay if you want. I will say nothing," he gestured with a smile. "There have been others."

"Jose!" and grabbed him by the arm to exit with him.

Brian turned to see Amalia with her eyes closed, dozing off to sleep.

Jose locked the door behind the two of them and continued down to the next floor and Brian's room.

"Thanks, Jose."

"No, thank you," he replied in his Spanish accent. "You may have saved me my job. If anyone had seen her, whoa! It could have been serious."

"See you tomorrow, Jose'."

"Chure," he replied.

As Brian closed the door, he could not help but feel the frustration that the night had conjured. How desperately he needed to be with a woman, but not that way. There was truly only one woman he desired to be with now, and she was right here in Belize, only a few short miles away; the only question being, where?

# THREE

*Dia uno (day 1)*

The sound of keys jingling outside the door forewarned Brian to the housekeeping girl's intent of coming in. Unable to move to cover himself, and with the notice of 'Do-Not Disturb' on the inside of the door, a curt shout, "later!" stopped them short. He could hear the shuffle of their feet and mumblings in their native tongue as they moved away from the door. As Brian rolled over to bury his face in the pillows, the sharp light entering through the curtains drew his attention to the strip of a perfectly cloudless, blue sky. In contrast, a streak of brown glass exposed a beer bottle sitting on the night table bringing back memories of the night before. The smell of the lone cigarette butt in the ashtray contributed to the stale taste in Brian's mouth; he could bear to lay no more.

Dressed in nothing more than shorts, housecoat and a pair of sunglasses, Brian followed the outside stairway down to the dining lounge. After a cup of black coffee and some fresh strawberries, the uneasiness in his stomach subsided and his head began to clear. There had been two telephone messages left for him at the front desk, his cell-phone had not worked; one, that Steve would be arriving that evening and would go directly to the restaurant; the second was from Maria, at the museum; Brian was to call her sometime before noon, he was already late.

As Brian emerged from the glass doors of the dining hall, the blue sky reflecting in the rippling water of the swimming pool looked clear, refreshing and inviting. Flicking the lid to his cell, he waited for the roaming signal-search to locate, but with no luck; the thought of heading to the telephones in the lobby took second place to the towels stacked neatly on a table by the pool. The water was, as he expected, crisp and cool, and after returning from a brisk swim to the floating bar, Brian laid back on the deck chair to soak in the warm sun. A busboy across the pool by the bar caught his attention and he made the notion with his hand for a telephone. The busboy acknowledged and disappeared into a side building, moments later he reappeared with a full tray.

"No thanks," pointing to the menu and taking the cordless-phone along with the bottled water.

Smiling, the busboy returned to the open doorway and disappeared.

Placing the call, Brian had learned Maria was temporarily absent from the office and left a message for her to call 'poolside' when she returned. Leaning back and replacing his glasses, he closed his eyes and became immersed in the sounds and fragrance that surrounded him, quite pleasant.

Within minutes, the sun had lifted the coolness from his skin and the familiarity of the occasion took him back to when Steve and he had spent their holiday, just north, on the island of Cozumel. It had been a little earlier in the season and with the countless students down for spring break, they had decided to cut their diving visit short and head to Cancun and drive further inland to visit the ruins. It was meant to be a great opportunity to expand his portfolio of photographs and familiarize the two with the local customs and brew; there was always the off chance of procuring some antique collectables to take home.

### Precursor - Six years earlier:

Guatemala and Belize, were the Mayan cultural centers of the area that housed ruins of the Classic Period (AD 300-600), apart from the ruins at Cerros that go pre BC. At the peak of the Maya civilization, the area had a large widespread population of relatively peaceful peoples with languages, and culture, essentially the same. The surrounding tropical rainforest, which covers most of the mid-peninsula, consists largely of giant Ceibas (wild, cotton trees), Spanish cedars, varieties of palm trees and mahogany. Rubber trees, once in abundance, still add, in a small way, to the economy of the north peninsula. The numerous ruins, which dot the area, are mostly covered with brush, grass and small trees. Unawares visitors climb the mounds and structures sometimes without a hint of what is lying beneath. Colorful orchids grace the jungle's damp boughs, along with liana vines that hang suspended from the trees. It is an area difficult to navigate, difficult to work and difficult to cultivate, but for some, ascetically pleasing all the same. Just north, at the tip of the peninsula, the soil is thin but nutrient rich, and in the rainy season comes alive with plants and insects. It is low, rolling country with heavy forests cut through by the occasional rivers, grassy savannas and swamps. It is still now almost uninhabited with no obvious governing body apart from the occasional game warden or local priest, whom on occasion, we needed desperately.

Where Steve and I ventured was the northern Maya region of the Yucatan, and the states of Campeche and Quintana Roo. This area becomes dryer the closer to the tip of the peninsula and not as visually pleasing as the rest. It is flat and has very little ground vegetation apart from the scrub and an abundance of rubber trees. The soil is very thin over a limestone base and supports very little in this almost rainless territory of the Yucatan. This area is renowned for its' great potholes (cenotes), some being as large as one hundred and fifty feet across. These are filled with collected rainwater that often flows freely between the holes through the porous, limestone aquifer and a network of underground rivers. It was the desire to dive these mini pools that got us into a regretful circumstance with the local 'Policia' and near deportation. The rental of a vehicle to haul our scuba gear, and the chance meeting of a local, amateur archaeologist, whom we gave a lift, started us off through this arid land on our first Mayan adventure.

## The tale of unrelenting embellishments:

Where on earth Steve got the jeep that was to take us on our travels, I will never know. He said it was a rental, but I expected he had purchased it from a local resident looking to make a fast buck. The necessary four wheels and windscreen were in place, and there was a wiper blade on the drivers' side just in case it should happen to rain; apart from that there was little else that could be said to be familiar.

"Come on Bri! Hop in," came the encouragement of my jovial and proud companion.

"You've got to be kidding," I slurred, lifting my scuba tank over the remains of a dented and rusty tailgate. "Does it have seat belts?"

"What do you need seat belts for?" he asked with a boyish grin. "We are close to the ground. Look, low-riders!"

As I bent over to look at the wheels, there was barely six inches clearance from the ground to the frame. I shook my head; in this terrain we would need double the distance to keep our muffler; that was, if we had one?

"Hear, listen to this," as he turned the key. 'Whomp, blup, blup, blup.'

No muffler.

"Won't be taking many pictures of birds and wild life this trip, will I?" I chided at him.

"At least not up close," he recanted.

As we made our way out of town, in a cloud of dust, I had my doubts we would make it to our destination.

An hour passed and we were almost half way to our hotel in the town of Valladolid. I had never heard of the place, but was content, at this point, in letting Steve handle the travel arrangements. This would, for the time being, allow me the option of having someone to blame if the situation became less than tolerable.

The roads, by all means, were better than I had expected, with the only real obstacles being the many bicycles laden with produce and family members. Their young children running alongside would yell through our open windows, trying to sell us anything they deemed salable. It was only when we had to turn off on the road's dusty shoulder, or on to the not-so-well traveled paths that the dust clouds that trailed us, billowed in leaving us choking and teary eyed. It became a continuous jockeying and choreography to out-do the relentless, dust clouds. Needless to say, when we arrived at our destination, none of the locals gave us a second look as tourists, due to our appearance resembling that of a number of workers on any given day.

Crawling from the front seat, I stood and looked about to the quaint colonial facades of the buildings that lined the perimeter of the main plaza. At the far end I could make out the cross-pinnacled spires of Cathedral de San Gervasio.

"All right, ay!" came the call from Steve as he stepped from behind the steering wheel to the front of the vehicle and started to brush himself off.

As I looked toward him, the billows of dust gently drifted away in the bright sunlight. With hat in hand, he banged his thighs releasing even more clouds. His teeth shone exceptionally white beneath a blackened upper lip that trailed in streaks to his nostrils. I began to laugh at his appearance till I realized I too would be painted with the same brush.

"Yeah, great!" I returned to his whimsical display of fortitude at our arrival.

"Now, if I remember," he stammered, "We have to find the 'el Meson del Marques'."

Turning around and pointing to the flat-fronted, stucco building, with multiple doors facing the street, just across the roadway, "Is that it?" I questioned, knowing full well the answer.

"Good aren't I," he boasted as he retreated to the back of the jeep.

Grabbing my camera bag from behind the seat, I slowly walked to toward the hotel brushing myself off all the way, trying to disperse as much of the dust as I could. On entry to the small office, just up several worn marble steps and off the main foyer, I approached the Mayan receptionist who beamed with delight at my arrival, but sobered instantly at my visage.

"Hola senor, may I help you?"

"Si, I have a reservation, I think? The name is Alexander."

"Ah, Si senor, we have you here for three days in a deluxe room."

"Deluxe! I responded surprised looking back toward Steve through the open doors. "Yes, that will be fine. With two beds I hope?"

"Si, that will be sixty U.S. pour favor."

"Now?"

"Si."

Steve came sauntering in with bag in hand and a weight belt strung over his shoulder.

"Couldn't you have left that in the truck?" I asked.

He shrugged, "It is better to be safe than sorry."

"Yeah, I suppose. We will have to bring all of the gear in for the night."

He nodded in anguish.

"Senor, your car can go in the compound at the back," the receptionist chimed over hearing our conversation. "It is very safe and is locked at night."

"Great!" I replied looking back to Steve and said quietly, "Perhaps we can cover our gear up with a blanket to hide it."

"Uno memento, while I see if the rooms are ready. If you will wait, I will have someone take you upstairs.

Within moments, a young man, not more than eighteen, grabbed several of Steve's' bags and nodded for us to follow him up the stairs.

Entering the foyer, we were overcome by the quaintness of the Old Spanish hotel with tall, pillared archways, and high ceilings that skirted the immediate dining area. Large, wooden candelabras, adorned with smoked-glass cups that hid the modern convenience of light bulbs, hung from unhewn, log, ceiling joists. An open, wrought-iron fenced-in courtyard, to the left as we entered the restaurant area, was filled with plants and a stone fountain that sprinkled and spattered its contents from tier to tier giving the ambience a romance beyond our need. Outside its perimeter, white, sheeted tables, adorned with candles and sculptured napkins, awaited the evening's patrons, with a crispness that was only surpassed by the two, young waiters posing motionless, attentive to their servitude.

"How much are we paying for this?" I asked, straining to see the swimming pool beyond the gated courtyard.

"What do you mean, we?"

That night, I sat down to a meal of tortillas, refried beans and a tasty concoction of tomatoes and jalapeno peppers that washed down well with some local beer. As we talked about our desired itinerary for the next day, at the table across from us, a lone, middle-aged, black man with a sparse mustache and beard that graced his bony jaw line, nibbled on salad and pieces of enchilada. Every time there was mention of cenotes, and how we would precede with the dive arrangements, his attention would perk in our direction. It was not long after the completion of our meal that he approached our table and interrupted us with an apology.

"Excuse me," he stammered. "I could not help but overhear your conversation. I assure you, I was not eaves-dropping, but in this open space it is hard not to hear the immediate conversation next to you."

"Oh, I hope we weren't talking to loud," I stated getting up from my chair, towering over the slight man to greet him.

"No, no," he stammered. "I have done much research in this area. The cenotes are a passion of mine and have spent many hours studying the artifacts and remains found in them."

Steve looked up at me with a glint in his eye.

"Would you like to join us for coffee?" I gestured, pulling a chair from his table.

"That would be nice, thank you."

"What exactly is it that you do?" Steve asked boldly, without introduction.

Getting seated properly across from him and looking at him directly, I reached out my hand, "Brian Alexander, and this is Steve Grayson," nodding to my brother-in-law.

He took my hand firmly and gave it a shake, then turned to Steve who sported a grin.

"Doctor Magnus," he stated directly, reaching out his hand, "but call me Magnus, if you like."

I turned to get notice of the waiter, who stood in the archway that opened to the bar and directed him to our empty, coffee cups.

"I was born in Buffalo," Magnus stated emphatically, thinking to assure us of his status, "and started doing work with the university, of the same name, many years ago. I came down to study the ruins and native culture. It has been most interesting for me, and my colleagues, to continue here, and have been back only on several occasions to deliver artifacts."

"Is that a fact," Steve returned, rubbing his chin.

Just then, the waiter came up, "Café?"

"Si, tres," I replied with a smile. "Gracias."

He poured the three and headed back to the arch to stand at his post.

"You will be diving here, did I not hear you say?" Magnus asked.

"Well, we are not all that certain yet, we have just got here, but we were thinking about trying to find a site and taking a look."

"Well, be careful if you do. It is against the law to dive the cenotes, and authorities are not as lenient as they used to be in regards to the archaeological sites in the area. You could receive stiff fines, or even jail terms now, if you are caught removing any artifacts, as insignificant as they may seem."

"I thought if you received permission, it would be OK," I asserted, sitting firmly back in my chair.

"At one time you could," Magnus stated with a low voice and little emotion. He took a sip of the black swill brimming to the edge of the small, ceramic cup, "but no longer, since all of the holes are now considered of archaeological value. But, if you know the right people," he stated with a bit of a smile, "there are still ways."

Steve and I looked at each other noting the

implication.

"So, there is no way we can do recreational diving in the area, "Steve asked, shifting slightly in his chair.

"Well, not here at any rate," he replied.

"How long will you be staying in Valladolid, Doctor?" I asked, taking a sip on my coffee.

"Till morning," Magnus replied, getting up from the table and leaving his half-finished coffee. "I am doing a little research in the jungle not far from here. Perhaps, we shall meet again. Thank you for the coffee." With that, he gave a gentle nod and left through the tall, rounded archway to the rear gardens.

"Well," commented Steve, swirling the coffee in his mouth. "What do you think?"

"It certainly changes things a little, but I would still like to take some photos, if at all possible."

"Good. Me too! We will have to leave early in the morning if we are to get any diving in."

Leaving several bills on the table, we gave the waiter a nod and followed Magnus out into the open garden and up the stairs to the rooms above.

It must have been barely four when the first cock-a-doodle-doo pierced the morning air. The sun was still not up as my feet touched the floor and I sat peering through the bamboo slats that graced the window of the room. The shutters, on the outside, remained open to allow a breeze and the odd mosquito through. Steve snored lightly and was oblivious to the morning's initiations. Grabbing my pillow, I lobbed it at the prone lump that lay across the room with no more of a successful response than a primordial grunt.

"Come on man, wake up!"

"Alright already," he replied from beneath the

sheets.

Not more than twenty minutes passed before we had loaded the necessary equipment into the open trunk of the jeep. Not wishing to arouse attention, we began pushing our vehicle out of the compound and on to the street. Along the narrow streets of town, we began to notice small groups of locals cluttered by the roadside. They watched intently as we pushed our way passed till we encountered another group of wayfarers wishing to give us a hand pushing our truck. Within moments, we had a dozen eager and willful helpers assisting us to get from the hotel area, unnoticed…..

The drive was dark and secluded, and within the hour we were driving passed the gated area of the service entrance to Chichen Itza with no sign of a guard to stop us. The road beyond the small, stucco buildings was very rough and almost not navigable in the low jeep. As the sun was beginning to rise, we turned the windshield wiper on to remove the dust from the glass and view more clearly the tall temple called 'El Castillo' (the castle). Looming through the trees to the right that separated the main compound from the service area, the shadow of the principal structure gave an ominous, foreboding aura to the surroundings. Shadowy structures of the closer 'Ball Court' played tricks with our eyes; shrubs and vagrant stelae peered back at us as if waiting for the summoned ancients that lay-in-wait to sacrifice the loosing opponents. With a scribbled, napkin map in hand, retrieved from a bellicose cab driver, we wearily proceeded down the rocky roadway. Not at all sure how far we could take the jeep, we knew if we persevered and got close enough to the cenotes, we could make a go of it. At the roads final end was a wooden building used to service the cenotes. Backing up as close as we could to the line of trees by the path, we crawled out of the short jeep and took a closer look at the exercise we were about to embark. Not knowing how far the site was from the edge of the compound, we loaded up as much equipment as we could. After two minutes of slugging over hilly terrain, we came across a small, stone building beside an open pit approximately one hundred and fifty feet across. As we peered over the edge, down some twenty plus feet, we began to wonder whether we were nuts.

"Did you bring enough rope?" I queried, not bothering to take my eyes off of the steep slope and overhang of limestone rock.

"Yeah, it is back in the car," Steve replied, sweat breaking from his brow.

"I'll go get it. Did you remember the security line?" I asked.

"Yeah, it's here.

By the time I returned, extra rope and camera equipment in hand, Steve had already prepared the scuba equipment on several blankets close to the edge. He had moved around a little further to the left in a relatively sheltered area with a few trees for protection. The sun was just breaking the horizon as we donned our light, neoprene suits first.

"Ok! Who goes first?"

"What do you mean?" Steve asked, as he struggled with his tank over his shoulder.

"One of us needs to go first to stack the equipment at the bottom so we can crawl down the rope." I suggested."

"That's a good idea. You go first."

Struggling down the near vertical face for some

time with my mask around my neck and fins draped over my arm, I eventually hit the water's edge, just below a thin ledge above the surface. I could barely stand on it, so I slid gently into the water and stacked the equipment on the ledge and waited for the tanks from above. Giving a shiver as the trickle of cool water found its' way down my spine, I laid back and donned my flippers.

"Ok Steve, start lowering."

One by one the tanks, belts and camera came over the edge and filled the thin out-cropping quickly. Once all was down, Steve slowly maneuvered the steep slope and came to rest alongside me in the water. I took note of the large knots down the length of the rope, secured at the bottom to ensure our safe return to the top some twenty-four feet above. Within moments, my tank was secured and the small safety-line, our life-line back to the surface, was in place. Bobbing up and down just below the surface to adjust my buoyancy, I looked down into the dark abyss, camera in hand. After a few moments of quiet reflection, Steve came along beside me. Signaling him back to the surface, we both ascended.

"Don't forget Steve, the floor of the pit will be very silty. Try and stay off the bottom and keep your legs up so when you scissor, you are pushing the water 'awayyy' from the silt."

He gave me the 'Ok' and we let the air out of vests to start the descent. It was difficult to tell visually how deep we were going due to the gentle slope of the walls away from us under the overhang we had previously scaled. The visibility near the surface must have been fifty feet, but no more, due to the greenish algae; as we got deeper, the light of the early morning sun faded quickly. I had always presumed the water in the cenotes was crystal clear, but I suppose that would be determined by the amount of current that flowed through the network of tunnels throughout the limestone rock, and that flow would depend on the amount of rain they had had lately, which was none. I lit the lamps to my camera, and watched as the tunnel became illuminated to an endless hole of blackness some yards ahead. Behind us, the little security-line floated aimlessly as we continued down into the further reaches of the hole. Our exhaust bubbles lazily floated up, growing larger like rolling donuts the further they ascended.

After several moments, the slope flattened out and it was as if we had entered a large cave. The silt and leaf refuse began to stir as we settled close to the floor. A quick look at my depth gauge showed we were close to forty feet below the surface and enclosed in complete darkness apart from my lamps illumination. Steve approached a stick extruding from the silt and attempted to pull it from its' resting place. At exactly that moment, the connection to the camera lamps faltered and we were temporarily in complete darkness. Within seconds, my fingers had found the delinquent connection and Steve was illuminated once again holding what appeared to be a femur bone. Startled by what he was holding, he dropped the bone and kicked his legs, which stirred, up a cloud of silt. Trying to avoid the cloud, I put my hand down into the silt and got my finger stuck on a rock and pulled it up only to find my finger was stuck in the eye socket of a skull. Panicking, I tugged at the skull and almost dropped my camera, which in turn loosened the connection, and once again we were in complete darkness. Looking up to the haze of light above us, I could just make out Steve bolting madly along the safety line heading for the surface. Hyperventilating slightly, I gathered my thoughts and played with the connection on the light yoke and once again was able to see. Nothing was visible through the eye of the camera apart from bright clouds of silt billowing lazily. Slowly, I proceeded to the surface behind Steve. The dive was over.

As we broke the surface, the sun was brightly reflecting off the distant wall. The shadow, cast below the walls, accented the severity of the overhang. At first glance, I wondered if this was the same place we had descended into, but the rope was still where we had left it. Steve was near the shore attempting to put his weight belt on the thin ledge. Still trying to catch his breath, he rested periodically floating on his back with his tank regulator dangling beneath his head.

"Did you see that?" he asked exasperated.

"Yeah, I have it on film. At least I think I do." I slowly swam to the shore to rest the camera on the ledge. "I think that is it for now." I submitted, securing the equipment to the outcrop.

"I didn't think there would be anything left after all these years, did you?" he asserted, slipping his mask from his face.

"I always suspected there was still stuff here, but not human remains!"

"Yeah," he responded. "I think we better get out of here." looking up to the overhang. "It looks a lot higher from down here, doesn't it?"

"Yep!" I sighed, the word whispering across the surface of the water.

"Here let me go first," he tendered.

Slipping out of his tank and supporting it on the

ledge, he grabbed the rope with both hands and slowly made his way up to the where the overhang met the wall. With his elbows supported against the wall, Steve tried to get foot leverage to force his way higher, but as he struggled, he bounced against the wall uncontrollably losing his grip on the rope. After several tries, he came crashing down into the water with a splash.

"Here! Let me try," I suggested.

Making my way over to the rope, I placed my weight belt and tank on the rocks and proceeded up the rope to the same point that Steve had achieved. Struggling to get beyond the point, I forced my hand between the rope and the rocks and pulled myself hand over hand. I had almost made it to the cusp of the wall when the rope gave way and I too crashed back into the water. Disappointed and wondering why the rope had given way, I broke the surface to the face of Steve looking at me with a sardonic grin on his face.

"Darn! I was almost there," I yelled at him, slapping my hand on the water. He just looked at me and pointed to the sky.

"Buenos dias amigo!" came from above.

Looking up, all I could see was the dark silhouette and the militaristic uniform of the guard who leaned over the edge; a knife clutched in his fist, glittered in the morning sun.

By the time they had hauled us, and all our equipment to the surface, it was almost noon. Chichen Itza had become overrun with tourist, and with the commotion of the police and military personnel, making us a spectacle was not difficult. They had loaded all of our stuff into the compact, rental truck that was gleefully driven by an officer, back down the gravel, service road. Steve and I, they loaded into a police jeep, and paraded us throughout the main plaza area for all to see. It was a long, dusty, sweaty ride back to the outskirts of Valladolid. Once inside the Police station, we were held separately in small, stifling-hot rooms with nothing to eat, and bottled water to drink; it was well into the evening before we knew at all what our fate would be.

"Buenos noches, Mr. Alexander," came a familiar voice. Looking up from the wooden, slat bed I had reclined on for the better part of the day, was Dr Magnus. "It appears to me you have some difficulty, you and your companero.

"Yes, it would appear so."

"I had a call in the field several hours ago that the police had picked up some poachers in one of the cenotes. I would have thought you had more sense than choosing a site as popular as that."

"Well, I suppose you are right, but I assure you, we intended no damage and would have been gone in half an hour when we were accosted and relieved of our equipment."

"You know, it is a serious crime that you have committed."

"Yes, I am aware of that and would ask you, where do we go from here?"

"Well, that depends on you, doesn't it, Mr. Alexander."

"How much?"

"How much do you have?"

Shaking my head, I spoke to the concrete floor, "How much?"

"Five hundred U.S. and they will release you

temporarily into my custody. Your passports will be returned later."

"How much later?"

"Let's just say in a couple of days."

"Why into your custody?" I asked, wondering as to the purpose and extent of our infringed liberty.

"From what I gather, you did not tell them much and asked to let you get in touch with the closest embassy."

"There was not much point in denying our circumstance, now was there," I replied.

"It is a good thing you had your camera with you. Poachers do not normally take pictures of their pilfery. It was not hard to convince them that I had hired you to catalogue some of the work sites in the area. You had just ended up at the wrong one."

"We are indebted to you, Doctor."

"Please, call me Magnus." He stopped and turned as he was about to leave the small room. "I will arrange to have you released temporarily till you return with some 'security money'. Mr. Grayson will remain here for the time being. Your jeep is being released to you." He disappeared from my sight.

We did not see him till the following morning when we were met at 7:00 a.m. outside our hotel with several of his work crew there to ensure our co-operation. Our equipment had been released to us, and all was apparently accounted for and kept in the compound overnight.

"Well gentlemen," he said with a tone of smugness, "you will be assisting us over the next several days with some excavating work. I trust you will find it very interesting and something you are familiar with.

Within two hours, we found ourselves in the middle of secluded area being lowered once again into several cenotes. Only this time, we had lots of company at the edge of the holes to help us up and down with our equipment. There were underwater floodlights run by small generators at the surface to give us plenty of visibility to work in. Small cages and buckets on pulleys were lowered down continuously and filled with debris from the sloping bottoms, and filled as fast as we could manage. I was a little startled at the lack of archaeological protocol when it came to excavating the artifacts that were found immersed in the muck. I managed to take some pictures of the excavation sites, but was directed in such a way as to not reveal the local. I was happy to do so for a while, but after several days was beginning to feel somewhat uneasy at the work at hand and the legitimacy of the projects assigned to us.

The following day, we were to go deeper into the forest and would be sleeping at a campsite with the local laborers. Some of them we had got to know and were friendly enough, but the majority held us with a level of contempt that bordered on hostility. The thought of spending a sleepless night on the hard ground, and in a forest that continually buzzed and croaked, did not appeal to either one of us. We had an alternate plan.

That evening, after the waiter had taken away the supper dishes, we asked him to send for Antonio, one of the bellhops we had befriended. We had noticed that Magnus had several of the local police as close associates, but notably no military or Federalis. After several hours, and a bottle of San Miguel, we knew what we needed to do. It was a simple plan and with a little luck we would be able to pull it off.

The day had been a tough one, and we were able to excavate a large section of a partially submerged pit and recovered a number of clay figurines and obsidian cutlery. We had packed away as much of our equipment into the little four by four as we could without being suspicious and returned with a case of beer and several bottles of rum that had been hidden in the back. For the next few hours, we had all the friends we needed, and even Magnus began to lighten up around the campfire. After several hours, a plate of refried beans and more than several drinks, we ran out of refreshment.

"Come on Steve, What say we head back to town to get some more beer."

"Sure. It shouldn't take too long, should it?" looking over to Magnus. "Why don't you come for the ride Magnus? You can show us the way."

He looked around to the others who stared back with glossy fixed eyes." Sounds like a good idea. I need to pick up a few things anyway."

Within several minutes, we were on our way out of the campsite close to Ek Balaam, bouncing on the trail heading toward the main road that would carry us back in the direction of Valladolid. Within twenty minutes, a half dozen military trucks heading in the direction we had just come, crossed our path. Without giving it a second thought, Magnus continued to puff on his cigarette staring out into the darkness beyond the headlights. Within the hour, we were pulling into the outskirts of Valladolid. Parking outside a well lit cigarette store close to the Police Station, we all entered in and picked up a few items. On exiting the store, we were confronted by a group of military personnel and an Officer de Archaeologic. Somewhat relieved at their sight, I noticed Magnus tense up and automatically reach for a cigarette. We were ordered back into our vehicle and directed to a parking lot a short distance from the station and cautiously got out of the truck. Within a moment, several soldiers surrounded us. The Military Commander approached us asking for our papers. Recognizing Magnus, he nodded in his direction and stood directly in front of us.

"Your papers please."

"Uh, they are in the station," I replied, looking in the direction of the building.

"Why are they not in your possession?" he quarried, without taking his eyes from mine.

"They are being held while a security check is being done on them," chimed Magnus.

"These gringos working for you?" the commander asked, looking toward Magnus.

"For the time being," he replied.

"I will need to see their papers. Does the 'principalmente' have them?"

"Si," replied Magnus.

The commander motioned to one of his subordinates to seek the papers. One of the Federal officers entered the station and returned outside after several moments. Striding up to the Commander, he handed him the papers and stood close to watch the inspection. "Are their papers in order?" the Commander asked the officer standing close.

"They appear to be in order," he replied, reaching for the papers to be returned.

The Commander without taking notice, stood glancing at the passports and then to us, and then back to the passports.

He handed them back to us with a nod, "You should not be without these."

"Thank you," we both replied simultaneously.

The Commander approached Magnus and stood directly in front of him. "There has been some illegal digging in the area," he stated, flipping his hand in demand of his papers.

Magnus pulled his leather pouch from his pocket and gave it to the commander. "We have just rounded up a half dozen 'escoria' about thirty miles from here. They seem to be working in the State Reserve without a permit. Would you happen to know 'anyting' about 'dis'?"

Magnus stood motionless, the commander inches from his face. "Non, Senior," squeaked from his throat.

The commander backed off and looked at several of the soldiers who began to laugh.

"He has been with us," blurted Steve.

"And where might that have been, Gringo?" came the bold retort of the Commander.

"We have been out site seeing for the day. We have all of our stuff in the truck," Steve motioned waving his hand in the trucks direction. One of the soldiers began to approach the truck, but the Commander stopped him short.

"It is your lucky day Doctor," the Commander laughed, "But I will keep these."

Steve and I just looked at each other in relief. The commander waved at his men to proceed back to their vehicles and the policeman back into his office. A small crowd of children and curious onlookers had gathered around the periphery of the cigarette store parking lot, and were beginning to approach the jeep.

"We'd better go," cautioned Magnus.

"But not to the site," chimed Steve.

"Non, Senor Steve, not to the site."

It was only later that we realized that the pouch did not hold Magnus' papers, but something persuasively more lucrative. We wasted no time in making our way to the hotel compound with the truck and upstairs to secure the rest of our belongings. We spent a number of hours in the cantina, having a few drinks and thankful we were able to get away from the exploits of the good doctor. We saw Magnus with a suite case and all his papers stuffed under his arm, leaving the hotel. When we saw him again, the following morning before our departure, Magnus voiced his gratitude for our support with the Commander, which in one way proved our supposed innocence to him, not that it mattered.

## Now

It was a pity things had not turned out as planned, and now, back in the present, years later, all Brian had on his mind was getting answers to the mysteries that plagued him.

Whether it was fortune or misfortunate that, once again, he would cross his path would yet to be determined. He was in need of answers to the questions of the jade bowl, and the disappearance and whereabouts of Shawna, and it was Magnus who would most likely have some of the answers.

As Brian lifted his head from the deck chair, he caught glimpse of an attractive, dark-haired woman in sunglasses, following the walkways to the pool. Her black purse swung militaristically beneath her arm as she strode in her black, platform shoes, dodging the cracks in the concrete floor slabs, her full thighs beat at the stretched sides of her tight, three-quarter-length, black skirt. It was Maria.

# FOUR

## *Dai dos (day 2)*

When Bart dropped Brian off at eight, the streets downtown were crowded with shoppers and fun seekers. As he approached, the many colored lights surrounding the tabled court gave the inn a festive atmosphere. Flames of candles on each table illuminated the faces of the many patrons enjoying the gaiety and intimacy. One slight man sitting alone in the corner, was Magnus.

"Buenos Noches, Senor," the host chimed, as Brian walked by the front counter.

"Buenos Noches," he returned, pointing to the rear of the courtyard.

The host nodded and went to collect a menu and his tray.

Magnus rose as Brian came close to the table.

"Magnus, thank you for meeting me. You look well."

"Thank you. I am pleased to do so," he responded taking a deep drag on his cigarette and reached forward to shake Brian's hand. "I was quite surprised at the notice that you were on your way."

"Yes, well I had little alternative but to come, and you are one of the very few people I know in Belize. Besides, if you are willing, as I mentioned in my letter, I would like your help in acquiring suitable locations for the filming. The documentaries budget is not too bad and could be profitable for both of us." Magnus took another drag of his cigarette. "Who else better to contact when in need, than the good Doctor."

He smiled at the attempt of humor. "Possibly," Magnus responded, taking another deep drag. He sat quietly and waited for the Canadian to continue.

Brian's calculation was to keep the doctor guessing and feed tid-bits to increase his appetite. Luckily, Magnus did not pressure him into more details, but by the sparkle in his eyes, Brian could see there was interest ignited. He was cautionary in regard to his true purpose; a 'wait-and-see' attitude was in order. Until Steve had arrived, and they had a chance to discuss a final plan of action, he would stay mum; not that they didn't trust Magnus; it was just, 'they didn't trust Magnus'.

The hour passed quickly. Having several beers, Magnus and he talked about the past adventures, excavations and photography projects they had individually been involved in. Brian gleaned some info about excavations going on in and around Belize, but steered clear of the mention the bowl. Altun Ha, and Cuello, and the area close to where the jade originated, were only short drives down back roads and through the forest. Altun Ha was not as secluded as some sites, but would still be a challenge for a 'gringo' to get to without a guide. Bart had offered his services, and after consideration, became the likely candidate.

A loud commotion by the door got every bodies attention away from their food and conversation. As Brian suspected, Steve had arrived from the airport and was feeling no pain. Dumping his luggage by the front door, he made his way through the tangle of chairs and tables to where the two were seated.

"Hi Bri!" came a near shout from several tables away.

Both Magnus and he stood to their feet to welcome Steve to the table. With one arm, he gave Brian a good solid hug, then reached for the hand of Magnus.

"Magnus, it has been a while," he said with a grin, then turned to see if the waiter had followed him to the table.

Taking a seat, he waited till the server approached, "Hola Amigo, he directed at the server. "Tres cervasa, por favor."

"Si, senor," the waiter replied.

Moments later as the beer came to rest on the table, the toasts and cordialities began and the mood became relaxed and festive.

Steve's continual gaze at Magnus was not one of contempt but more of surprise. Magnus' hair was noticeably grayer, and his build even more slight than it had been in the past, but his eyes still held that worldly sparkle that ignited at the prospects of adventure and money.

**Fact:**
Magnus was a character to deal with, but once his intent and desire was understood, he was very easy to figure out; at least in part. One thing Brian had discovered, as the conversation became less guarded, was although he did not always agree with Magnus's

methods, he had a heart for archaeology and a love for the Mayan people. As Brian was to later learn, money gleaned from his not so honorable exploits was often funneled into local colleges and schools to help with educating the local youth. The poverty and drug problem that raked Belize's moderate and low-income earners, and the rural-regions, had hindered the young men from breaking the cycle of poverty. The artifacts, as far as Magnus was concerned, were a natural resource to be gleaned, from time to time, and the benefits channeled back to the descendants who needed it most. The government, recently well established and stable, struggled with the lack of capital to help support the infrastructure that was required to sustain a consistent level of growth, technically and economically. As required by the World Trade Organization, this growth was to be active and relatively stable if a country was to reap the benefits of its association. Without a consistent tax base to feed the 'machine', the first programs to suffer were, and are, the social ones. Within the Government, there was noble intent, but with much corruption in many of the departments struggling to maintain budgets, there was little progress. For the Department of the Interior, field archaeology at many of the sites, and the selling off artifacts was a cash cow, bringing much needed money to a struggling economy trying to survive and save a national identity. There was much illegal trade, more lucrative than the licensed and traditional methods of distribution that has sent many pieces to the international market. This is where the good Doctor seems to have fit in. He never spoke openly of his official relationships, but one could tell there was a great deal more to Magnus than met the eye.

"Well gentlemen," Magnus chimed, swigging down the remainder of his beer, "I have a young lady waiting for me, and it is time to take your leave."

"Thank you, Magnus for taking the time to come," Brian stated, standing to take his hand. "I will be in touch with you in several days to discuss the details of the operation."

He nodded and looked over to Steve, who also stood to bid farewell. Both watched as he sallied around the tables of the crowded little restaurant, out past the gated eat-in portion of the inn, to the street beyond. A tall woman in a colorful shawl met him just beyond the gate, grabbed his arm and walked with him out into the playful darkness of the street.

Magnus, strolling with his lady friend, brought memories to Brian of walking arm in arm with Shawna through the woods near Ossette, all those months ago. He could still feel her hand grasping his arm as they struggled over the gnarly, root-laden pathway; her curt laugh that pierced the air as they almost fell to the side, sent shivers of delight down his spine even then. His mind wandered to sitting in Vincent's office, gleaning his papers for leads to the jade bowl's whereabouts and thinking of her. He had more questions than answers. If it had not been for the chance sighting of her in a group picture with her colleagues at Cuello, near Orange Walk, here in Belize, he would never had discovered the connection to the University of Albuquerque, and the on-going work here. From what Brian could gather, she was quite the respected archaeologist with ties to several universities. She had been involved in a number of sites in the area years ago. Working with several notable, female archaeologists, Shawna had helped them to uncover discrepancies in the theories, put forth by their predecessors. Lifestyle and origins of the preclassic Mayans, became more precise and remodeled after solid evidence. The jade bowl, by not so great a stretch, could have been a part of that scenario, not so much in the present tense but the antiquated one. Regardless, the two, Shawna and the bowl, were connected, and if he were to find the one, he would find the other.

The ride back to the hotel was a quiet one. Block by block, as they drove to the Haulover Creek Bridge, Steve watched out the window of the cab as the streets and people of festive disposition drifted to the more somber. There was very little affluence in this part of Belize City, and what little existed was well hidden behind high walls. The hurricane that had swept through the area, all those years ago, had left its card in the guise of quickly, rebuilt buildings and sprawling, slum-like neighborhoods.

When they arrived at the Royal Reef Hotel, Brian had discovered Maria had left a message stating a possible location west, by the Mayan mountains, close to the Guatemalan border. Caracol, an active dig of which Shawna could have been a part, was several hours away, and not easy to get to. If not there, the only other possibility would be Xunantunich, closer to San Ignacio, but less likely. From the staff photograph Brian had offered to Maria, found in Vincent's office, she had not recognized any of the undergrads, but all their names had come across her desk at one time or another; Shawna Brook's had not. In passing, Brian asked her if she could recall any extraordinary packages having had arrived, via a courier, from the States approximately a month ago. Maria remotely recollected muted excitement from the director of the museum, over an artifact that had been placed in the vault at the Department of Antiquities in Belmopan. She could not elaborate on the incident but noted that every month, or so, there was always a find, or locate, that would send the office into jubilant celebration. This information had not been all that promising, but a lead that could be followed up at any rate. He was to visit her again the following morning to get written permission from the Department of Archaeology, and also from the Forestry Department in Augustine. Brian had been depending on the indiscrete episode of their first meeting to get information and now decided that Maria had paid penance; besides, she had turned out to be quite genuine in her dealings with the counterfeit doctor, and went more than the extra mile to prove herself, which meant friendship, not obligation. Brian would meet her in the morning.

Jose' greeted us near the front door to the restaurant. "Hola, Brian," he half yelled toward him, then looking over to Steve with his bags, "Allow me Senor, and let me take dose for jou."

"Could you take those up to the room Jose," Brian asked? "I'd like to take Steve out the back for a nightcap."

"Jure," he replied, "I'll catch up with jou a little later."

"Thanks Jose'," Steve chimed with an appreciative smile.

They walked back around the side of the building

from the front. Several of the hotel employees leaned up against the stucco wall by the service entrance and puffed away on lighted cigarettes. The air was warm and the sky void of clouds, as they continued to the boardwalk along the ocean's edge. The bright, star-sprinkled canopy overhead, along with Ichtel, the mythical, moon goddess, lit their way. A gentle breeze played the palm trees back and forth in the rhythmic motion of the Caribbean.

"Why don't you sit here and I will get us a couple of beers," Brian suggested, motioning to a bench at the edge of the walkway.

"No thanks Bri. I think I've had enough." He seated himself by the water's edge. "I would just like to sit for a while. It has been a long time since I've been able to relax and breathe the tropical air." Taking a deep breath, "and this is great."

Sitting down beside him, Brian stretched out his legs and watched as a shooting star arched the sky.

They sat without talking for some time, taking in the moment.

"Have you been able to find Shawna yet," Steve finally asked?

"Nope, not yet. I have only one lead to follow, in Belmopan. Hopefully, with Magnus' help, I will have some luck."

"She appeared to be quite a woman," he sighed. "at least from what I remember. She seemed to know what she wanted."

"Yeah, very independent," Brian grunted as he bent over to search for a blade of grass to place in his mouth.

Steve, noticing his motion reached in his pocket for a small pack of tipped cigars, "Here!" handing one to Brian. He just looked at it in surprise. "Yeah, I know, I was hoping to find some good cigars while I am here."

Leaning over to take a light from Steve's sheltered hands, he sat back and puffed. At a distance, from in front of the bar, a commotion began to stir and within five minutes, a scuffle had broken out. At a glance, Brian recognized the one fellow as Amalia's friend from the previous night, who now broke away and slowly staggered his way towards the front of the hotel.

Throwing the remains of his cigar into the surf, Brian got up and motioned to Steve, "Let's go."

Steve, with the short remains of his cigar still stuck in his mouth, followed without hesitation. In through the foyer, Brian met Jose', slipped him a fiver and motioned him to follow with them passed the elevator to the stairs leading up. All three followed the drunk at a distance, up to the third floor and stood back unnoticed.

'Knock, knock, knock,' the fellow pounded on the door of Amalia's room, a cell phone visible in his other hand. After another series of knocks, the door opened and they could hear the recognizable muffle of an argument. After some loud, objectionable screams and what appeared to be a white shirt thrown in his face, the door slammed and the fellow walked down the opposite way and disappeared down the elevator.

Steve, taking a short puff on his stogie, looked at Brian, "What was all that about?"

"His cell phone worked." Brian chimed "Com' on, let's go to our room. I'll try to explain."

"Good night, Jose'"

"Good night, amigo."

### *Dia tres (day 3)*

After an almost sleepless night and a hot shower, Brian left Steve, still snoring, to go visit Maria at the museum. Bart quickly met him after a phone call, out in front of the hotel foyer; within minutes they were on their way to the downtown area.

There was a multitude of locals and tourists milling about the streets, doing their early morning shopping. Bart, with his window open, slapped the side of his car and honked his horn repeatedly to encourage slow, encumbered pedestrians out of their way. A half hour passed till the cab cleared the shopping area and pulled up to the gates of the museum, 'an approximate fifteen-minute walk from the hotel.'

An ambulance and several police cars blocked the entrance through the gates while a small group of people crowded the steps up to the doors.

"Boy, I wonder what's going on here," Bart voiced, as they slowly pulled passed the stopped vehicles.

"Yeah. Could you pull up ahead and park while I find out what's happened."

"Sure," Bart replied, without hesitation.

Climbing out of the car and walking over to the steps and the people waiting there, Brian snuggled in beside several American looking women waiting in line for the way to clear.

"What's up?" he asked openly to the two of them but looking to the policeman at the top of the stairs.

"We are not sure, but we think someone has been hurt in a robbery," the eldest of the two replied.

"Oh! That is not so good, is it?" he returned.

They both shrugged and went back to waiting patiently in line.

Looking around for a way to by-pass the police, Brian thought of the back entrance he had used to exit at his last visit. Slipping passed a guard, waving his camera case and a portfolio as a purpose, "Delivery!" He walked boldly by and headed directly for the souvenir shop without a second look. Brian could see the guard through the glass portion of the shop's inner door and waited for him to turn so he could slip out, unnoticed, and up the stairs to the left. Once there, he could see no people at the end of the hall; the door to the butterfly storage area, where he had first met Maria, was closed. Feeling a little confused, he re-entered the stairwell and faintly heard voices from below. Waking down the two flights of stairs, he was confronted by a plain clothed officer at the entrance to an office in the basement.

"Parada!" came the command of the fellow at the door.

"Is everything alright?" Brian questioned, wondering about the situation inside.

Just over his shoulder, Brian could see Maria being cared for. She was sitting in a chair facing him, talking to a young man while an attendant gently patted her face with gauze. He could see that she was flush and had been crying. Her face appeared bruised and her clothes torn as if she had been in a struggle. Maria's young companion, of several days ago, lay prone on a gurney, talking with an interrogator.

"I am afraid you will have to go," the sentry cautioned to Brian in English.

A young man, a national, with a Department of Tourism identity card attached to his lapel, said a few words to Maria and darted out between the two of them.

Without hesitation, Brian retreated out passed the clay statues, and figurines, as they watched from their glass tombs and cluttered shelves.

Outside once again, Brian observed as the young man that had just blasted by the guard and he, climbed into an older, blue, pickup truck and speedily drove off. Realizing this fellow might know the circumstances of Maria's assault, Brian signed Bart to where he stood. Hopping in, they immediately took chase. Within moments, they were once again surrounded by early morning shoppers, and carts loaded with produce, and watched helplessly as the little, blue pickup headed west across Haulover Bridge and out of sight.

"Darn!"

"Where to," Bart asked?

Defeated, Brian replied, "The Royal Reef."


Steve lay by the pool, sipping on a coffee, covered in sun block. He looked touristy in his shades and sun hat, an oddity if you considered his style back north. He looked very relaxed, and Brian was reluctant to crash into his party-for-one, but felt it necessary if they were to locate Shawna. Brian felt disturbed at Maria's demise, and with the young man in the pickup, a greater sense of urgency was now setting in.

"We have to get in touch with Magnus again, Steve."

"Oh! OK!" he replied, without moving a muscle.

"Maria, at the museum, has been hurt, I think a robbery. I have a sneaky suspicion there is more to come. We need to get to Belmopan, and talk to some people at the ministry. We have to get some answers."

"Ok!" Steve replied again, shifting uncomfortably.

"I'm going up to the room to get the number. Why don't you come and get some of the equipment packed."

"Ok," he replied, unmoving.

Impatient, Brian turned back and motioned him to get going.

"Do you think you could give me a hand?" Steve sheepishly asked. "I'm stuck to the chair!"

Magnus was unavailable by phone and knew by this time of the day, there was little chance of finding him. They would have to venture off to Belmopan with little more than a phone number and a pocketful of concern.

The compact, yellow car the two had rented, stuck out like a sore thumb as they navigated the crowded streets of the city. For the most part, they looked like a couple of garish, red-faced tourists down for some fun…The backseat and trunk were loaded with equipment, along with bags of chips and beer, the necessities of tropical traveling. The sun had not been particularly friendly on Brian's northern skin and Steve was just beginning to pink-up from his morning session at the pool. The road was busy with fully loaded, produce-trucks and taxis, their drivers trying to avoid the many potholes that dotted the worn pavement. Further out of town, the Western Highway, became smoother and more navigable, the scenery more pleasant. The journey to Belmopan would take an hour.

The beer had gotten better over the last few years, but still carried that underlying taste of skunk. After draining the remains of the can, Brian tossed the crushed ball into the back seat with the others. It was extremely hot and with the air-conditioning not working in the car, a slight dizziness was all that could be accomplished by drinking the fluid. The mountains had steadily grown in the distance as they headed inland. The road, for the most part, carried very little traffic and they often found themselves the only vehicle on the open two-lane highway. The mangrove swamps either side only added to the monotony, but gave, from time to time, the distraction of work-crews hacking away at the gnarly encroaching branches. Steve, the conversation king, slept in the seat beside and gave no entertainment except to grunt when they encountered an intrusive bump in the lengthy road.

It was mid-afternoon by the time they entered the outskirts of Belmopan. The Canadians had not decided on a plan of action, but knew they would have to visit the Government Archives, and Department of Archaeology. Driving the streets, they were astounded by the appearance and size, or lack thereof, of Belmopan. It was rather unassuming and totally out-of-character for a city, let alone the Capital of a country. Within twenty minutes, they had driven around the city, gotten lost, and found themselves again at the cities' entrance from the main highway roundabout. It was pleasant enough, but not at all what the two had expected. Returning back by the main road into town, they passed the bus-station and turned right into a well-manicured open field. There was a large stately building at its rear with several, three-story, older buildings to the right, but nothing to denote whether these were indeed the Government offices. With Steve straining to see whether the structures held titles adhered to their walls, Brian navigated the newly paved and curbed roadway.

"Yes, this must be them." Brian attested, reflecting

on the nicest roads they had encountered since their arrival in Belize.

"Wait! What's that over there?" Steve pointed out another three-story, brown building.

Swinging around, they followed the roadway to an unpaved, gravel parking lot and slowed to view any inscriptions that may denote the nature of the buildings purpose. There, above a narrow doorway leading into the building, was a faded, unobtrusive sign, "Archaeology Department".

They slammed their car-doors simultaneously and curiously walked toward the building that was, supposedly, to house some of the most valuable artifacts the Mayan Civilization had to offer. Upon entering the narrow entrance way, they proceeded up a short flight of stairs to a cramped foyer and a wooden door with a plastic "Archaeology" nametag below its frosted pane of glass, and back-in-a-few-minutes note stuck crudely on the side with masking tape. With a what-can-we-loose look on his face, Steve tried the door and found it unlocked. Within, was a high counter barring their way from entering further, several chairs were located off to one side. A 'please wait, we will be with you shortly' sign on the counter-top directed them to 'wait' and they took a seat.

After several moments had passed, Steve asked, "What are we doing here?"

"I'm not sure."

After several more minutes had passed, "Do you think we should ring a bell or something?"

"I don't know." Brian replied.

After several more minutes, Steve got to his feet and stretched as far out over the counter as he could to see into the far reaches of the office. Hearing no sounds within its confines, he slid the rest of his body over the counter and proceeded deeper into the area.

"What are you doing?" Brian screamed.

"I'm not sure." he replied.

"What are you looking for?"

'I don't know,"

"Then get outta there."

He continued to look about the paper-laden desks spotted throughout the office till hurried footsteps were heard coming down the stairs from the next floor up.

"Steve!" Brian shouted, alerting him to the possible intrusion.

Without enough time to clear the countertop, he tucked himself beside a filing cabinet just out of sight.

The door opened, "Hello, can I help you?" came the question from an elderly, graying clerk.

"Ah, well yes, ah, I would like to get permission to take some pictures and film one of the archaeological sites."

"Which one, the number in your party; what equipment will you be taking? Do you need guides, or will you be supplying your own?" He looked down at the dumb expression on Brian's face. "You will have to fill out a form and submit it tomorrow; we are just about to close. I will have to get it for you."

He exited the office door and then out through the front, foyer doors. At that moment, Steve bolted from behind the cabinet and jumped the counter without so much as moving one paper out of place. The clerk entered from another door beyond the counter and came to face them from behind the counter; with a form in his out-stretched hand, he looked at Steve, then to Brian and then back to Steve. He began to say something, but shook his head and continued with his instructions to Brian.

"You need to fill this out and bring it back to me. You will also need police clearance and approval from the Park Warden of the site you wish to visit. I can arrange that for you."

As they left the building, from the distance they heard the sound of thunder. It sounded quite odd and within minutes saw an army helicopter skimming the trees. Approaching from the west, it began to make a landing in the clearing just beyond the building. Both the Canadians leaned on the car and watched as the helicopter slowly touched down. With its radials slowing down, the side-door slid open and its passengers exited from below the drooping blades. As they walked closer, in single file, their faces became more visible, and to Brian's surprise recognition of one of the individuals. Amalia's American husband, or boyfriend, whoever he was, was walking with his secretary close behind a military official of high rank. They talked intensely taking no notice of anyone, or thing, around them and did not observe the waiting two.

### Dia quatro (day 4)

The next morning brought little encouragement when the proceedings of the day started at the Police station. A fax from Interpol, to complete their clearance-application for the permit to film the ruins, seemed to take forever. Hind-sight is always 20/20, and if Brian had kept his intentions quiet, entering the sites as a tourist, camera bag in tow, Steve and he could have shot film and investigated to their hearts content without a second glance or hindrance. But, fate always has a way of bringing all of us onto a path, or occurrence, that staggers our intellect as to whether life is truly random, or predestined (they both sat callously regurgitating the experience of six years ago).

On their way back to the Archaeology Building from the station, they passed an expensive, but beat-up SUV, with a familiar face behind the wheel, 'Magnus!' Both their heads turned at the same time and watched intently as he pulled into the gas station they had just passed.

Awestruck and elated, Steve accidently drove off the shoulder and into a stand of bushes. Just out of sight, they eased themselves from the car to view the damage. Keeping one eye on Magnus only a few hundred yards away, they got on all fours to view the undercarriage. Luckily, there was no visible damage to the car and only broken branches to the bushes. Able to back out almost as easily as they had gone in, Brian reversed the car to the other side of the road and waited till Magnus had finished his transaction. Pulling out and following him at a fair distance, they watched as he circled the round-a-bout heading for the Western Highway and San Ignacio, a small town near the border of Guatemala.

"What shall we do?" Brian screamed at Steve.

"Brainwave, we have to go back to the ministry. Our names are on an application we are about to submit, remember."

"Oh, yeah!"

In silence, Brian drove the round-a-bout several times considering the next plan of action until Steve elbowed him and pointed in the direction of town.

The parking lot at the ministry was full of police and army personnel-carriers. Entering slowly, they found a parking spot sheltered between two large vehicles.

Recollecting, once again, the incident of six years ago with concern, they came to the frightful conclusion the police were here to arrest them. "What do we do, run for it?"

"And go where." Steve asserted. "Interpol came up with our names from the diving we did before in Mexico."

"Then I suppose there is no reason for running?"

"No, I guess not." Steve replied.

They both got out of the car and headed for the office.

'In Her Majesty's Service' royal emblem, gracing the sides of the vehicle's doors, a number of British soldiers waited on the grass, and side-glanced the two as they proceeded up the walkway to the rear door. With dry mouths and beads of sweat on their brows, they entered the office now crammed with a variety of people and one reporter.

They were met with the glance from the clerk of the previous day, waving them over to a vacant corner of the counter. He gestured Brian to give him the application.

"Thanks, you will have to go now," he asserted. "As you can see we are very busy. Just go ahead and if there is a problem, we will let you know."

"Let's go!" whispered Steve, elbowing Brian once again.

"Waite! Let's see what is going on."

Once outside, the comparatively cool air eased the tension from their imaginary plight.

"If they're not after us, then who?"

"Or what?" Steve replied.

Just then, the news reporter came out and tucked

himself by the wall to light up a smoke. Slightly greying with age, and a little frumpy from too much desk work, he searched all his pockets. Not having a lighter or match, he came over to where they were. Steve reached in his pocket and produced the necessary lighter.

"Thanks," he sighed, taking a deep drag from his cigarette. "May I offer you one?"

Steve reaching for one, smiled; Brian, with the wave of his hand, declined.

"Boy, this is mayhem, huh."

"Yeah," the reporter replied, shaking his head in disapproval. "I didn't introduce myself," taking Steve's hand. "Owen, James Owen, from the Provincial News."

"I'm Steve, and this is Brian.

"Look at these troops," Steve attested taking a drag on his smoke, scanning the army personnel and trucks filling the parking area. "British-to-boot."

"There has been nothing like this since a huge shipment of cocaine was intercepted several years back." James cited.

"Another one?" Brian interjected."

"No," Owen responded, "search and rescue. Or should I say recovery. A woman archaeologist was abducted from one of the sites just this side of the Guatemalan border. She won't make it though. They never do. They'll never find her."

A bad feeling began to well up inside Brian. Steve took a noticeably, deep drag from his cigarette.

"Oddly enough, yesterday there was an attempted abduction from the oddest place," Owen continued, "the Museum of Natural History, in Belize City."

The blood drained from Brian's face. Maria wasn't

robbed, she was almost kidnapped.

Steve took a last drag and flicked the stub against the brick wall, sending sparks in all directions.

"Thanks for the smoke. We have to go."

Steve grabbed Brian's arm and directed him to the passenger's seat. "Let's go. We have one chance to get a go at this, and he's left already."

Startled by their quick retreat, Owen intuitively decided these two knew something, and he was going to find out, 'a morsel of truth could feed a feast of speculation'; the game was a-foot.

# FIVE

*Dia tres, temprano (day 3, early) Dr. Magnus*

The candlelight highlighted the dark, moist skin as Magnus caressed the thigh and hip of his young, sleeping companion. Covering her nakedness with the bed-sheet, he silently crept over to the desk that housed his personal belongings and paper work. He had not been all that comfortable with his meeting earlier with his Canadian acquaintances and wondered at their true purpose. His instincts told him that they were not being entirely honest; but then again, who was? For that reason, and that reason alone, Magnus had been able to remain active in his pursuits and a step in front of the 'functioning' law enforcement. He didn't consider the Canadians a threat, but understood the nature of these two men, as haphazard as it may have been. Then, there was an urgent call on the message machine the day before from San Ignacio, a student he had befriended a number of years back, needed information and would call again.

Looking through his journal of past meetings and

events, nothing stuck out that could refresh his memory as to the true purpose of their being in Belize. Concerned, but not overly troubled, he got up from the desk, looked over to his beautiful friend and preceded down the stairs to the gated courtyard that led to his workshop. Several dogs barked ominously in the distant, but that was all that this sleepy hour aroused.

Freeing several locks and loosening the bolts of the door to his lower warehouse, he swung it open exposing a room full of artifacts. Miniature, stone stelae welcomed him from their precarious perches above cupboards full of other clay figurines. Colored etchings of popular Mayan cave paintings and glyphs adorned its walls, while others lay strewn across a large worktable. Shards and chips of clay lay on the floor beneath a small, round work-stand; a chisel and hammer lay across its table as if ready for use.

Magnus crossed the littered expanse to a potter's wheel in the corner and sat down to scrape the hardened clay from its table. Surrounding him on either side where low shelves cluttered with small bowels and vases in the likeness and period of the classical Maya. Uncovering a pail, he reached in and pulled a fresh clump of clay and began to work it to the wheel until it formed the smooth likeness of a bowl. Placing his slippery, wet hands on his knees, he stared down and watched as the kicking-stone slowed the piece to near standstill. Sitting motionless for some time, he stared blankly as the piece became lob-sided and slid out-of-shape with the slowing momentum; he had a clue. Without washing his hands, he turned off the lights and re-secured the doors to the room. He silently walked upstairs.

The half empty bottle of rum attested to the condition of Magnus as he slept, His head propped back on the shoulder of the armchair, his closed eyes staring blindly at the fifty dollars BZ that lay on the coffee table under his feet. The young woman now awake, got dressed, gathered her few things and left down the narrow stairs into the fresh, morning air.

Magnus' sleep had been fitful. He dreamed of a dark presence, an entity that haunted him and would often return to him during times of trouble and uncertainty. In his dream, the day was bright and colorful. A stunningly beautiful woman and a young child ran frightened, aimlessly through the large courtyard of a familiar ruin. He was of younger age then, and watched from a distance as the woman, his wife, fell and reached toward the young girl who continued to run towards him. Kneeling in close embrace, the two of them watched helplessly as the earth opened up and swallowed his prone wife. Turning to run away with the girl in his arms, the psychic force of the gaping earth followed them as they tried to escape through the maze of the ruins. He usually awoke at this point in a cold sweat, heart racing, but this morning, he was still too drunk to get out of the chair.

In early-life, Magnus' studies had taken him to the ruins in the northern, Yucatan forest, just north of Chichen-Itza. Ek Balaam was still an obscure, isolated ruin that had remained unnoticed and out of the scrutiny of foreign archaeologists. It offered an excellent chance for local teachers and students alike to dig and study without the bothersome intrusions and interruptions that notoriety would bring. Treasure hunters and site-seers, oft-times would descend on these unsuspecting delights and unknowingly remove or destroy valuable threads to the woven fabric of the early Mayan history. It was close to here that Steve and I paid our dues to Magnus for orchestrating our liberation from the local Policia all those years ago.' His wife Angelina, had been helping him with his studies and had accompanied him on many of his outings to the ruins. They were very much in love and had a daughter, who although quite young, accompanied them on their excursions.

The Ek-Balaam ruins were similar to most of the others in the area apart from the many alcoves and stalls and what some would consider for horses and mules. The great pyramid was a grand edifice that had at its crown, a small-courted area for a lookout. From its heights you could span the peninsula to the other sites in the area, Chichen-Itza being the most prominent.

Magnus had spent many of his scholarly years gleaning through the ruins and ancient texts to determine the true nature of 'Lord Balaam'. For most intents and purposes, the lord of Ek Balaam was not unusual and was, in folklore, considered one of the original four sons made by the Creator. There were several facts that intrigued Magnus, one of which was this individual never married as the others did, and also had the ability to command 'nature' at will (directing a gourd to bring forth bees that debilitated a throng of disgruntled subjects). Iqui-Balaam had traveled through the Quiche-Maya relatively unambiguously, remaining close to the other prolific brothers, who began to father nations, but in obscurity. The ancient text of the 'Popol Vuh' (not complete) records the lineage of the other three brothers, but not of Iqui-Balaam.

Magnus' studies took him worldwide to Ethiopia, the Middle East, Bosnia and other countries. He spent years trying to locate the sources of related folklore, along with the sources of foreign coins found in the Maya-ruins. He studied the texts of these civilizations in regard to the sacrificial ceremonies and the origins of the Canaanite god Baal. The evidence he gleaned began to point to a small group of individuals, or perhaps even one, who traveled from place to place throughout the world, bringing their sordid beliefs and ceremonies to an unsuspecting populace. These beings, through civil rebellion of their subjects, would eventually be routed and forced to relocate to another unsuspecting community hundreds, or thousands, of miles away. To an ignorant, subservient people, these individuals would appear as gods, perpetuating their awesome and grievous acts on naive people; if these were, as the Scriptures suggest 'fallen angels", then these would be immortal beings, having a wealth of knowledge that would far exceed anything known on earth. Only after the coming of individuals like Quetzacoatl (feathered serpent) from ancient Mexico, and the mysterious enlightened Cuculcan, often regarded as one and the same, was there any relief or teaching away from idol worship and sacrifice. It was through Magnus' inquisitiveness and initial publication of his findings, that he began to receive the threats to his life and that of his family. Unrelenting, he continued with his work and publications which unfortunately brought about the disappearance and eventual death of his wife. His daughter, who is now a physician, remained safe and the two of them, out of the country, pursued careers at a northern university only later to return to Central America, and for Magnus, to continue in the search for his wife's murderers.

Reaching forward to the front-edge of the chairs' arm, Magnus pulled himself forward to sit spread-kneed before the coffee table. His red-eyes scanned the surface noting the ashtray, half-empty rum bottle, and the now absent fifty dollars. Rubbing his eyes and running his fingers through his graying, thin hair, Magnus staggered to the small washroom that housed nothing more than a stained sink and a soiled toilet. The dripping tap spurted a few streams of brownish water before it released a clean, clear, usable flow. A wet towel hanging from a wall-hook attested to its use earlier that morning and was discarded to a pile of soiled linens in the corner. Water dripping from his face, Magnus re-entered the living room only to discover the remains of his wallet scattered over the bed where she had left them. A yellow, happy-face button and a ceramic-clay dildo were all that were left in the indentation where his companion had lain. A smile came to his face. He had enjoyed the company last night but not as much as meeting his daughter earlier after supper. The meeting with the Canadians, and then several hours with his daughter, had stirred emotions and concerns he had not felt for a while. His young friend of later that evening was nothing more than an attempt to return to a younger and perhaps more happier time; at least that was what the rum helped to convince him of.

The joyful shrill of a morning-bird brought him from his self-induced stupor and focused him on the task at hand, Belmopan.

Loading the few tools and papers he had hastily prepared into his vehicle, he turned to take a quick scan of the property to ensure he had forgotten nothing. The elderly lady from the house next-door peeked through the bars of his courtyard to bid him farewell. There were few people he could trust with his belongings; not that he would expect her to foil an intrusion to his property, but trusted her to do the right thing should there be an occurrence. Besides, Magnus was a bit of an oddity and an enigma to the people in the neighborhood. Some thought of him as an eccentric, old professor, others a crazy, old pervert, but regardless, he had the respect of the majority for his work with the local community.

The inclement weather of the night before had missed the area and had passed further west along the mountain range running from the south. Reports of downed trees and flooding in the low-lying, reclaimed areas would not affect the traveling to the capital. The roads leading from the southern suburbs were dry and Magnus left billowing clouds of dust in his wake as he drove hastily from their outskirts. The road to Belmopan was bumpy, but well paved, and the quickest. Magnus had thought of taking the back route, but this would have added several hours and he needed to get to his old friend Henry, at the office in Belmopan. There was an uncertainty he had felt when he considered a bowl that had been recovered in the northwest some months previous, and wondered whether there were a connection with the Canadians.

The bowl, he knew was of Olmec origin and had read the brief article in a scientific journal published only weeks previous, about its discovery at Ossette and its known history to date. The brief mention of a 'foreign group' lobbying for its release gave Magnus metered concern for the circumstances surrounding the artifacts repatriation, so obviously native to the area. He would run it by Henry.

It was later in the afternoon when Henry finally made it back to his office. The police had requested that he and his staff be made available for the search and rescue of an archaeologist who had become missing the previous night. Henry knew of the circumstances relating to her abduction but his staff was not, and was to accompany military personnel, more for protocol and ensuring the sites and surroundings were not roughshod with troops and gear. The search would begin in Belize, but would more than likely enter Guatemalan territory. Logistics would be left to the military that had the authority to enter Guatemala.

"Magnus!" Henry blurted on entering his upstairs office.

Magnus rose to his feet to take his friends hand. "Nice to see you again; it has been what, two years?"

"At least that," Henry replied, smiling from ear to ear.

He could see that the years had not been good to Magnus. His graying hair was slightly matted to his skull, and his eyes were dark and set deep within their sockets. His suit was wrinkled and worn at the elbows, but his dear friend still had the dignity to wear a tie even though the knot was no more than an attempt.

"It is a bit crazy around here at the moment. The military have requested, or should I say the Policia, that we accompany them on some excursions into the mountains along the border."

Magnus raised his brow but enquired of nothing.

"Apparently, there is a girl missing from the dig at Caracol. They think she was kidnapped, and I'm afraid I would have to agree. She is an American, the woman who was responsible for the Olmec bowl being brought back."

Magnus shifted in his seat, Henry noticing it, "Why what's up?" he asked.

"Well," Magnus started, taking a deep breath, "that's why I'm here."

Surprised, Henry took a seat across from his visitor and shook his head, "How do you do this?"

"Do what?"

"Always come into my office, somehow knowing what is going on when no-one else does."

Magnus returned a blank look, "All I know is some acquaintances have come a great distance to do some business, and am not all that sure they aren't involved in something that ultimately should include us."

"You know my friend, I almost lost my job and was threatened with deportation all those years ago in Mexico, and I have finally put all that behind me and have started to make a difference for the people and the industry in the area."

"Yes, I know Henry, and I will never be able to repay you for your kindness to me and my daughter after my wife passed away."

There were a few moments of silence as Henry got to his feet and reached for the stack of papers on his desk, "You see this Mag, I have two weeks work in my hands and a dozen more in the file cabinet over there, I would give it all up, job and all for a month in the jungle with you and a crew."

"Magnus smiled, 'Thanks, Henry, all I need is a little info on the bowl and the lobby group that wants it."

Henry busied himself with papers and said nothing for several moments then finally stated. "You know there have been several attempts to steal the bowl from the vault."

"Obviously, they were not successful."

"No, not so far, but they are persistent." He continued. "People are being paid off and there is no reason to believe it won't happen again."

"Any clues or suspicions Henry?" Magnus asked, getting up and walking to the window.

"No, not really. But there is an American businessman who has been floating around since the bowl's arrival. He keeps popping up at the weirdest places."

"Talking about popping up in the weirdest places; here are those acquaintances I was telling you about."

Henry skirted the desk and joined Magnus by the window just in time to see the two disappear along the sidewalk to the rear of the building. "Where are they from?"

"Canada," Magnus returned, "I met them in Mexico a number of years ago when I helped them with some problems in Valladolid. I helped them out and they in return did me a favor."

"Why don't you come down with me and"

"No," Magnus protested, "I do not wish to see them at this time. It is best they do not know I am here."

"Well, I best go down and see to them. There is no-one tending the offices, and I am the only one available"

Henry disappeared out the door, his steps echoing through the hollow stairwell; Magnus continued staring contemplatively out the window.

Magnus watched with solicitude from behind the tinted glass as the Canadians retreated to their car and ducked out of sight just in time not to be spotted by an army helicopter that appeared over the rooftops. It precariously swung and hovered in the air before landing on a grassy knoll not a hundred yards from the parking lot. Magnus patiently watched as the passengers disembarked and proceeded to approach the rear of the building. Amused, he watched, as Brian and Steve, stayed motionless behind their vehicle to avoid notice by the entourage. Still giggling from their predicament, Magnus was startled by the appearance and vague recollection of the businessman that anteceded the Military Officer. He too began to wonder where to appropriately disappear, not out of fear, but with realization that the information that this man knew would flow more easily with fewer ears to listen. Henry was a good friend, but Magnus did not wish to jeopardize or compromise their relationship, at least not openly.

Magnus cold hear a brief conversation being held in the open stairway, and then after, several doors opening and closing. Footsteps came once again clamoring up the stairwell and Henry entered the room like a whirlwind.

"Would you like to come with me Mag?" Henry

asked without looking up from his dutiful hands as they gleaned the clutter of paperwork on his desk, "You might find the debriefing interesting."

"No, I don't think so," Magnus replied without taking his eyes from the Canadians as they slowly drove from the parking lot below. His mind drifted to the rear of another car, some eighteen years earlier, and the dust cloud it left behind as it sped away; his wife's fearful and teary face darting back and forth between the shoulders of her captors as she strained to see from the window her beaten husband left for dead.

"Waite a minute Henry, maybe I will, but can I just listen-in without being noticed?"

"I suppose so Mag. But why?" he questioned, as they prepared to enter the stairway.

"One of the fellows was an associate of mine from a few years back, and let's just say, if I were there the conversation would be muted."

Henry shrugged his shoulders while Magnus held the door for him.

"I'll fill you in over dinner later."

"OK!" Henry returned, taking the lead down the stairs. "You slip in there," pointing to an enclosed area backing onto the offices beyond. "You should be able to hear it all from there."

"Thanks, Henry," Magnus murmured as he disappeared behind the door.

"Heh, Mag," Henry whispered, with his mouth close to the closed door, "I'll see you at eight. I'm in the book."

Magnus sat quietly and waited in the dark for the briefing to begin. His mind began to wander to events he wished would stay unremembered.

The suns' rays beat down hard as Angelina carried the water jugs to the cool of the alcove close to where they worked. Felicia had been left for the day with the neighbor two doors down from their apartment, who also had children. Magnus and Angelina loved Felicia with them, but understood it was equally important for her to interact with other children her own age, so it was convenient on all accounts to leave her once in a while to play as a child instead of a budding preschool archaeologist.

Magnus had just picked up the few chards of clay findings extracted from the overlay of the terrace half way up the temple face when he noticed a cloud of thick dust pluming up above the tall grass that lined the long laneway into the dig. The road was at the best of times unnavigable at any speed, and at mid-day he was not expecting visitors. Thinking of the chance something may have happened to Felicity, he dropped his tools and descended the awkwardly steep stairs that led to the grassy courtyard below. Approaching the area where Angelina was preparing their lunch, he could see two men rummaging through his personal belongings while Angelina sat crouched down on the ground beneath a man that towered above her; a large, black car sat idle some distance in the background, its rear window down several inches alluding to scrutinized proceedings. Walking from Angelina and into the alcove where the coolness sheltered their perishables, the one fellow began to throw the water cans and ice packs from with-in. Realizing they were there to do harm, he screamed and ran toward the intruders. Being a slight man, he was no match for the assaults that were wielded upon him and with a severity that left him unconscious and bleeding. Barely able to move when he awakened in the hot afternoon sun, he turned his head and watched as the rear of the black sedan disappeared in a cloud of dust. Magnus strained to lift his head and was able to catch a glimpse of his wife's face in the rear window just before they disappeared.

When he came to once again, he was able to roll over and drag himself to the alcove that had once housed the foodstuffs for the day. Prying open a canteen of water, he brought it to his lips and swirled its cool contents in his mouth and spewed out the pinkish fluid. His lips were swollen and cracked, and hurt when he once again brought the canteen to his mouth. He drank deep and rested his aching head on the cool limestone wall behind him. He looked down to his swollen, dislocated knee and plied his surely broken ribs, wondered who would perpetrate such an attack and why. His fist was frozen in a half closed position, bloody from a knife slash that nearly opened an artery. Protruding from between his fingers was a bone, or at least what he thought was a bone. Spilling drops of precious water from the tin, he watched as the blood dripped away to reveal a colorful plume of a Macaw. It was confusing to see such an oddity at first, but as he began to comprehend the implications, he began to cry. Unable to move his swollen and broken body, he could think of only one thing, saving Felicia, and then he passed-out again.

The morning brought the sun and the end to a restless, pain-filled night. With more strength, he was able to shuffle himself along on his wrists to the edge of the clearing near the ruins. The little Austin, that had been his first car since college, was almost a half mile away and remained untouched by the assailants.

Magnus felt that if he could make it to the vehicle, he would somehow be able to drive. It took over an hour to crawl to the little car but once he was there, he was unable to use his damaged hands to pull the chromed lever to unlock the door. Exhausted, he rested with his back to the car door and the blood that had covered his hands now streaked the light turquoise paint. The sun began to sting his already scorched flesh. The canteen he had dragged with him had somehow lost its lid, and the contents gone. Magnus no longer had the strength to return to the shelter of the alcove. Defeated, he rested and listened to the buzz of life in the grassy lands surrounding him. He fainted.

After what seemed an eternity of sleep and agony, "Magnus" echoed in his ears. Was he hearing things?

"Magnus!"

Lifting his head and squinting from his swollen, dry eyes, he could barely make-out the familiar face of his good friend and colleague. "Henry," gasped from his lips.

"Magnus!"

There came a gentle tap on the door.

"They're here, buddy."

Magnus leaned himself comfortably against the wall in the closet and emotionally steadied himself from the dream he had just had. Feeling uneasy at the predicament of his surroundings, he encouraged himself that this was the right thing to do. Reaching in his pocket, he silenced his cellular, it was always better to be on the safe side.

The conversations were faint but audible.

## *Dia tres, al final de (day 3 evening)*

Belmopan was no audacious place. It was quaint with paved roads and few sidewalks. No high-rise buildings blocked the rolling vista that crested with low mountains to the south and evaded to meadows and slow-moving creeks to the north. A large, playing field in the middle of town was center-stage to a variety of events and celebrations. The main street circumvented the main body of the town and made navigation quite easy apart from the lack of readable street signs, especially at night. By the time Magnus had found the austere bungalow along Trio Street, it was quite dark and passed 8:30.

"Hello, my friend," as Henry opened wide the door to allow Magnus to pass.

Magnus brushed by his friend with a warm hand gesture and removed his shoes to an alcove in the wall. The tiled foyer opened up into a large, sunken, living area with wall-to-ceiling windows that faced an open valley. A small number of lights below signified the scant population of farmers in the area..

"You have a beautiful view," commented Magnus as he found a place to sit amongst the paper-laden chairs and couches.

"Yes, thanks," he replied, gathering up enough paper-works to find a seat for himself. "Let's have a drink, shall we."

Magnus winched slightly at the thought of it, but before he could refuse, not that he would have, Henry handed him a glass of dark rum, ginger and ice.

"Did you get much of what was said this afternoon?" Henry asked."

"Well not as much as I would have liked to, but tell me about the American? I recognize him, but cannot remember the exact circumstance of our meeting."

"He is the businessman I alluded to before in my office, who has been turning up in odd places in connection with the Olmec Bowl." Henry stated. "He was implicated in a looting incident a while back, but was acquitted."

"I remember that." Magnus replied, taking a sip of rum. "Do you think he is the one trying to steal it? It would be a nice prize."

"I can't be sure mate, but he's right there with whoever it is, and he certainly has enough money and pull. Since the bowl has made its way to the archives though, things have settled down."

Magnus crossed his legs and took a gulp of his drink. "And what about the girl?"

"The girl is a Native American from the north," Henry replied. "The British do not want the Yanks interfering with the delicate balance of political power should the troops have to enter Guatemala. But then again, the kidnap victim is an American; the Embassy will insist on the full co-operation and involvement of some US Forces. The American, I guess his name is Doug, Doug Baldwin, suggested the temporary alternative of a grace period to allow the ground forces already in place, time to search and recover the girl."

"And what do you think Henry?"

"It really doesn't matter what I think. The American insisted that it was appropriate for such a request." Henry's voice lowered in pitch when he stated the fact. "I suggested the American Consulate be informed and to stand ready should there be a request made for a ransom."

"Do you really think they want to give her up?"

Magnus asked.

"I'm sure they want something," Henry affirmed.

That statement caught Magnus's attention. "What did you mean by that? Do you know that there will be a request?"

"I'm no fool Mag, and either are you. Just because the bodies are rarely found, does not mean the ancient rites are not still practiced. We have seen the signs."

"Henry, can you get me a private meeting with this Doug? Magnus requested. "I know this guy from somewhere." Henry nodded in affirmation. "It might be twenty years, and another country, but I recognize him."

Henry's intuition warned him of the emotion Magnus had for this man, but Mag was his friend. Hesitating for several moments watching the doctor's cool, blank stare, Henry finally released, "Of course I can."


Just then a short, native woman with graying hair entered the room by the kitchen and brought a basket of bread to set on the table. Startled by the intrusion, Magnus put his drink down and put his feet firmly on the floor.

"It's OK Mag," Henry blurted almost spilling his drink. "She's my house-keeper, Elisa. She has been with me for years," fondly looking over to her. "We are quite close."

Magnus eased his mood, relaxed back in the chair and picked up his drink again.

"Sorry Mag, I forgot how sensitive you were to uninvited guests, whoever they might be."

"It's OK Henry; I'm a bit shaken up. These Canadians, and this American, have rattled me with their presence, and it has brought the past flooding back to me in such force that I have not felt this anguish since the death of my wife."

"I understand Magnus, I'll help you as long as you promise me one thing." Magnus looked up. "That when all this is over, you help me to recover as much of my career as can be salvaged."

Magnus dipped his head as if remembering the past.

"Come-on Mag, let's eat."

# SIX

*Dia dos (day two)*

Amalia awoke late in the morning face down on the pillow. She was naked from the waist down, legs spread wide; her right hand was nestled in her groin. She perspired slightly from the closeness of the room; there was no ventilation; the drapes had been drawn closed. Thoughtfully, she rolled over to stare at the ceiling, reflecting on what had or had not happened the night before. Amalia's body hummed, but she could not determine whether the feeling was residual of the previous night's drug abuse, sexual arousal, or both. She thought for several moments but could not bring to mind the man belonging to the face she had last seen in her room the previous night. Bewildered and frustrated, she replaced her hand and tightly squeezed her thighs together enjoying the release of tension. She fell back asleep.

Late in the evening there came a knock on the door.

"What do you want?" she screamed. Her voice

muffled from beneath the pillow.

"Si, Amalia." came a low, male voice. "It is Juan."

"Go away!" she returned, throwing a pillow at the closed door.

"Senior Doug is on da phone for jou. He has been trying to reach jou all mornin."

"What does that bastard want? To apologize for another night he didn't show up!"

"Please Senorita, you must talk to him."

Amalia got up from the bed and stormed to the door. Opening it quickly, she grabbed the cellular from Juan, "Leave me alone, you bastard, she yelled into the phone. "You did it again to me last night, and I have had it with you leaving me with this lackey you call a bodyguard."

She threw the phone at Juan, the culprit, and attempted to close the door behind her.

"You take that foot of yours out of the door, or Doug will get an earful of what you did last night."

"But Senorita, I meant no harm, just to make you happy."

"Get the hell outta here, "she screamed, throwing a towel and slamming the door. Locking it and replacing the bolt, she crawled back to the bed and covered herself lightly with the sheet.

In the early years, Doug had showered her with gifts and money, but now all she could think of was how wrong it had all gone. The abuse she had received from Juan when she was barely twelve years old, was foremost on her mind. She had been physically mature and beautiful for her age, although naive. Amalia was thankful to Juan for the attention he gave her and removing her from the poverty she experienced with her family. He had promised her clothes and an education in the big city and relished the attention flouted on her by his friends, but it was not long before his attentions turned to ulterior motives, and then came the favors he would ask her to do for the men he brought home. Juan had beaten her once, and that was all it took to be convinced that the occasional playful hour with a drunken stranger was better than losing the one asset that would get her from this bondage, her looks. He had continued to keep her in drugs and money; it helped to mask the mixed feelings she had for her life.

One evening, Juan brought back an Americano, who had previously been quite enamored with her and offered to take care of her. Juan adamantly opposed, and the men accompanying this handsome, older man, helped persuade Juan of the opportunities that would open up for him, should he agree. She watched in glee while they continually encouraged him for an hour until an agreement was reached. Amalia had the impression that Doug, the Americano, was not desirous of a relationship with Juan any longer, but was convinced by Juan that the antiques, gleaned from the local forests would not be so readily available should he not be there to mediate. A deal was struck and Juan would continue, but now as an associate, of sorts, to keep an eye on local business proceedings. Doug had friends in the Government of Belize, that could pull many strings; including the one around Juan's neck should he have rebellious thoughts. Juan would solicit Amalia's services from time to time, but to no avail; she would play with him. He still found her very attractive and would use the drugs in an attempt to have his way with her. She hated Juan for what he had done to her, but had pity for what she considered a lost, lonely soul. Everything in the triad was kept functioning as long as she played the game with Doug, but, she was at her wits-end with both of them. She took care of herself, as best she could with Doug's money and dressed in the finest clothes he bought for her, but she wanted more, a future. She was tired of the drugs and partying, the gaps in her memory, and all the men's faces that drifted in and out of her mind; and now there was one more.

A slight thud on the door stirred her from sleep. The lights from the walkway outside the door silhouetted the figure that entered the room. Barely awake, she swung her legs to touch her feet to the carpeted floor.

"Why did you not call me back? I have been worried about you all night." Doug's voice was low with no hint of rebuke.

Amalia said nothing as he closed the door and approached the bed where she sat. Easing himself beside her, he sat motionless and watched the faint sparkle in her eyes that darted back and forth as she searched his for the reason of his inconsideration. She was quick to raise her hand against his face, but his hand caught her wrist and forced it to her side. Again, she raised the other hand in retaliation, but he caught it and forced it down to the bed, inclining Amalia at the same time. She forced her knee up to meet his groin, but he was able to deflect it. She was helpless as he nestled his face down into the crevice of her neck and shoulder; he gently kissed.

"You bastard," Amalia protested, as the sensation brought shivers to her body. She giggled aloud in response to his continued impetus. She struggled to get free from his grip but the attempts exposed her vulnerability. He pressed himself against her nakedness.

### *Dias tres (day 3)*

A sharp knock on the door woke them early from a deep sleep.

"Who is it?" Doug shouted, releasing himself from Amalia's embrace and grabbing for the gun he kept close in his jacket.

"Juan, Senor Doug."

"Just a minute!" Doug responded, pulling a sheet to cover himself and proceeded to the door.

"What is it Juan?"

"There has been trouble Senor, in the jungle."

"Why, what's happened?"

"The girl," he whispered. "The girl, she escaped."

"What!" Doug returned, opening the door to allow him in.

"Si, Senor. The girl has gotten away."

Doug closed the door behind Juan and leaned up against the wall to consider the news' implication. Juan's eyes scouted the room and came to rest on Amalia's half exposed body on the bed. He continued to look her way until Doug's attention turned full back to him.

"Change of plan," he declared quietly under his breath looking over to Amalia.

"We talked about the woman at the museum, remember?"

"Si Senor. It will be difficult."

"Take one of the new figurines and use it as bate to get her from the museum. Tell her we have several items she may be interested in, including a butterfly."

"Ok! I'll do my best."

"No!" You will do it."

Doug let Juan out through the door and proceeded to the shower. Amalia could hear the water as it splashed in waves against the walls of the enclosure. Her eyes darted back and forth as she considered what she had just heard and the affects it could have on her life.

She pretended to sleep on, but Doug turned to her as he donned his clothes, "I will send for you later. We will be spending some time in Belmopan."

Amalia grunted a reply in recognition, and went back to sleep.

Juan's light, brown van blew plumes of bluish smoke as he drove through the cramped streets of the old quarter of Belize City. He was having a difficult time deciding on whether to enter the museum, or wait in the parking lot. The gate to the parking lot was attended, but knew from previous outings that the guard left the gate open while he did the rounds of Government buildings. If he could get to the clerk during this time frame, the kidnapping could be possible.

"Museum," Juan stated to the guard who flagged him by. He pulled passed the checkpoint and around to the far side of the tiny, two-story museum.

Taking the small, leather pouch from the glove box, he unwrapped the contents to view a small, clay, stylized figurine. The little man had a plume that emanated from the top of his head and a large belly that protruded from above his folded feet. It was one of Juan's favorites, acquired from a dig several years back. It would do the job nicely.

There had been no one at the entrance to greet him, so he slowly walked to the stairwell. Not knowing which way to go, he chose up the stairs to the exhibits, watching for Maria along the way. From the top of the stairs, he could see down the long, exhibit hallway to an open door. There, as he'd hoped, Maria could be seen walking back and forth through the opening, carrying papers and boxes.

"Buenos dias, Senorita," Juan announced, entering the room.

"Well, hello!" replied Maria, surprised, not expecting visitors. "I do not believe we are open yet. Was there no-one down at reception?"

"No there wasn't, but it is you I wished to speak to," Juan answered with a quiver in his voice. He looked at her full breasts and shapely hips and felt delight at the prospects of the abduction.

"It really should wait till later," she replied, returning to her duties. "I am just about to leave."

"No wait, please!" Juan insisted. "I have something that may be of interest to you," reaching for the leather purse in his jacket pocket.

"May I be of assistance to you sir?" came a voice from just outside the door.

Startled, Juan slipped the purse back in his pocket and turned to face an unfamiliar, security guard.

"Well, no thank you." He turned to Maria, "may I contact you later?"

"Perhaps, but you must make an appointment if you wish to submit a piece."

"Thank you, miss," Juan responded. "I will return later."

Frustrated, Juan retreated down the hallway to the

stairs with the guard close behind.

Bewildered as to how to accomplish the deed at hand, he sat in the van and watched as the seagulls danced and sallied on the sea breeze that whisked its way through the maze of buildings surrounding the parking lot. The guard from the gatehouse slowly walked the perimeter of the lot and disappeared into one of the buildings. Taking the leather pouch from his jacket, he opened the side door of the van and placed the figurine, along with the bag, propped on the wipers of the sporty, compact next door. Sitting with his feet on the ground, he pondered his next move.

Five minutes had not passed, when he heard the familiar sound of high-heels on the walkway close to the van. Squeezing by the open van door, Maria stopped, surprised to see the package on her windscreen.

"Interesting isn't it?" Juan interjected, startling Maria.

"Where did you get this?" she questioned, easing further around the open door.

"Not so far from here. Would you like to see more?"

"No thanks!" feeling uncomfortable with his reply.

"May I have it back please?" Juan asked.

Wanting nothing to do with it, Maria reached out to hand him back the piece, when all of a sudden he grabbed her arm with great force. Swinging hard with her free hand to strike him, she grazed the top of his head and lost balance. Taking advantage of the move, Juan dragged her into the van. Pulling as hard as she could, Maria's footing slipped and she fell hitting her head on the sill of the van. Seizing the moment, he grabbed her hair with both hands and pulled her in.

With one quick blow, Maria was unconscious. For several moments, she lay motionless, but when she came-to she was lying on the pavement between the two vehicles. Inside the van, the young guard was overpowering Juan, holding him down to subdue him. Grabbing the nearest thing he could, Juan struck out. A short screwdriver wedged between the guards ribs. Falling back in pain out of the open doors, the young man tripped over Maria and fell against her car. Juan, taking advantage of the break in momentum, jumped into the van's front seat, started the engine and drove over the grass to the open driveway. The tires screeched on the hot pavement and the doors flailed back and forth as he sped out the exit and down the narrow street. Unable to respond quickly, Maria and the guard gathered themselves; the young man pulled the stubby screwdriver from his side and noted the bloodstained shaft. No one in the area had noticed the mishap; no one came to their aid. Getting to her feet, Maria put her arm around the man and they both limped down the walkway and into the cool of the museum. Downstairs, in the office, they dialed for help.

Panicking, Juan sped from the downtown area and out passed the city limits to a familiar spot in the mangrove forests. Sitting a short distance from the road, well hidden in the dense underbrush, he sat in the makeshift hut he had escaped to from time to time. Amalia was familiar with this place; he would bring her here to get her drunk, stoned and have his way. He was frantic in his mood and considered what could be done to ease the dilemma. Cracking open a bottle of rum, he sat and contemplated his next move. He would ditch the van and make his way to Belmopan to kill Doug, this was all his fault; or better still, kill Doug, find Amalia and run away. He dug for his gun beneath a stack of soiled burlap bags. He reasoned to keep the van for now, his only mode of transportation. He knew Belmopan would be the next stop. The message earlier to Doug, about the escaped girl in the jungle alluded to ample opportunities to do the deed. He needed a foolproof plan.

Grabbing the half bottle of rum, Juan climbed into the old van and turned on to the highway heading west toward the mountains.

It must have been mid-morning when a sharp rap came on Amalia's door.

"Who is it?" she requested from the bathroom.

"Jose, from room service."

"I didn't order anything."

"Si, Senorita. I have been asked to order a cab for jou."

"Oh. OK!" she returned. "Uno momento."

"Si, Senorita. I will wait for jou."

Amalia gathered a few things and her small, luggage bag and opened the door. She slowly passed Jose and gave him a concerted look, "Were you in my room the other night?"

"No, Senorita," he affirmed, his temperature rising slightly.

"Are you sure?" giving him a second look.

"Si, Senorita."

She fluffed it off. "Ok, let's go."

"Si," replied Jose, picking up her bags to follow.

Out front of the Hotel, he placed her in the cab.

# SEVEN

## Dai Uno, por la tarde, (day one, evening) (Edmundo)

The road out of Caracol, was a disaster of rocks and potholes; racing as fast as he could, Edmundo steered frantically to avoid the obstacles that would ultimately end up with a bent rim or a busted ty-rod end. All Edmundo could think was Shawna; time was of the essence. He had been given the task of caring for Shawna, by the Ministry of Tourism by direct order from the National Forensic Science Service. The Department of Archaeology, had been involved with encouragement from the Director of Antiquities, so with the outstanding pedigree of command, he was in deep do-do.

Edmundo had trained with the Belize Defense Force, and had spent over a year with a special British ops-team making forays into Honduras, down to the border of El-Salvador. Media exposure to victimized civilians during one of their covert missions, created irreversible, collateral damage and an ill-feeling for the work that was going on, so he felt the time was right to leave the force with anonymity instead of disgrace. Archaeology, and collecting artifacts had been a boyhood hobby he shared with his sister Maria, that continued through to college; she now worked with the ministry in Belize City. With these credentials, Edmundo became the prime candidate for this cushy appointment of securing Ms. Brook's safety.

With Edmundo's mind clicking into operation's mode, options began to pop into his head; the one most realistic, under the circumstances, was of his companeros in special-ops, that was, if they were still working the area. If he could make it to Makah Bank, close to the Mountain Pine Training Area, within two hours in this weather, and locate their field command, he may be able to elicit more assistance from the specialized group; if he couldn't find them, another hour to San Ignacio, with few options left, he would need to talk personally with friends at the Defense Force in Belize City.

The time it took to get to Spanish Water Hole, was relatively quick, but the changing terrain with more severe up-thrusts to the foothills of the Mayan Mountains, and less travelled, winding roads drastically slowed progress. Entering Makah Bank from the south-west was like entering a maze. Further up the Bank, there had been more civilian developments and better roads to facilitate tourism, but in this area where the military staged outings, it was still pretty secluded. Trying several times on the field radio, he was not able to raise a response. Slowing and doing short forays up several, familiar ravines also showed no signs of occupation and concluded in this rain, it would be like finding 'a pottery chard in an acre tell'. San Ignacio, and a land-line telephone, was the next plan of action.    Edmundo had suspicions that the abductors had no intention of taking Shawna into Guatemala, but right here, not too far distant. If he was right, and the celestial planets were lining up, the time would be right for another ceremony. He considered consulting a  Doctor of  Archaeology, he had met in college, a bit off the wall, but the doctor believed in the continuance, not reemergence, of the Jaguar Cult; it was from this man that Edmundo had developed a keen eye for artifacts and also the desire to be able to protect ones' self, and their family.

San Ignacio, a small town, was situated just east of the Guatemala border. At this time of night, even though the rain had stopped, navigating the slippery streets that terraced the north side of the town would be tricky. The streets followed no particular grid and led, at one time or another, to one of two bridges that crossed the river eastward to Santa –Elena, and on to Belmopan. Edmundo had frequented a local hotel called the Aguada, and befriended the American owner and his Belizean wife. At this time of night, he was hoping his friendship would hold firm.

Banging softly on the front door to the restaurant of the inn, he hoped only to waken the Butlers and not their guests. Luck would have it, Jackson was in his office just off to the left down a short hallway leading to the ground floor rooms and pool. He did not have to knock twice, a tall figure of a man of middle age sallied through the dining tables to the glazier, front door.

A muffled barrage of metaphors could be heard as he played with locks just on the other side, "What in blazes do you think," then stopped short. "Edmund!"

Jack spurted. "What on earth are you doin here? Come in! Come in!"

Edmundo swept inside and stopped short, "I need a huge favor Jack. There has been a girl kidnapped from the Caracol dig. I believe they are making their way close to here, and I need to use your telephone."

"Sure, sure, but you look terrible. Can I get you some coffee?"

"That would be great." Edmundo replied.

"You know where it is," Jack directed to the telephone.

Edmundo gave a nod and turned left into the overcrowded, cramped office of the Aguada.

"Sure you wouldn't like something a little stronger?"

Without a word, Edmundo dialed some numbers and after several minutes was only able to leave a message on one.

"Rats!" retorted Edmundo, as he reentered the dining room. To the right stood the long, drink service bar with Jack at the far end by the patio door, preparing the coffee. "Perhaps I'll have a shot of rum."

"Sounds good to me," Jackson poured two.

### Dai dos (day 2)

The morning light came early as Edmundo jerked awake from a deep sleep. Being convinced by Jack that a few hours' sleep would do him no harm; the rum eased his racing brain long enough to shut down for several hours. The bed covers had hardly wrinkled under his weight on the firm mattress. Splashing some tepid water on his face and rinsing the film from his mouth down the drain, he grabbed his light leather jacket and silently left the room. Passing the palms that overshadowed the open pool, and the large thatch covered dining hut, he exited through the steel gate, careful not to let it clang. The only soul to bid him farewell was a restful iguana warming himself in the early morning sun; the roosters had already performed their early morning arias.

Within the hour, Edmundo had passed the Hummingbird-Highway-turnoff for Belmopan and contemplated a visit to the ministry, but considered what little could be accomplished by the bureaucracy and without more thought continued on the Western Highway. The good doctor would be his first bet for starters, and if he made good time he could be Belize City for brunch; the second, some commando friends.

Magnus's front gate which led to the stone steps to his upper floor rooms was ajar. Edmundo could faintly hear the singing of a women coming from up above. Confident in knowing Magnus would not object, he climbed the stairs and entered the open area and looked about. The woman's voice emanated from the kitchen at the rear of the apartment. The work desk was cluttered with papers and drawings of stelae; clay figurines lay chipped and scattered.

"Hello!" he yelled, vying for attention.

A middle-aged woman appeared in the doorway, startled by the intrusion. "What can I do for you?"

"Oh, I'm looking for Mag. I phoned earlier but did not get an answer, so I dropped by to say hello. Any idea when he will return?"

"No," she replied. "He is in and out all the time. I never know when he returns or when he goes. I hear his gate open and close. I don't know whether he is coming or going. He does not…"

"Thank you," stopping her in mid-sentence. "I will

drop by later."

By the time Edmundo got to the museum close to Eve Street, lunch-hour was over and Maria was still not back. Sitting patiently in his pickup, he watched the pedestrian traffic pass the entrance way leading to the guard house. Eventually, a bouncy, well-endowed brunette in high-heels struggled up the incline past the gate-house. The guard leaned out the window with a smile on his face, "Hi Maria," and watched as her buttocks and full thighs wrestled beneath the fabric of her tight, black, knee-length skirt.

"Hi sis," Edmundo chanted from behind the wheel of his truck.

Startled, Maria turned and lifted her sunglasses with glee, "Mundie!" She toddled the few yards to where he was and stuck her head through the open window to give him a kiss.

"What on earth are you doing here?" she asked surprised. "Weren't you just in Caracol?"

"I drove almost all night to get here," he stated, climbing from behind the wheel and slamming the door. "Is there anywhere we can talk?"

"Sure, follow me. My office is downstairs."

The coolness in the basement of the new, museum addition was welcome as they made small-talk about family matters and the need to get together more often. Closing the door behind him, Edmundo asked whether the fellow from Canada had returned.

"Well, as a matter of fact, I have just come from seeing him at the Royal Reef. I did as you asked and found out a few more things about him and, well, he's not a doctor. He just said that to try and get me to tell him what I knew about Shawna, which was nothing," tilting her head sideways in thought. "But I did tell him there was a chance she could be in several different sites."

"You didn't tell him that she…" Edmundo stopped Maria short.

"No, no, no, that she was with you?" Maria interjected.

"Well, she's not anymore." He said with head hung low. "She was kidnapped from the site yesterday. The Military are out trying to get on the trail, but I don't think they'll have much luck without some further help. I've been trying to get a hold of Dr. Magnus without much luck."

"Is he that archaeologist that lost his wife all those years ago and went kinda, nuts?"

"Well yeah, but he's not nuts, just a bit eccentric. He knows more about Mayan anthropology than anyone in the area, which is why I need to see him and Man Ocho. I need to get hold of Ocho; he will know where some of the guys are."

She thought for a moment, "I think he's dating a new girl, a dancer working at the Tigris."

"Thanks sis," he motioned to get up and leave. "I have another favor to ask."

"What is it?"

"Could you put me up for the night? If I get stuck with Ocho and the guys, I'll never make it back to Santa Elena tomorrow, a least not in one piece."

"Sure." she replied. "I can put up with you for one night."

"Thanks Sis, by the way, what happened to your arm?"

"Oh," looking down at the slight bruise at the crease of her elbow. "I donated blood a few weeks ago. Does it look that bad?"

"No. It's just that Shawna had the same thing done a while back, a letter in the mail about a shortage of blood."

Then Maria thought for a minute, "Yeah, and then a funny, little man with glasses came a few days later and asked if I'd heard about the shortage. I just went to the clinic he suggested and thought nothing of it."

"Odd," Mundie asserted walking toward the door. "I'll catch you later."

Club Tigris was a wild sort of place. The patronage was younger and reflected the more affluent class of Belizeans that decided to go slumming for the night. There were some drugs, but mostly alcohol was the intoxicant of choice, which flowed abundantly. The interior décor was reminiscent of the many previous owners that had occupied the building. Spanish stucco, adorned with Caribe murals accented with pottery shards and clay figurines, lined the walls. A bamboo canopy over the bold, garish, mahogany bar remnant of years of British influence, was tucked far on the back wall; an ethnic variety of patrons perched on tall, bamboo, steel re-enforced stools adorned its perimeter.

The British Army contingency had commandeered the Tigris as its own with a few Belize Defenses intermingling in the crowd to add some local flavor. The Belizean girls were beautiful, with Spanish, native Creole and black mixed together to make a long, shapely, seductive, irresistible, mocha desert that few could refuse. The fair skinned, British and American girls that found themselves here, were in short supply and never long without someone vying for their attention. Scantily clad, bronze, slippery dancers dotted the bar area encouraging patrons to the open floors to dance and mingle; they kept the atmosphere alive till the wee hours of the morning.

At the bar sat a broad-shouldered, fair-haired, muscular, young man with his back to the festivities. Strategically placed in front of glass shelves with a mirror behind that reflected all who entered and left the establishment, he watched. It was not his job, it was what he was trained to do; by nature, he sized everyone up to determine 'shield or friend', with zero tolerance to anyone who did not obey the unspoken code of conduct. Passing-out, stone drunk was acceptable.

Man Ocho was a special-ops member of the elite 'Jungle Jedi, renowned for their skill in close hand-to-hand combat and forays into the hostile jungles of a number of countries. The girls he knew and dated, gave him the nickname Ocho for his 'special-ops' equipment. Not restricted to the discipline of fidelity, he usually kept his girlfriends for only months at a time and moved on when things got too possessive. Mundie, (Edmundo's nickname) got to know Ocho while serving together in the Jungles of Honduras on the lookout for Contra Rebels near the Salvadorian border. Ocho was cool-headed and had the ability to execute operations and strike in a quick, orderly fashion with no trace and little, collateral damage. Respect for his years of service and skill, had shown up in his record with commendation and no casualties under his command section; a great feat under extraordinary circumstances. If anyone would be able to find Shawna and her abductors, it would be Ocho.

Edmundo talked briefly with Ocho at the bar, the two retreated to a less audibly, intrusive area of the club to drink beer and strategize.

"You know we have no mandate to do this

Mundie." Ocho argued, taking a sip of his beer.

"I know, but some of the guys are already on the hunt, a least I think they are. A Gazelle flew over the area before I left, and I could swear I saw part of the team."

"You're probably right. Some of the guys are on a training run in the western mountains. I'm not sure who the commander is; Gizmo should be there, but I can go to Price Barracks and try to dig up some info." Ocho thought for a moment and grabbed up his beer. "I'm owed a few favors," he announced, with a sly grin from one corner of his mouth while he strained a sip of beer through the other.

"I'll see you in the morning." Edmundo sighed, grateful for his friend's involvement.

### *Dia tres (day 3)*

The noise and traffic along Albert Street, was exceptionally loud for a Thursday morning. The sun was noticeably higher in the sky than he would have liked. Realizing he had slept late, Edmundo reached for the clock temporarily placed on the coffee table in front of the couch and read, "8:30." The beer from the night before, and two days of nearly no sleep had caught up with him; he was getting soft. Reaching for his cell, he flapped it open to see if any messages had been sent; none. Grabbing his duffle bag, he rummaged through till he found his toothpaste and a change of underwear and socks; the rest would have to wait. Splashing some water over his face and running his wet fingers through his hair, Edmundo ran down the stairs of the quaint, centuries-old, second story apartment building to the bustling street below. His blue, pickup truck had remained untouched for the night and threw his bag into the passenger's seat. Wheeling around the corner, he headed down toward Haulover Creek and then over to the museum. Within ten minutes, Edmundo was entering the lane to the museum and was confronted with a lineup of cars and a small crowd of people. An ambulance and several foot-patrol Police were blocking the way and helped to direct the cars and pedestrians away from the area. Parking the pickup as close to the museum as the traffic would allow, he edged his way, by foot, to the security gate and the officer inside. Recognizing Edmundo, the security guard waved Edmundo through and then gave the police guard a nod in approval. Allowed to pass, he entered the rear of the building and down the stairs to the offices below. Outside Maria's office stood a plain-clothed officer who barred him from entering.

"I'm Edmundo DelaCruz, Maria's brother." He flashed his Ministry badge and looked toward the attending officer in the room. The police Sergeant noticing Maria's motion of recognition, looked at the officer by the door, and nodded for Edmundo to enter.

"What happened?" Edmundo quarried, as he walked by the young, museum security guard on the gurney, to Maria waiting on a chair.

Maria's face was scratched and bruised, her knuckles raw from contact with a rough pavement or object. "We were attacked," she said emphatically. "If it hadn't been for Romi," nodding to the young man wrapped about the ribs with gauze, "I would be gone, Lord knows where."

Mundie looked toward the young man with a nod of appreciation, "Thanks."

In like, Romi nodded in return.

"Did these guys try and take you?" Mundie asked.

"He offered to sell me a figurine, and when I said no, he left and waited for me in the parking lot. He forced me into his van and punched me." Tears started to well up in her now distraught face.

"Don't talk about it now sis. Are they taking you to the hospital?" Edmundo quarried.

"Yeah, I guess so."

Mundie squeezed her hand gently and kissed her cheek. "I have to get back to Santa Elena, and find out what is going on." With that, he hurried by the guard officer and another onlooker by the door, out into the street above and back to his pickup. He had to get in touch with Ocho, and find-out what he'd come up with; trying him on the cell, there was nothing. Pulling out into the pedestrian traffic, he turned and headed west toward Haulover Bridge and the Western Highway.

Once over the other side, his cell chimed, "Mundie? Ocho. We've got some intel on a camp in the Mountain Ridge that was recently deserted."

"Great!" Mundie replied.

"The trail leads deeper into the jungle. Satellite shows two light vehicles there two days ago; they're working on make and model; should have more later today. I've contacted a couple of guys. We have a go, but keep it discrete. I'll meet you at Jack's." The signal went dead.

Slightly relieved, Edmundo pulled over to an ABM machine, pulled some cash and headed in the store for supplies.

In one of the rooms on the upper floor of the Aguada, Ocho had laid out several, aerial maps on the bed. Smaller, satellite photos pinpointing the target camp were being passed around to several other participants waiting patiently in the room. A final determination would be made shortly. All were dressed in civilian clothes, with their togs and kit in duffle bags skirting the perimeter of the room. Mundie wore the standard issue kaki of the tourist department, only now a firearm was strapped to his hip, also standard equipment in certain areas of the Petén and jungle. A gentle tap came on the door.

"All's ready."

Oz opened the door a crack with his foot automatically placed at its base to restrict a forced entry.

"Your tucker has been placed in the Rover, and all the rest in the Humvee," Jack offered through the opening.

Let him in Oz," Mundie requested. "Jack will cover surveillance here, San Ignacio, and up to Del Carmen. We're expecting the abductors to cross the river near San Jose Succotz. Jack's wife's brother's best friend operates the ferry there. Should they decide to cross; he will contact Jack.

Jack nodded to the remaining team, Knobby and Gizmo. Jackson had met Ocho with Mundie on previous occasions here and at some of the clubs in Belize City. They had become well acquainted, exchanging stories of Ocho's previous forays into Malaysia, and Jack's into the jungles of Vietnam. They cried as much as they laughed and had still moments of cool reflection over some of the things they were required to do; some things they mentioned not at all. It was in Malaysia that Ocho had met Oz and Knobby, and all requested to be come apart of the same special ops regiment under the Command of a kiwi, Major Tully, of the British Army Training Unit Belize, stationed at the Price Barracks near the Belize Airport. Gizmo, the medic and Zoologist, was assigned later.

Gathering up the papers, photos and bags, they quietly headed out the door and down the stairs to the parking lot and the waiting vehicles. Mundy's blue pickup was nearly dwarfed by the camouflaged Rover and the flat-forest-green Humvee (a gift from the yanks), and was left behind. Not a word was uttered until they were underway and spoke briefly over hands-free, satellite phones and ear-pieces with wire microphones that bobbed rhythmically with the contours of the road. The GPS embedded in the dash along with a myriad of sensing and other locating devices, spoke in a seductive, female voice directing them inland from Buena Vista, into the mountains toward Black Rock. Ocho, Mundie and Gizmo, took up the rear in the Humvee, while Oz and Knobby in the Rover, took lead with the specialized coded GPS called Wanda, the seductress.

Once they got off of the more traveled trails and onto the less, they apologetically turned off Wanda and proceeded with eyesight and wits. Within the hour, they bounced and jogged into the clearing that had been located by satellite previous. Several monkeys chatted briefly in the ceiba tree-tops, but became still and quiet as they watched the intrusion from their lofty height. A scarlet Macaw took flight toward a stand of mahogany and disappeared into the foliaged canopy that shadowed the secluded, jungle coppice. Orchids adorned some of the trees but were noticed little by the determinable team; if not for the task at hand, this would be a restful, appealing place.

Careful not to disturb any clues that may lead them to the perpetrators, they crept in stealth through the heat and dense humidity to search the half dozen wood and bamboo buildings. Several green, vinyl, lawn chairs scattered the area along with make-due tables of planking and tree trunks. Certain that they were alone, but cautious, always mindful of misplaced ordinance and booby-traps placed for unsuspected visitors, they searched with calculating diligence.

Within minutes, the soldiers had secured the area and Mundie was called over to a thatched, bamboo hut with a swinging door. Together with Gizmo, he knelt to view blood-stained gaze and a pair of women's soiled shorts. Haphazardly thrown to one side, was a hand-carved, wooden bowl, its contents long evaporated in the jungle heat.

"It looks like we have an ID. Do you recognize these shorts?"

Mundie gave a sigh, noticing the small killer whale embroidered on the rear pocket, and nodded to the affirmative. "Yeah, they're Shawna's."

"Captain!" Knobby shouted. "Come look at this." Oz strutted over to an area just in front of and off to the right of the hut. "Look!"

Oz bent on one knee, and turned the three foot log over in his hand exposing a dark stain and a clump of black hair caught in the bark. The broken stems of the foliage and bald areas devoid of plants, pointed to a struggle and presumably, the ultimate assault with the small log.

Gizmo crept over from the entrance to the hut and knelt beside Oz to examine the ground area. "I do not see any signs of a body being dragged away, in fact," looking off a short distance to the west and down a declination to the dense forest, more broken fern fans. "Knobby, go take a look and see what you can find."

Oz taking the hint, "We'd better scout the area a little more to see what we can find.

A few short moments later, above the din of the now clamorous jungle, Ocho's voice could be heard. "Captain, you'd better come look at this."

Lying face down, just beyond the clearing towards a shallow creek canopied by bamboo and palms, was a hulk of a man. Starting to stink, the body must have lain for at least a day; its outermost extremities were gone. Chunks of his lower back and buttocks were missing just above his faulty trousers that rested at half thigh; a jaguar had already made its claim. On closer examination, the remains of a severe edema protruded from the upper-rear-right quadrant of his skull; the skin and hair absent, matched that of the log.

"We have our victim," stated Oz, kicking the booted foot of the corpse.

Knobby came up from behind and stated emphatically, "We have a trail."

"Good," returned Oz. "Get ready to move out."

"What do we do with him," questioned Ocho.

"Leave im! He'll keep the jaguars and critters busy for a while."

Without a second thought, they returned to secure the vehicles and prepare for jungle-trekking.

The trail was easy to follow and appeared to have been forged by a herd of cattle. Whoever was in pursuit of the original two had no cares or considerations as to who may follow. Panic and desperation appeared to be the driving force behind their pursuit. Travelling fast and light, they were able to determine that a group of no less than eight men were in chase. Oz took the lead position followed close by Gizmo, the zoologist, handy for snap decisions on snakes, edible bugs and plants; following up last was Ocho, making sure they missed nothing. When the general direction of the chase was ascertained, Mundie and Knobby would drive the vehicles to as close a proximity as the jungle and terrain would allow. Wanda was coming in handy again.

Within two hours of flight south-west, Oz came across the cramped clearing that had sheltered Shawna and the Mayan woman. Scouting the perimeter of a hundred yards in every direction, Ocho had determined that the original pursuants had routed, or altogether missed, the hideaway, but also found evidence of another trail that led directly to the shelter. Returning to the center of the area, Ocho found Gizmo fingering a delicate, feather needle; the obvious remains of a blow pole, the weapon of choice of the Mayan in hunting monkey and small game. The area showed signs of much activity but little lasting damage to the surrounding foliage. This group was not the original band that had followed them from the compound. The soil depression in some of the tracks was very light and almost unrecognizable; following these tracks would be difficult save for one set of tracks, larger feet.

"We will have to hurry, clouds are rolling in," sighted Ocho, face to the sky. Luck has been on our side with no rain so far, but if she rolls in, we'll get eaten alive with the bugs."

"It will hold off for now," Oz replied. "Move out!"

They scurried along keeping close eye on all possible evidence of passage, whether it be a broken twig, fern leaf, parting of foliage, a print in the mud, or even a piece of moss dislodged from a rock lining the allusive path. They travelled like this for three hours, radioing intermittently to the tracking vehicles till they came to a well-worn path strewn with bodies. A mixture of Mayan natives, of slight stature, along with Creole, lay scattered throughout the small area. The Mayans had been shot at close range as if in hand-to-hand combat. The Creoles had been darted and then hacked with machetes to finish off the paralyzing effects of the drug-tipped assault.

"Come here Cap. I think this one's still alive." Gizmo suggested.

Oz, who came to examine the body leaning motionless against the tree, gave it a nudge and pricked the lifeless soul with his knife. "Are you sure?"

Not responding, the victim sat motionless, his left arm hanging from its cleaved socket, a dart dangling from his neck just behind his ear. "He's not cold, and there is slight reaction in his pupils. He must be breathing ever so lightly."

Felling his cool, clammy skin and looking into his eyes, Oz came to the same conclusion as Gizmo, "We can't leave him like this."

Oz, pulled out his revolver with its silencer muzzle, and pushed it to the man's temple. A slight pop and recoil, and it was over. His head tilted to one side and drool spilled from his mouth. A delicate, light-pink orchid, perched effortlessly above his head, reached down with its tendrils as if to capture his escaping soul, a blue morph butterfly transported it to the ethers.

"The rest are all dead Cap," uttered Ocho.

"Numbers," Oz questioned?

"I counted four hunters and six Mayans, and maybe six hours ago."

"Which way, Oz asked?

"They are heading east along the path here; I would say just four remain."

"Radio Knobby, and tell him to get on this road stat. It's going to get dark soon."

"Yes, Cap."

As the team approached the remote village at dusk, made up of no more than a dozen huts and lean-tos, they could hear crying and waling. There had been obvious signs of a fight, with a young, boy victim placed on a table surrounded by a group of women, young and old. Close by hung the carcass of a small, half -butchered pig-like peccary, obviously abandoned, put aside in time for the unpleasant task of preparing the boy's body for burial. Startled and frightened, they scattered to warn others; the elderly remained fearless to face the indignity of another assault. Several dogs approached with bared teeth, uncertain of the team's intent and stood their ground, retreating only at the request an elder. Oz bent down on one knee, with his rifle pointed away, horizontally across the other. As a gesture of peace, he nodded his head and looked in the direction of the prone boy. Ocho and Knobby lay their fingers beside the triggers of their SA 80s and scanned the area for hostiles. They noticed a group of young males with blow pipes, behind several, grass huts near the outskirts of the hamlet; they made no effort at aggression.

"Who did this," quarried Oz?

"Banditos," he replied, head slowly drifting to his chest.

Oz got to his feet and came before him. Raising his hand to the old man's shoulder, he replied, "Let us help you."

Within the hour, Mundy and Knobby in the utility vehicles, had entered the small borough and began the task of retrieving the bodies of the villager's fallen friends and family several miles down the trail.

### *Diaz Quatro*

By early morning, with only a few hours of sleep, Mundy and Oz began the process of retrieving whatever information they could glean from the elder. His English was very broken, but they understood Senorita, Americano Indian. The old Mayan could speak some Spanish, so translation was slow, but effectual. By his words, after the banditos entered their village, they were met by more 'cobarde' (cowards), in a white truck and left with the senorita. They drove fast and north-east, and perhaps, back through the mountains

"If they are in hurry, they may choose to stay on the main roads," Mundy suggested, hopeful that they might catch them in an unpopulated area.

"Knobby," Oz yelled. "See if you can raise one of the teams in operations a bit west of here. Perhaps if we can get one of those choppers to give us a hand, we might find them sooner than later.

The teams that had been near Caracol, were brought closer and began setting up a drag net from Guacamalio, to Baldy Beacon. The area was immense with treacherous terrain, but it is what the forces were trained to do.

# EIGHT

## The Custodian

Not far distant from Henry's office in the Ministry of Archaeology Building, a well-groomed and manicured, grass field of approximately four acres, lay vacant beside the Governor General Field. Thirty feet below, in the aft of the Government Buildings, a single, aged figure walked the polished floors of the porticoes that formed the historical archive. Housed within its many rooms that branched from the maze of corridors, were the wonders and riches of a nation barely recognized. Apart from a select few civil servants, along with some closest to the National Forensic Science Service, very few were aware if its existence. Driven underground, well hidden from the previous occupying British, the treasures of a hundred, Spanish Galleons sparkled within locked rooms. The pottery, statues and figurines of a lost civilization once plundered, now crowded the many storage alcoves far within the reaches of the original caves. This was an awesome but quiet place, where few spoke but in whispers. The souls who did enter these halls were escorted quickly and quietly, to and fro, from the resource alcoves, by a small group of custodians that rarely exited the catacombs except on ritualistic occasions. All supplies and correspondences were screened by one of several guards that never entered the complex beyond the outermost receiving rooms. It was a mysterious place that over the years had remained obscure and definitely unknown to the general public, but on several occasions some of the visiting souls went missing.

A lone, stooped figure that stayed out of sight, shunning attention was a hideous sort of man, hiding his gnarled features beneath a draped hood that fell loose above his shoulders. His voice, quiet and deep was his only seeming attraction, giving a soft and seductive sound that mesmerized those in attendance. His eyes, when exposed, were piercing and slightly bloodshot, as if sleep deprived, and hidden deep within the puffy flesh that surrounded them. He had been there for what some say was an eternity, and given full authority over the institution by some previous administration; no-one could remember which one, for no-one had seen the vaulted documentation, or had seen any other, apart from this odd creature, sweeping and walking the halls of this sacred place. He quietly did his business through the wee hours of the morning, and left late from the corridors after viewing hours. No one had ever seen his living quarters, and he spoke only to the few assistants who appeared to hold him in great regard, for they were never seen to question or refuse his requests. He had always been quite generous with his donations to the Red Cross and supported the Medical Sciences wing of the University of Belize, with few strings attached apart from the occasional request for reports on certain blood-type screenings.

Unbeknown to the others, several rooms were his favorite. He would sit for hours and gaze at the Mayan reliefs that had been reclaimed from overseas and crumpling ruins, relocated to this safe place to stifle irreversible decay. Clay vases and plates depicting sacrifice and bloodletting lined the walls and were dusted almost daily and cherished as if personal heirlooms from his past. Small clay and jade figurines from Canaan, Middle East, and Central America adorned the shelves of his private sitting quarters along with woven blankets and mats that were strewn about accenting the sparse furniture, and used as if possessed. Often, he would shut off the security cameras to some of the main storage rooms and take the key that opened the most sacred of the sanctuaries. The custodian, sat for hours amongst the Chocmol and other sacrificial altars and artifacts. Some had been repatriated from far civilizations of the world, previously plundered from the jungles of Central America; the most recent, a small, jade bowl, with the Mayan calendar etched on the lid, seemed his favorite.

He had held the jade bowl in his hands once before, many years ago. It had been a slight thing then, and for the most part was still not all that entrancing; but people had always desired to have it as a keepsake. The bowl had been a delightful, little trinket, given as a gift to a woman who had shunned his advances. The betrothed daughter of a king, would have nothing to do with the arrangements made for her procurement. He had only wanted a tiny piece of her heart, literally. She held within her genetic pool, the purity that would sustain him for a more lengthy time, a hundred years or so, maybe two, perhaps more; he was not sure. It would depend on the quality and directness of the lineage of her ancestry back to the original one. She was the purest he had been able to find for some time in this decaying world. The Custodian had continued to use less superior subject tissue for his medical procedures, but with the inevitability of more frequent operations, came of course, the need for more donor tissue.

He gently fingered the embossed sides of the bowl, and stroked the calendar lid; the bowl was a pretty little thing, a gift to capture her heart. Love and hope, the two psychological pillars of mental strength, were used as tools, endeared by this insignificant creature called man. These were illusionary emotions, like the light of the moon, reflective, and not of pure essence; just like him. He had hoped to entreat the princess with this gift to steal her heart away; but, understanding the true nature of his gesture, she escaped from the top of the temple at Xunantunich. The local Mayans at the time, considered her disappearance a miracle, and she was placed in the pantheon along with the other gods. The princess was remembered for her act, and all that remains to this day is an embossed slab of stone, the 'Stone Maiden', present in the secluded alcove where she had fled. The Xunantunich ruins, soon thereafter, fell into disarray and decay. Knowing her mortal nature, he continued to search for her offspring; they somehow evaded his many efforts of finding them, till now.

The special sacrifice of all those years ago had slipped his clutches, but he had another. She would be arriving soon, and how ironic, she delivered the bowl, now called 'the Pillars of the Moon', back to him as a gift. He placed the bowl back in its place and continued down the hall to his private quarters. He was still uncertain whether to bring her entire body back or just the important parts. He would need to have the cooler sterilized along with the bags to contain the ice. Xunantunich was not far distant, but he could not take the chance of any deterioration. A cooler was always less conspicuous than a body.

A story had circulated among the facility's guards, that at one time, he had been a talented, medical surgeon of international renown barred from continuing his research. After little debate and much to-do, death-threats eventually drove him from Europe, and underground to continue his work. Organ transplants, and trials of cell regeneration had not been imagined yet, let alone practiced, so he had left the Mediterranean area by boat to continue in obscurity. All this, he considered a slight thing, and many years later, he has been left alone to go on with his research in absolute privacy. No one has lived to tell the tale of the true nature of his work, but one individual has pursued his career, from a distance, slowly putting the pieces of the puzzle together.

### Dias tres (day 3)

Time passed and stories being just stories, the crumpled, old man had become as much a part of the archives as any of the historical papers and artifacts that are housed here. Few outsiders ever had audience with him, seemingly protected by those closely associated to him and silenced by the riches he bestowed them. No one outside the inner sanctum knew where he had originally come from, or in most cases did those in his attendance ever seem concerned, for he had always been there. Today he had a visitor,

Doug , the Americano.


Doug Baldwin was a cool, calculating character, whose good looks and savvy had kept him a step ahead of all those who would trip him up. During the Second World War, he had been young and had a good nose for opportunity. While his buddies were out shooting and defending the front-lines, he was in the background procuring weaponry and souvenirs for the boys to take home on convalescence or leave. He always seemed to be there when all the accolades were being doled out. He was a well decorated man, and appreciated for the efforts he had made in making his superiors look and feel good, at all costs.

After the war, the mercenary life did not appeal to him, so he entered the Caribbean stage running goods and rum from the eastern seaboard of the states, south to the islands; lucrative to say the least. His desire for power and money eventually led him to the antiquity trade and a variety of relationships with individuals like Juan (Amalia's friend from the Royal Reef bar). Cut from similar cloth, the two had been able to forge a workable relationship that generally served them both well as long as the artifacts, drugs and money flowed abundantly.

Juan, on the other hand, scraped his way through life being the only son of an alcoholic father, who regularly beat him and threw him out of the house. One such night, his father drunk, chased after him into the nearby mangrove forest. After evasion, Juan has chosen to hide out and watch for his father. After some time had passed, Juan had heard muffled screams and his father's cursing, and had found him with a young girl. Fallen from his drunken state, he had hit his head on a branch. Shouting and cursing at Juan as being useless and threatening to kill his mother, Juan took destiny into his own hands and ended this barrage of threats and insults with a log; the belligerent drunk never came home again; they never found the body. The young girl, who was barely twelve years old, half naked close by, obscured by fallen trees and scrub, witnessed the whole episode, her name, Amalia.

The news Doug had to bring the custodian was not all that good. His prized genetic pool had escaped custody, and even though they were confident the search would recover her, trepidation crept the halls before him. Shawna had found temporary freedom, and if necessary, since the custodian's second choice was still a possibility, there was hope the momentary lapse would not unleash morbid retribution. As a last token of appeasement, there was always Amalia.

The gates clanking loudly reverberated throughout the halls of the complex. Every section of the security ring had its own set of doors that the American would enter through. Each gate had protocol that had to be adhered to with signings and photo recognition, or shutdown would be initiated and the complex would be frozen till proper procedures and assurances were met. The closer Doug got to the archives, the fewer security personnel he saw till eventually no-one came. The halls were very brightly lit from overhead and seemed endless apart from the intermittent gates. The sound of his footsteps echoed from the hard, bake tiled floor to the white-washed walls giving an unnerving, delayed, audio response adding to his uneasiness. Upon reaching the last gate, Doug was welcomed by a rather scholarly looking spectacled man of slight stature, who bowed then handed him a damp, hand towel. A smile and hand motions that indicated he was to use the towel for sanitary reasons and discard it into a bin. The man directed Doug to sit on the nearby chair, bowed once again, and disappeared down the hall and through a doorway.

The reception area was rather nicely decorated with exotic wood and burgundy, leather chairs and setae. Artifacts lined the walls on shelves and tables. Figurines and vases from notably different areas of the world were on display and in pristine condition. Doug was tempted to lift and view these treasures, but was ever aware of the dark, smoke-colored domes that covered the security cameras. He began to wonder at the odds of being able to route the security and enlighten the archives of just a few of the copious treasures.

In the background, whilst he was daydreaming, he slowly became aware of a shuffle and a light knock that became progressively louder. Inquisitive, he stood erect just in time to see a stooped figure enter the reception area and stand at the threshold to one of the halls.

"Greetings," escaped quickly from Doug's lips, more out of nervous reaction than cordiality.

The figure stood for some moments without utterance and stared unflinching in Doug's direction.

"I hear there has been a setback in procuring the specimen."

"Umm, yes." not wishing to contradict the custodian. "I'm confident she, I mean it, will be found in short order. The British have started the search just across the border and the US military are on standby should they fail."

"For your sake, I hope they do not." The custodian slowly shuffled to one of the chairs and took a seat on its front edge. "My time is coming soon; I only have days for the procedure to take positive effect." He shuffled a little in his seat; Doug remained silent as the custodian appeared to want to continue. "Have I not been good to you?" the custodian asked, his voice in smooth, low tones. "You have a lovely estate close by."

"Yes, my Lord, more than generous."

"We have been together for a number of years now, have we not?"

"Yes, Lord."

"Do you remember all those years ago when we first initiated the terms of our agreement, and you went to the northern palace and took care of an inquisition that had begun to plague me?"

Struggling to remember back thirty years to the Yucatan, Doug began to falter, "I think so."

"Perhaps, I can refresh your memory." With that, he taped his cane on the floor and the portrait of a face came on to the monitor embedded in the wall opposite where he sat.

The face on the screen bore a familiar resemblance, but he could not be sure.

"Ek balaam, some thirty-two years ago, you procured a specimen for me; a woman who has served me well these years, but you were to remove the obstacle that plagued me somewhat, from previous years."

"The young archaeologist and his wife!" Doug entreated, remembering a younger Magnus.

"Yes, you were to take care of the situation, and yet I find him on the compound not several hours ago."

Sitting silent for mere moments, he then tapped the floor once again. The sheepish, spectacled man appeared in the reception area and stood off to one side silent. "Thank you, Andreas."

Not sure what to say or do, Doug walked over to a sealed, glass case which supposedly housed one of the lost books of the Maya.

"Do you still have the ring?" asked the custodian.

"Yes, I do," Doug replied, looking down to the jaguar face, black embossed on gold.

"Then wear it well." The custodian turned and slowly returned down the hall he had previously come, the aid by his side.

"It will be done my Lord," Doug replied. "It shall be done".

# NINE

**Diaz Quatro (day 4) Santa Elena**

It was hard to figure where Magnus might go. He knew the area well and Steve and Brian had no idea where to begin. Magnus had many friends and could be in a number of areas, he was no fool and they figured that he knew as much about the little jade bowl as anyone; Magnus had access to most of the archaeological sites in Belize, if not formally, then by attrition and association. He also must have ideas as to who kidnapped Shawna.

Santa Elena, was a quaint town on the banks of the Macal River, which divides it with its sister town San Ignacio. Driving through the town center and across the draw bridge to San Ignacio, they watched and waited for someone or something to point the way to Magnus. After an hour of perusing the sloping, hillside streets, they continued through and around the downtown area of San Ignacio watching the quaint shops and outdoor merchant stalls.

Agitated by their lack of resolve, Brian and Steve

decided to re-cross the river and spend time in the sister. Tired, they grabbed some beer and enchiladas at one of the local restaurants and headed down to the little park by the secondary bridge over the Macal. Sleepy after their meal, they lay considering their options and drifted in and out of sleep while the sounds of playing children, birds chattering, and the babbling water as it washed the shore-line pebbles, lulled them to serenity. The sun dodged the clouds and started to lift the moisture from the grass forming a blanket of steam that dispersed in the breeze, as trailing wisps.

Memories of French's Beach, on the southern coast of Vancouver Island, drifted into Brian's mind; a peaceful place he visited on occasion to take photos, write and relax. The sound of the pebbles being washed in the stream reminded him of the surf and warmth of the sun that beat on his face as he lay on that far-away beach, and of quieter times. Cardinals, instead of squawking seagulls, sounded their arias in the immediate trees. The Olympic Peninsula panorama of Washington State, to the south of the beach, was etched in his mind. Below Cape Flattery, at the peninsula's tip, was the site of the ancient Makah tribal village of Ossette, where the Olmec jade bowl had been recovered nearly a century ago. The night of self-discovery, with the native, hallucinogenic tea for him, and the 'circle of stones' that brought back unsettling feelings, were culprit. This had been the last night he had seen Shawna. Agitated, he woke from his day-dream with a renewed energy to continue in the search for her.

"Wake up. Let's go!"

With a grunt, Steve was up and back in the car preparing to drive the spacious, back streets of Santa

Elena's suburbs.

The dusty roads offered nothing of interest to the two who were resigned to heading further up out of town, toward the Guatemalan border, when a blue streak caught the corner of Brian's eye. Down at the end of one of the sun bleached, gravel streets, with a quaint, hotel-like building beside an open field, was the familiar, small, blue pick-up truck.

"Steve, stop! Back-up a little."

As they pulled alongside the pick-up, Brian realized that they had indeed found the truck of the young man that was visiting Maria at the museum. A Department of Tourism sticker, affixed to the corner of the windshield, confirmed his suspicions. Easing himself from the car, Brian slowly paced around the blue spectacle and wondered at the man's relationship with Maria.

"Is there something I can help you with," came an abrupt question from behind the shade of the screen-door of the Aguada Hotel?

The door opened slightly, and then remained stationary while Brian withdrew from the vehicle. Approaching slowly, but unreserved, he responded. "I was wondering if I might talk to the fellow who owns the truck."

Jackson remained quiet behind the shelter of the door and fingered the handgun hidden in his pocket. Not certain how to reply and wondered at the peculiar, language accent, he waited for a further response.

"We are from Canada, wanting to film some of the archaeological sites. We needed a guide and noticed the tourist sticker on the windscreen. Is this fellow available?"

Steve peered from the driver's seat with his elbow

resting on the sill and gave no response to the lack of rebuttal apart from raising his sunglasses to his forehead.

Silence hung for several moments. "I'm not sure if I can help you," Jackson replied from behind the screen.

"May I come in," reaching his hand to the door?

Backing away, Jackson made no effort to welcome Brian in and moved to the side to allow him entry to the cool interior of the restaurant. Reserved but confident Brian harbored no ill will, he turned to the bar area at the rear and asked, "Can I get you something?"

"No, we are not stopping for long. You have no idea when the Tourist rep will be back, I'd definitely like to talk with him?" Brian could see through the window, that Steve was out and leaning against the side of the car; Jackson continued behind the bar.

"What sites would you like to see?" Jackson asked in his southern US accent, scrutinizing the two from mirrors at the back of the bar.

"We would like to see Caracol and Xunantunich, but not sure of the directions. What's your name by the way?"

"Jackson, but you can call me Jack." Thinking for a moment as to how to answer the first part of the question, Jackson had to consider the search party, and the fact Edmundo had asked him to watch for anyone suspicious coming through the area. He had pairs of eyes everywhere throughout the twin sisters, who, for the price of a couple of beers, were diligent. His brother-in-law's friend could keep tabs on, and perhaps glean more info from, these fellows on the trip across the Mopan River at the crossing to Xunantunich. There was also Magnus, who had taken a room, and had left at once, having been told that Edmundo had returned from Belize City, looking for him. Magnus had dropped his bag and left in a hurry with directions for Edmundo to wait for him. Perhaps Magnus could figure these two out. It was odd that they were here right when the girl was kidnapped, Edmundo and the commandos where on maneuvers and Magnus, who he had not seen in years show up, all at the same time; not a coincidence.

Steve came through the door. "I think I'll have another beer Bri. It's getting awfully hot out there."

"Yeah, OK. Sounds good," Brian replied. "Dos cervasa, por favor," he yelled at Jack.

"Would you like an American Beer," Jack questioned. "I have Bud and Coors, sent down once a month.

They looked at one another, "Sure, one of each."

Jack dropped them lightly on the table just as Steve began to speak in private. "So you think the guys that tried to get Maria are the same as Shawna's."

Jackson not hearing all the conversation caught the name Maria only, and strained from behind the bar to hear the rest. In low tones, Brian and Steve carried on the conversation and sipped on their beers. Contemplating the unlikely chance of another coincidence, Jack waited for them to finish. "You guys got a place to stay for the night?"

Steve looked up at Jack and then whispered to Brian, "You know, that guy in the pickup has to come back sooner or later to get his vehicle, right."

"Yeah," Brian considered. "Maybe we can at least find out what he knows." Steve nodded in agreement.

"Do you have any rooms?"

"Give me an hour and I'll have clean linen and towels in a couple of rooms," he replied.

It was midafternoon when the two left the Aguada, and headed south out of San Ignacio towards the Guatemalan border. Within twenty minutes, they were at San Jose Succotz and crossed onto the small hand-propelled ferry. Driving down the steep incline onto the wood-planked ferry, the operator gave greeting and started to crank the wheel.

"Where you from?" he quarried, pumping the wheel with a smile.

"Canada. My brother-in-law and I are here on a holiday, taking in some of the sites," Steve replied. "We were in Mexico a few years back, but never made it down here. The ruins here are just great."

"How many have you visited so far," he asked?

Stammering unprepared for the question, "None, as of yet. I just arrived yesterday, but with any luck we'll catch a few more and," turning with a smile toward the upcoming shore, "we're here now!"

The Mopan River was a short crossing that had sharp tree-covered banks on either side. Bamboo and swamp Cypress trees canopied the shallow river that disappeared in either direction into damp, dark jungle. Brian prepared his camera and checked the batteries before they bounced off the ferry and started up the mile-long laneway to the parking area of Xunantunich. Surprised at the number of vehicles in the lot, they stopped first at the kiosk and shop, to relieve themselves of the incumbent beer. Perusing the copied artifacts that adorned the glass covered case, Brian retreated to another display area that highlighted archaeologists and excavators of the past. Interested in the history of the site, he was intrigued by the written fable of the Mayan Maiden who had been betrothed to a prince from a distant region, and had chosen to escape the union by disappearing into the temple, never to reemerge. To the by-standers and local priesthood, this was deemed a miracle and the young woman was deified as the 'Stone Maiden', and the site was eventually renamed in her honor, Xunantunich.

The pathway, of several hundred yards to the temples and courtyards, led steeply up, but was paved making the incline manageable. Entering the grand courtyard from between two lesser temples was impressive. The largest temple was at the far end which, apart from its rear, was excavated and somewhat rebuilt to reflect the enormity of the architectural undertaking. Its towering pinnacle stood high above the forest and was adorned with an ornate frieze. Around the outer court of this large edifice there were no less than six other lesser temples still in disarray, but showed signs of defoliation and excavation. This was considered a lesser site of the preclassic period, and was not as popular as others, but within time it too would yield all its secrets from centuries past. Neglect of these sites was in some ways a saving grace and kept the mystery and romance of this civilization alive.

'El Castillo", the largest of the temples receiving most of the attention, was rebuilt with some measure of proficiency and showed ongoing signs of excavation. Its face was cleared with the large stones being replaced in their original foundations. Other areas around the sides were cleared, but were in disarray with some of the walls and hallways being partially rebuilt. The temple's facade was grand with a wide stair case ascending to a central plateau, and holding rooms for sacrifices of animals and defeated ball players who gave everything they had to the sport, including their heads. Above that, the temple rose to a band of frieze that skirted the upper plateau, then extended up to a crowned pinnacle that overlooked the entire area for miles. This lookout area was crucial for security of the region and doubled for celestial reading and mapping.

As the sun came out once again, the air became heavy-laden with scents from the orchid blossoms and the thick underbrush that adorned the perimeter of the clearing. The trees were alive with the songs of birds and the drone buzz of jungle insects, outdone only by the musicians and dancers that paraded in native regalia celebrating at the foot of the large temple. The two Canadians sat, out of breath, drenched in sweat, watching and enjoying the ambience and quaintness of their surroundings.

Only a few short miles away, at another archaeological site, an acquaintance sat, sipping on a bottle of water. Waiting for the arrival, and perhaps the ending, to a decades long enigma that had haunted him

### Magnus' endeavors:

Cahal Pech was a well-preserved, ceremonial, archaeological site of the late preclassic (200AD). Just a twenty minute walk uphill from San Ignacio, it was an ideal spot for the doctor to scrutinize and manipulate the greedy Mr. Doug Baldwin, into an area deeper in the jungle not so far away, where he could do away with this parasite. Doug's blood-letting, now recognized as an enigma to Magnus, had through the years skimmed enough profits from Belize's natural and manufactured resources to bring the small Caribbean country up to relative prosperity. Doug Baldwin, had been implicated in the court proceedings by looters that were caught and tried; he, of course was exonerated, but the name Baldwin and the proceedings stuck in Magnus's mind. Apart from this, up until a day ago, Magnus had not been able to place the familiarity he felt for this American businessman. He had recognized Doug's voice from the televised political wrangling that had occurred ever so often from this shoot-from-the-hip country, but was never able to place the familiarity to a particular occurrence; it was only when he heard his natural, vocal cadence whilst inside the darkened closet at Henry's office, that he recognized the fine details and accent the voice instilled. From the shrouded, painful haze that encompassed him twenty years ago, he remembered lying semiconscious, helpless and listened while that voice stripped him of the very reason he rose each morning and went to bed at night; it was Doug Baldwin that had been present at the kidnapping of his wife Angelina, at Ek Balaam.

At three thirty, an hour before the closing of the site, Magnus grabbed his leather briefcase from the front seat of his jeep and headed up the slick walkway to the ruins that had once housed royalty. Henry had arranged for Doug to meet an antiquities dealer from the area who needed backing to finance an unexcavated tell within the Mountain Pine Ridge Reserve, close to Black Rock. Within his briefcase, Magnus carried several, miniature, clay figurines and obsidian cutlery to embellish the ruse to an acceptable level of trust and finance: a small revolver, wrapped in thick linen, was also there to ensure the proceedings developed into a fruitful and rewarding encounter. If he was able to lure him away into a reclusive area, all the better, there would be a chance his greed would be the catalyst to his own demise; if not, the meeting could end right here.

It was quarter to four and a large black Escalade pulled into the parking area below. The light drizzle of rain had stopped from the passing low, cloud-cover. Magnus watched as the driver and a front seat passenger opened the rear doors for the occupants in the back to exit. Doug Baldwin, and a young woman gathered composure and stroked the wrinkles from their light-linen clothes. Slowly walking the sheltered, but slick, walkway with lush foliage to the upper reaches of the complex, they entered and exited his line of vision. One of the front-seat passengers, obviously a bodyguard, followed close, scanning the area for security. Cool and composed, Magnus sat near the top steps of the temple and waited for the couple to enter the courtyard. From the far end of the ball-court, they walked arm-in-arm; the woman's sunhat drooped and danced as she aggressively clutched his arm, trying to navigate the grassy area in her stylish slip-on shoes. Their heads moved from side to side visually taking in what the lush, colorful surroundings had to offer. For a moment, Magnus almost imagined them as the Royals that once graced the complex, but not unlike the kings of the past era, there was much contempt for the opulent and lascivious lifestyle that this duplicitude embraced. In seeming slow motion, the two stepped onto the stone, tabled area that was positioned at the bottom of the half-dozen steps at which Magnus sat perched at the top.

Slowing, as he approached the bottom step, Doug looked up to see the shadow of the man he had witness beaten all those years ago and recognized from the visual he had seen in the custodians presence. Uncertain as to motive, Doug gave Magnus reasonable doubt as to intent and proceeded up the steps to greet the prospective without alluding to his recognition.

"Thank you for coming to meet with me," sighed Magnus, gently releasing the pent-up tension from being face to face with his nemesis' apprentice. It felt odd for him to be in Doug's presence at this moment. Looking directly into his eyes, he could feel all emotion ease from himself as if a drain cock had been opened and all pressure had been released. Magnus felt no emotion at all; he could have killed him at this moment and not felt a thing, a coldness surged through his veins. Looking toward the young women at Doug's side brought back a fleeting moment of recollection of all those years ago in Ek-Balaam. Magnus's young wife of similar stature and complexion, stood before him as if to warn him of the coming calamity. Emotion began to leak its way into his psychic and he began to flounder. Setting his briefcase down on the top step, he fumbled with the latches and before he could open the case, a severe blow came to the side of his head. Tumbling headlong down the remaining stone steps, Magnus found himself prone and aching. Fading in and out of consciousness, he once again heard the familiar voice echoing through the dimness while he stirred to wakefulness. Screams through the numbness and haze, alerted him to the cool metal that had been pressed to his temple.

"You are supposed to be dead," came the growl to his ear. "I'll deal with Henry later."

Not moving, and forcing his consciousness to surface from the haze, Magnus wiped the blood that dripped from his bruised nose and rose to one elbow. Above him, Doug looked down at him through dark, cold eyes that shined with a desire to kill; the young women beat on his back profusely till he stood erect and swung the full length of his arm and weight across her face; she went sprawling onto the grass not two yards distant. Looking to the contents of his briefcase scattered down the cascade of steps, and his revolver now in Doug's hand, Magnus, on all fours, collected the chards and figurines he had purposed for his scheme into the open case.

"You bastard," Amalia screamed, as she turned back to Doug, he cocked the gun ready to shoot.

Magnus ignored the threatening sound and continued in subdued dignity to pick up the scattered remains.

"Boss?" quarried the guard that had slowed from a run across the open court.

Doug realizing the sensitivity of the situation and the openness of the site, grabbed Amalia by the arm. Dragging her to her feet, he forcibly pulled her in the direction down the path to the vehicles. "Bring him!" he commanded the subordinate.

Snapping the briefcase shut, Magnus staggered in the direction that Doug and Amalia had taken to retrace their steps back to the parking lot. Within the dense underbrush along the path, a lone, dark figure waited patiently for the return of the couple, and the opportunity to strike.

Juan crouched low, and waited with bated breath to make his assault on the lives that had so impressed his. As Doug strode by with Amalia dragging behind,

Juan noticed the revolver being slipped into his pocket. With the guard-house and shop that were now closing due to the late hour, and with no tourists noticeably about, now was the time to act. He was about to pull the trigger when the shuffle of feet, and low voices, could be heard from up the path in the direction of the ruins. Juan, lowered his weapon as Magnus and his captor walked by, another revolver was visible and the likelihood of the attack being successful had halved. Juan recognized the slight figure of a man being corralled, and was curious to the purpose of this clandestine meeting. Time and opportunity were on his side, so for now, he would watch and wait as Magnus was shoved into the backseat of the oversized SUV. Doug's black Escalade drove out of the lot heading in the opposite direction to San Ignacio, into the jungle.

After twenty minutes of riding the rough, gravel road, and following at a safe distance in his van, Juan watched as the Escalade disappeared down an obscured laneway out of sight. Pulling off to the opposite side and into the underbrush, he shut the motor off and crossed the road to listen and determine the distance the truck had travelled. In the near distance, he could hear the slamming of vehicle doors and orders being shouted. Through the foliage, Juan could make out a break in the density of trees and the bright sun reflecting off of the bleached gravel in a clearing. Quietly, he crept to a vantage point and watched as Magnus and Amalia, were shoved through the doorway of a large, tin-covered building that looked like a warehouse for road building and maintenance equipment. Several other vehicles were in the lot, along with a white van now cream colored from all the dust and mud. Not noticing any guards posted, he crept through the ferns and bushes to a window along the side of the building to take a look. Thinking twice about accidently initiating a shadow of light to the interior, he chose to peek through a slight rip in the joint of the vertical, tin siding, close to the opening.

While his eye adjusted to the light, Juan listened intently while one of the captors argued and cursed while he relayed the story of their demise at a jungle camp. The chase through the Macaw Bank, down past Spanish Water Hole, and the loss of most of his men had been difficult. He was demanding more money and raised his hand to assault another young woman bound and gagged till Doug, who was confronting the man, stopped him. Pulling a pistol from his waist band, the assailant jabbed the barrel against the woman's head causing it to tilt away from the strike, and stood motionless in a fit of rage. Backing up immediately, Doug lowered his hands and began talking again. The pistol lowered from the woman's temple and the man retreated momentarily, appeased from what was offered; the two continued in conversation. The bodyguards that had accompanied Doug and Amalia at the Cahal Pech ruins, were near the front entrance with Amalia now by their side; Magnus was bound and seated on the hardened, dirt floor by the door.

Realizing he was greatly outnumbered, Juan decided to back away and wait for a more opportune moment to make his assault. Returning to the roadside, he restarted his vehicle and repositioned it to follow the Enclave when it reappeared from the sheltered drive.

"You idiot, do you not realize what will happen if we do not deliver her tomorrow!" Doug half yelled at the kidnapper as he held the gun to Shawna's head.

"We will get squat and all of this will be for nothing if we fail to deliver."

The Mestizo thought for a moment, and lowered his gun to his side. His three compadres in the rear of the garage lowered their weapons also, but watched intently the movements of the two guards by the door, who had their semi-automatic rifles presently pointed at them.

"Everything will be fine," Doug encouraged. "We will get you more money, just be patient. We have worked for the ministry before and have always been paid well."

Doug retreated to the doorway and nodded to one of the guards who nodded in return. Leaving Magnus on the floor, Doug, Amalia and the remaining guard retreated from the doorway back to the SUV and left the graveled lot down the drive to the road leading back to San Ignacio.

Shawna exhausted, sore and tired, began to weep.


### San Ignacio:

"Brian, get your ass over here!" Steve half yelled, as he folded his sunglasses, straining to see in the early evening light. A young woman, he thought he recognized from the Royal Reef Hotel, was slowly walking up the hill away from them. "Isn't she that woman you told me about, and waited for, while that guy was at her door?"

Having just exited from the sheltered doorway of a curio shop on Buena Vista Street, Brian caught a fleeting glimpse of Amalia's facial profile as she disappeared behind a palm tree along the lighted

161

walkway to the front entrance to the San Ignacio Resort Hotel. "Yeah," he replied as he watched her being encouraged by Doug to continue walking.

A short distance behind them, but staying out of sight, was a shadowy figure that remained close to the edge of the walkway.

Brian motioning with his finger, "I think that's the guy that was harassing her at the bar, and at her door."

They watched him disappear into the bushes as another pedestrian entered the walkway and followed in the same direction as Amalia and Doug. As the clandestine figure re-emerged from the darkness looking in the direction of the hotel, it was clear he was up to no good.

"Let's go ask him what he's up to," Steve suggested, without stopping for Brian's approval.

"Ok," Brian replied to the vacant sidewalk, and followed several paces behind.

On seeing the two Canadians approach from the opposite side of the road, Juan made no effort to run or hide, and stood almost defiant with his right hand in his jacket pocket. Noticing the fabric of Juan's coat being stretched toward the pocket, Steve became cautious and aware of a heavy object being manipulated within its confines.

"Buenos noches, senor," Brian uttered as he came up from the rear behind Steve.

Juan stood dazed as he wondered at the boldness of these two gringos. Without a word, he stood motionless, and stared at Steve who towered over him, in the protection of the palm trees. Once in the shadows away from the direct sunlight, Brian's face became familiar to him.

"What you doin here," Brian questioned,

motioning his head in the direction Amalia had walked.

Through the haze that remained in his head from the half-bottle of rum he had drunk while in pursuit of Amalia and Doug, Juan became cautious at the inquiry, and wondered at the purpose of this confrontation. Motioning to pull the revolver from his pocket, Steve had pulled back and jabbed his fist, with all his weight behind it, toward Juan's face. In the split second before contact, Juan lowered his brow and the full force of the punching fist landed on his forehead. Staggered from the sheer force of the blow, Juan fell back into the bushes and remained motionless, prone to the sky.

"Yeoww!!" howled Steve. The unfortunate motion of Juan, brought bone against bone, and Steve hopped in agony as the center knuckle of his hand shot agonizing pain up his arm.

"Wow, I'm impressed!" Brian crooned, walking to where Juan had disappeared into the shadows of the bushes complimenting the walkway.

"He had a gun," shuddered Steve as he joined Brian's side. As a bluish egg began to rise on Juan's forehead, Steve kicked him in an attempt to rouse him. With no response evident, the two looked about for witnesses and then toward each other, "We'd better leave him." Dragging him a little further into the flower bed, the two retreated across the street from hence they had come and headed back to the car.

"Let's get back to the Aguada, and get changed," Brian suggested, thinking of the resort and dinner. "Perhaps I can get Amalia alone and ask some questions."

**The shack:**
The storage shack had become dark, and the only

163

light to be seen was emanating from the antiquated, kerosene lamp that dangled from a beam above the square, wooden table where the four men intently played their card game. Shawna, released from her chair, snuggled close to Magnus trying to extract whatever heat she could from his frail body. The men had moved them toward the center of the room away from the exterior walls, and tied them to the support post. The crickets chirped to a near deafening volume and the rustling of mice and other nocturnals kept the two from nodding off into complete oblivion. Shawna had been able to get several hours of sleep after Doug had left and the leader of the Mestizo collapsed onto a slat bunk to sleep off the rum and the chase of the last days. Every once in a while one of the guards would look in their direction and quickly scan the interiors perimeter.

"You are the girl that half of the Belize army, and British contingency, are looking for," Magnus stated, shifting his numbing legs on the hard floor.

"Yeah" Shawna sighed, taking some comfort that she was no longer alone.

"You're the Canadian girl that brought the Olmec bowl down from Seattle, aren't you?"

Without lifting her eyes or her voice, she sighed a "yes," and then interjected, "I am Native American. There are no borders for me."

Securing his arm around her and cuddling her close, "You know there are a couple of Canadians fellows down here looking for you, and they are very persistent."

Shawna glanced up to his face wondering at the statement.

"Yeah, a couple of guys I met a few years back in

the Yucatan; Brian Alexander and his brother-in-law Steve.

At the mention of Brian's name, Shawna went slack. "What did they say?"

"Nothing about you, but said they were down here taking photos of the ruins." He looked down to her tears that were slowing edging down her face, "They couldn't fool me though. Mr. Alexander was much too intense when he came to see me; I knew they were up to something."

Shawna said nothing and wiped away the tears on his shirt. After several moments, she gathered herself and began, "If it had not been for Brian, the bowl would never had been recovered and made its way back to Central America." She fell silent for several moments. "My ancestors were kind of, guardians of the bowl and it needed to come back home to Central America.

It started a long time ago as my grandmother told us, with one of my ancestors, a Mayan, receiving the bowl as a gift from a prince who wanted to betroth her. She did not like him and escaped while he was waiting in the procession at the ceremony. She liked the bowl and kept it; he was pissed. It was eventually lost when a mudslide buried our village. Throughout our family's history, there have been tales of kidnappings, killings and intrigue with no other reason, or evidence of purpose, than that of the bowl. The latest attempt by the Jaguars, almost killed my cousin Peter, and my Uncle Daniel was possibly killed by them when he was a young man. This bowl has brought much unhappiness."

"You know, there may be an explanation to all this that you may consider," Magnus interjected. "I do not think these Jaguars are after the bowl, I think they are after you and your family."

"But, why?" Shawna questioned, looking up to Magnus's dark, but caring eyes.

"I cannot be sure, but it is what you carry inside of you, that he needs."

"What do you mean?"

"I think he needs your DNA, and maybe more."

"What!" Shawna half yelled, and turned to the guards to see if they had noticed. "How do you know this?"

"Because, whoever this man or thing is, he took my wife from me years ago, for the same reason."

"Do you think your wife and I were relatives?"

"I don't know, he replied looking toward the corrugated, steel ceiling of the shack. "There is a possibility."

Shawna, shocked, looked up at Magnus's face to search for a line of jest or doubt, she found neither. She hung her head and whispered, "Where he finds the bowl, he finds us."

Outside, the rustling of the trees in the wind became louder, and in the distance, thunder could be heard from the approaching storm - or was it something different.

They both cuddled cold and shivering, silent in the darkness.

# TEN

**Daiz quatro, tardes (it comes together)**

By the time Edmundo and Ocho had returned to the
Aguada, the sun had just set. Gizmo had taken up with
Oz and Knobby, and were taking up the rear checking
several, abandoned, military camps in the foothills of
the mountains just north of Santa Elena. Exhausted,
they entered the restaurant and placed their gear bags
by the archway that led to the pool and their rooms.

"Magnus arrived a few hours ago," Jack piped
from behind the bar, just loud enough for Edmundo to
hear. Surprised, Mundie and Oz leaned in close and
grabbed for the beers that Jack had instinctively put
within their reach.

"There were a couple of fellas asking for you as
well, this afternoon."

Edmundo straddled one of the chairs and placed
the bottle on the table. "What did they look like?"

"You can see for yourself, they just pulled up."

Innocent and tired from the days ordeal, Brian and

Steve entered the near, vacant restaurant through the screen door, only to be faced with a rifle pointed at them from no less than ten feet. Steve gently rubbed the raw and swollen knuckle on his right hand, more out of nervousness than comfort. Brian stood motionless, hands raised slightly looking to the man he had seen the day before coming from Maria's office in Belize city, only there was a revolver sitting on the table with its USP.45 muzzle pointed at his privates.

"Let's not get hasty," eased from Brian's lips. Jack behind the bar stood motionless and watched. "Can I have a beer?"

"What about me?" Steve squeaked, keeping his eye on the rifle held in Ocho's clutches.

"That depends," eased Edmundo, watching Brian's hands as he lowered them and slowly approached the table.

"Can I take a seat?"

"What do you want with Shawna?"

Brian, unsure how to answer, wondered at this man's involvement with Shawna, and did not reply.

"You were at my sister's office yesterday morning. Why were you there?"

Putting the pieces together, "You are Maria's brother?"

Not answering, Mundie watched closely Brian's eyes and autonomic reflexes to determine his intent.

"I had asked Maria for some information on a colleague of mine from Canada."

"So, both of you are from Canada." Edmundo stated, looking over to Steve who had not changed position or expression of face. He picked up the pistol and waved Steve over to the table and holstered it. "Maria got the impression that you were alright and," he stopped momentarily, "Shawna has mentioned a friend whom she owed her life to from Canada, many times. I know it is you."

Brian caught a momentary show of emotion in his inquisitor that could have signaled regret. This fellow had feelings for Shawna.

Ocho had lowered his rifle and collected up the bags holding communication devices and headed through the back archway. Jack brought a couple more beers to the table.

"What can I get you fellas to eat?"

### San Ignacio

Owen had eased himself from the shadows and crossed the road to where the two Canadians had left the fellow in the bushes. Creeping into the flowerbed and to the spot by the wall, he half shouted, "Are you alright?"

With no response, he crouched low and nudged the prone figure, then gave him another stronger shove.

With no warning, Juan lashed out with his fist just grazing Owen's shoulder.

"Hey, whoa, I'm just trying to help," Owen returned.

"Outta my way, gringo," spurted from Juan's foul and rum fumed mouth.

Owen backed away and protected his bag and camera that was silently snapping pictures of the brute that was now struggling to get to his feet. "I'll get those bastards," flowed from his mouth along with a barrage of Spanish, flavored metaphors.

Owen watched as the pitiful creature staggered toward the downtown area, retreating to the shadows of the dark, under-bellied nightlife that this man was apparently accustomed. Scanning the direction the Canadians had gone in, it was obvious he had lost them for the night. He approached the Hotel that the couple had entered earlier and decided, this was as good a place as any to spend the night, in fact quite luxurious. The American, who he had seen earlier with the British contingency in Belmopan, was an interesting lead. He would get to the bottom of this. The foyer was delightful.

## The Aguada

The chicken enchiladas, refried beans and salsa were delicious, and disappeared as soon as they hit the table. Ocho and Mundie kept one eye each on the Canadians and the others on the patrons and strangers that flowed through the tabled area. Patrons that were staying at the Aguada, freely filtered in and out of the dining area to the outside bar that thrived beneath the grass-thatch roof that covered the open and rough-hewn beams that supported the structure. The music had started, and the colored patio lights hanging from the bar's beams gave the open air place a mood of gaiety, some bongo drums and a steel-pan sat idle on a make-shift stage in the corner.

Brian, while eating, talked of his past involvement with the jade bowl and the escapades that had brought him to meeting Shawna, Peter and ultimately down to Belize. He spoke briefly of Vincent and the studies he had spearheaded along with theories he held for the intrigue surrounding the jade bowl. Edmundo intently listened and interjected with his own archaeological involvements once in a while. He had also mentioned Magnus, which of course initiated a whole different line of stories and humorous embellishments. Ocho had disappeared after supper and undoubtedly wished to confer with his men in the field. A young, vivacious waitress had kept the table in snacks and nonalcoholic beverages for the duration of their meeting while Edmundo, who described his earlier involvement with the military in Belize, told of how he came to be at Caracol, the site of Shawna's abduction.

"I have a meeting at the San Ignacio Resort," Brian stated getting up from the table. Steve looked up as he finished the last morsels of nacho chips in the basket center-piece.

"Would you like some company, "Edmundo asked?

Brian looked at Steve who replied, "I need to get this seen to." referring to his now swollen hand.

"Yeah, it looks broken, Mundie stated. "Why don't you get Jack to look at it. He was pretty good as a field medic in his day. He'll fix you up."

Steve got to his feet and approached the bar where Jack was busying himself with drinks ordered from the patrons outside.

"We'll have to get changed. We can't go looking like this."

"I don't have much, but I'm sure I can scrounge something," Edmundo returned.

They left through the rear archway that led to the pool, and rooms, where they all had accommodations.


The entrance to the San Ignacio Resort Hotel was well lit up and flash. Light-colored, marble tiles adorned the floors throughout and shined impeccably in the evening light. The wrought-iron railing that skirted the stairs along the eastern wall, led to the second floor and suites. Various ferns and tall, potted plants adorned the perimeter of the walls and accented the already bright and colorful foyer. Through the glass wall and doors, that exposed the exterior to the back, a scent-laden, gentle breeze blew from rear to front and up to the upper floors. The tops of palm trees, and the colorful bushes accenting the pool area, highlighted the deepening evening sky with its surrealistic, violet hue. To the right, the calming sounds of a waterfall, that delivered the clean, filtered water back to a pristine, aqua-blue, freshwater pool that rippled with the motions of patrons within.

Feeling a little underdressed, Edmundo and Brian passed the front desk and through the foyer to the lounge in its anterior. They found a table that would afford them a panoramic view of the main floor, and ordered drinks from the passing waitress. Brian proceeded to the balcony that overlooked the exotic pool and surroundings below. Scanning the lounge chairs, he caught a glimpse of Doug, the Americano, perusing a paper that lay across his lap as he reclined. At the water's edge, a black trail of hair floated on the surface and lay down on the shapely, muscular back of a woman he vaguely recognized. Her lean, dark shape edged out of the water with a quick sweep and up onto the deck with one motion. Her lean body and leg muscles rippled under the direct lighting from the lower balcony. She reached for the towel that rested on the chair beside Doug who paid no attention and began to gently towel dry her shoulder-length hair. Amalia stopped, as she noticed Brian watching her from above and felt his eyes upon her. She was stunning.

While Edmundo had watched Brian watching

Amalia dry herself off, he had withdrawn to the upper foyer to determine where she and Doug would have rooms. Brian returned to the table and waited patiently while Edmundo made the rounds of the hotel, taking note of the patrons, and who might be guards, or look-outs. Doug and Amalia had entered one of the balconied state rooms on the top floor, off to one side. Edmundo returned to Brian at the bar.

"Did you find what you were looking for?" Brian asked, swirling the ice in his empty glass.

"Yeah, they're upstairs. I'm hoping they'll be down soon for food and drinks."

"Did you know you had company all the time you were walking around?"

"Yeah, a fair-haired fellow around five-foot-eight, carrying a small camera!" retorted Mundie.

"A guy after my own heart; I've more or less given up on any camera shooting. He was watching you while you were wandering after Amalia and Doug. He's a news-paper guy we met in Belmopan when Steve and I found out about Shawna."

Mundie nodded his head and looked around to see if he was still present.

"I think he is following Amalia and Doug. This could be difficult if I can't get Amalia alone for a few minutes."

"You leave it to me," stated Mundie taking another sip of his drink. "Just let me know when you are ready to make your move."

### The shack

Nodding off lightly, Shawna and Magnus were kicked awake by a pair of size-ten work boots.

"Get up! Get up!"

One of the guards pulled them to their feet and corralled them by the door. The other had exited and was searching the sky, turning in circles with his rifle directed upwards. In the distance, Magnus heard the sound of the continual, thumping cadence of helicopter rotors. Inaudible to the average person's ear, the sound blended in with the surrounding noise ambience of the forest's natural resonations. The guards new the sound well.

"Get to the truck!"

Hesitating slightly, Shawna yelled above the din of the wind, "I have to go to the bathroom."

The guards looked at each other and then to Magnus, "Get in the truck!"

With the butt of his rifle, one of the guards forced them to the waiting, open doors and paused while Magnus helped Shawna onto the deck. Scanning the sky for the last time and noticing shafts of light emanating from behind low clouds, he cursed and jumped into the back with them. The doors slammed.

Grabbing a loose bottle of water that rolled aimlessly within the trucks confines, the rear guard took a long gulp and screwed the lid back on. Looking toward a cowering Shawna and Magnus, a little more defiant, the guard tossed the bottle to him and nodded to Shawna.

"I have to go pee," Shawna stated once again only with more urgency. The bumpy ride was doing nothing for her self-control.

"We have to stop; even for just a couple of minutes," Magnus requested with longing in his voice.

The guard considered for a moment and called to the driver to find a secluded place to stop. Within minutes they had pulled off the gravel, side road into a sheltered, wooded clearing. The treetops swayed and the leaves rustled as she squatted low, trying to ignore the eyes that watched through the shadows to her nakedness. Magnus tried to block her from their vision and sidestepped on occasion as the two sallied back and forth to watch her movements. As he heard her zipper being pulled up, he took a deep breath and charged for the guard closest to him. Completely unprepared, the fellow doubled in pain as Magnus, head dipped and butted into his solar plexus. With a quick sweep of his rifle butt, the other surprised guard cracked Magnus between the shoulder blades, and sprinted after Shawna. Lying on the ground, Magnus watched as the pursuant, chased blindly into the darkness after Shawna; then all went dark.

When he came to, Shawna was sobbing in the corner at the rear of the truck. He could see by the light of the street-lamps that flashed through the rear, door windows that she was covered in mud and blood. The scrapes on her legs and arms showed that she had given a good fight, but had failed to escape. The half-empty bottle of water continued to roll aimlessly throughout the rear of the van.

**The resort:**

It took another half-hour, but from his concealed, seated position, Brian could see Amalia, with Doug by her side, in the reflection of the glass, front doors. Carefully, she sauntered down the stairs in her ankle-strapped high-heels, exposed as she lifted the hem of her gown. The full-length, aqua-marine, satin dress that hung loosely from her shoulders barely covering her breasts, clung defiantly to the crevices and contours of her taut body. Her muscles rippled flawlessly beneath the cool fabric that shimmered provocatively as she walked slowly and gracefully toward the dining area. Large, silver and turquoise, pendulum earrings swung rhythmically as her body swayed with each step, her neck long, exposed from her hair secured high upon her head with enameled hairpins; a few, wispy strands fell loosely, caressing her shoulders.

"Wow!" escaped from Edmundo lips.

"Yeah, I know. She looks just as good naked."

Edmundo gave a side-glance to Brian that echoed reams of innuendo and gave a sigh.

Within moments of Amalia and Doug being seated at a table, the duplicitous Owen crossed the foyer and entered the lounge. Making no moves to interfere with the events unfolding, Brian and Edmundo watched from the distance as the two ate their sumptuous, seafood dinner unaware of the intrusion to their privacy of two tables over. Owen had taken several photographs of the unsuspecting couple.

Brian and Edmundo were just about to order another drink when two burly, coarse fellows entered the foyer, almost knocking a potted fern over; they headed to the dining room. A young bellboy ran forward from his station by the front entrance to stop them, but was swept aside with the regard of a small dog entreating them with a nip. Forcing the door open with a sweep of the hand, one entered the room and approached Doug with no concern for atmosphere or countenance, the other stood off to one side of the doorway as sentry. Few words were spoken at the table with the intruder standing ominously above an embarrassed Amalia. Doug, wiping his mouth with a linen napkin, and rising from the table, appeared to give Amalia an apology and retreated from the room with the stranger. Once out into the foyer, Doug and the other two slowly walked to the front doors. Out into the night air, they slowly walked to one side of the decorated pillars and continued their conversation; the bellboy cowered to one side.

Brian and Edmundo looked at each other inquisitively, and then back to Amalia, and Owen who was indiscreetly looking toward Amalia, then out to the doors again that Doug and the two had retreated. Brian sat for several moments, obviously torn between the two arenas; a decision would have to be made.

'Want to lay a bet?" asked Edmundo, looking to the three outside and Amalia sitting impatient and alone at the table.

"Oooo! Tough one," retorted Brian, considering the two scenarios. "I bet he goes for the girl."

"You're on."

Owen looked toward Amalia, and then out to the doors again and reached back to lift the chair from under his weight to get up. Amalia simultaneously got up from her chair, reached for her purse and made a move to exit. Owen intercepted her half way to the door and tried to make conversation, but Amalia brushed him off and struggled with the weight of the doors. Ephemerally, she swept across the foyer to the ladies room just off of the lounge area to the rear of the foyer. Side glancing the sitting area, she noticed Brian at the table and hesitated at his recognition. Owen pursued her through the doors and wavered due to her swiftness.

Taking the opportunity of the separation of Amalia and Doug, and her transitory response, Brian rose to his feet, but she continued and disappeared through the door to refresh herself. Edmundo, taking the occasion of Owen's diversion to advantage, he slowly edged his way along the wall to come up behind Owen should he choose to pursuit Amalia. Reaching in his pocket, Owen looked toward the slowly closing door and thought of his dwindling chances and took a cigarette from the confines of its package. Looking toward the front door, and then back to the where Amalia had disappeared; he turned briskly and headed for the front doors. Edmundo slowly shadowed him as he proceeded out into the fresh, cool night air.

Brian looked toward the bellboy who had disappeared from the front doors and scanned the area as he crossed the marbled floor to the alcove that housed the doorways to the washrooms. Confident the slow evening would allow him several moments alone with Amalia; he entered the women's quietly and looked toward the shapely woman as she bent forward over the sink to highlight her makeup.

"Well," she sighed as she side-glanced the movement to her left, "You have a lot of nerve."

Without saying a word, he quietly slid over to where she stood and leaned against the next sink and watched as she continued. Struck by her beauty and the openness of her dress as she leaned forward, he caught himself becoming aroused.

Sensing his attraction to her, she gently licked her lips and laid her hand upon his arm.

"I know you, don't I," she stated, with a measure of uncertainty.

"Yes, the Royal Reef."

"Ah yes. You and that little pervert Jose, who likes to watch me."

"He's no pervert. He's just enamored with such a beautiful woman as you."

Her gaze softened at his words and dropped her hand from his arm, "And what about you?"

"I am equally as smitten," he replied, with a slight smile that showed the whites of his teeth.

She gently moved closer toward him, lightly rubbing the firmness of her breast against his arm. Her eyes sparkled slightly as she looked up to him; her breasts reacted to the light caress and became firm beneath the silk fabric. Brian lightly laid his hands on her hips and gently squeezed the muscles that lay beneath. She responded by leaning against him and wrapping her arms around his waist. She laid her head against his chest as she could feel his hardness against her belly and gave a sigh.

She hugged him close for several moments then eased herself from the embrace, "What is it you want?"

Hesitating, taking note of the discoloration of skin beneath her make-up and a slight swelling in the area, "I need your help."


As Doug exited the front doors into the lighted portico, he could feel his anger building. "Why would you come here and jeopardize the operation knowing full well you're wanted by the San Ignacio Police." He felt his hand form into a fist, but was able to restrain the urge to strike out. "What happened?"

"Choppers in the area! We heard choppers and thought it best we move to another area."

"What! Did you guys move the girl and the doctor?" Doug felt his anger welling up inside again to an uncontrollable height.

"We have them in the truck."

Doug ran his fingers over his face and then

through his hair, "Ok, it will be alright. Just let me think." He stopped short and fumbled in his pocket for a cigarette. Just then, a guest from the hotel walked out and lit a cigarette, not three feet distant. One of the big fellas slowly walked over and stood in his way until the patron moved to the opposite side of the entrance to continue smoking there. Just inside, off to one side, another fellow stood looking through the glass to the foliage and the road beyond.

Just ahead, a little further up the hill away from the resort, Doug noticed the dirty, white van sitting motionless. "Let's go for a walk."

After a short ten minutes of Brian trying to explain the situation, a gentle rap came to the door alerting him of a change in circumstance. Giving Amalia a lasting hug, he cautiously returned to the sitting area of the bar and watched as Doug returned through the front doors without the two thugs; the bellboy peeked from behind the desk and stood tall in response to their absence. Looking through the glass door of the dining hall and noticing Amalia's absence, Doug did a quick 360 glance around the foyer and came to rest on Amalia as she re-entered the area. She gave Brian a shy smile as she walked arm-in-arm with Doug back to the dining lounge. Within moments, Owen entered from the front and continued to the dining lounge and the remainder of his dinner.

Edmundo, smiling from ear to ear, sat down across from Brian and questioned, "Well?"

**The Aguada**

It was late when Oz, Gizmo and Knobby returned. They looked exhausted and wind-blown, grubby from their two-day trek. They entered in through the back entranceway, away from patrons that frolicked and lazed in the chairs of the colorful, pool area. Thunder echoed as a chopper retreated back to base in the foothills of the mountains a short distance off. In the shadows, they crept unassuming, quietly without a sound, to the rooms that Jackson had provided with multiple, unimpeded access. Once in their rooms, they waited patiently for Ocho, who was aware of their arrival and would return shortly.

Bottles of water were passed freely around as the men unloaded their gear to be cleaned and serviced. Cold beer and food would have to wait until the necessities were taken care of and a plan worked out for the next day. Ocho and Mundie, listened intently while the men gave their reports of the encounters with the loggers and natives that worked in the area, and of the abandoned work stations they had cased and searched. The most intriguing, a fueling and maintenance shack that was positioned not more than five miles west along a gravel service road. Brake lights flashed as a van had retreated through the jungle, and out of sight of the pursuant Gazelle due to the low cloud cover. A close inspection later showed evidence of occupation and some measure of disarray at a quick retreat. They could not be certain, but scuffs in the dirt floor, cut plastic pull-ties and blood stains by a central support post, gave them enough cause to determine that someone had been held here against their will.

Edmundo gave a report of the couple at the San Ignacio Resort, and the implications that the American, and his girlfriend's involvement conveyed. Ocho agreed to the Canadian's plan to follow the two, and report to Edmundo as long as they stayed out of the way of military operations should the situation demand intervention. Edmundo also explained the possibility of a ceremonial service to be held at one of the local archaeological sites close by; most likely Xunantunich. He would do reconnaissance at first light; he would explain the situation to the Canadians.

The cocks crowed before the break of dawn, and the dogs replied in their usual back and forth bantering. Garbage can lids began to open and close as the kitchen staff began their early-morning breakfast routine. Brian's feet had barely hit the ground before he was rousted out of his second floor room. Steve followed close behind pulling on the remaining boot, unattached laces dangling from each side of vacant, boot-lace eyes.

Out on the deck beside the pool, duffle bags and rifles lay in order, guarded by Gizmo, who yawned and stretched toward the rising sun. Quietly, as the rest of the crew emerged from the shadows, all the paraphernalia was transported to the parking lot and loaded into the vehicles with silent precision. Steve and Brian followed Edmundo as he headed to his blue, pickup truck. Their yellow, subcompact car sat idle at the edge of the lot. A layer of accumulative dust covered its exterior initiated by the traffic of the heavy vehicles.

"Whoa!" came Steve's cry as he eased the driver's door open.

The smell of stale beer and cigarettes, wafted out from the interior. Half-full bags of stale chips and nachos littered the back seat, baked stale by the hot sun in the enclosed space. An opened beer can sat perched by the emergency-brake handle, green and yellow mold grew from its hole and tab; several lay empty and crushed in the foot-well of the passenger seat.

"Come-on Steve," Brian encouraged, opening the window all the way down and climbing in. "We have to keep up with Mundie."

The yellow subcompact, trailed the small, blue pickup in a cloud of dust out onto the street that led back to the highway from Santa Elena; the large SUVs headed out the other direction to the foothills, the military base and the choppers.

The ferryman was yet to be at his station when they drove up to the docking area by the Macal River. Pulling the retrieving rope that dangled precariously close to the water, they tugged the small, one-vehicle barge back to its station and loaded the pickup. Encouraging Mundie to continue on ahead, Brian and Steve cranked the ferry back to its eastside moorings and loaded the car. After a few short speedy cranks, they were following the jungle, encroached road to the parking area, and Edmundo, near the Xunantunich ruins.

To their surprise, there were already several vehicles parked near the kiosk, and a few more up the trail to the left that approached the rear of the Castillo temple not visible from the lot.

"Let's go up to the courtyard and see what's going on," suggested Mundie, pointing up to the hill and path. "If there is something being prepared, we'll know."

The three gingerly headed up the paved, steep path that led to the six-temple ruins that made up the ceremonial city of years past. Turning to check that all was well with the vehicles, Steve noticed motion in one of the vans that was parked close to the wooded trail and decided to check it out.

"Hey guys, I'll catch up with you in a minute. I just need to check something out at the kiosk."

Nodding without opposition, Brian and Edmundo continued up the steep hill in the direction of the ruins.

Trying to stay inconspicuous, Steve quietly walked around the cars just in time to hear the gentle slam of the van door. Poking his head around the rear of the van and looking up passed the large, backup mirrors, he saw the familiar build and hair of the fellow he had cold-cocked the night before. Checking in the vans windows, he noticed several, large shapes in the shadows of the interior. Two men had been taped together and were motionless. He could see slight jerks of discomfort; they were still alive. Quietly following behind, Steve stayed fifty feet at his rear and watched from his distance the movement and tried to determine his intent. A large, heavy object stretched his right jacket pocket, and all Steve could imagine it to be was the gun he had held in reserve the previous night. His heart began to pound as he thought of the repercussions that could ensue should this fellow recognize him. Pulling his hoodie low over his brow and donning his sunglasses, Steve continued along the path careful not to step on a stick or dry leaves. The enormous sound din of the jungle would cover most of his clatter, but there was always a chance this guy would turn at any moment to cover his trail. No sooner had the thought entered his mind, when Juan turned and noticed Steve behind him.

"What you doin here mang," he yelled at Steve, taking hold of the object in his pocket?

"Take it easy dude," Steve yelled back, not sure whether Juan had recognized him.

Juan did not move as Steve slowly sauntered up to within eight feet of him. Face-to-face they stood for several seconds till Juan slowly began to recognize the form that stood before him. Steve's heart pounded hard as he stood before Juan and took note of the bluish welt on his forehead.

"Nice egg," cited Steve as he stood motionless before Juan.

Juan bewildered, strained to see behind the glasses and then glanced down to his wrapped right hand. "Jou're the bastard that hit me last...."

Before Juan could finish, Steve took a lung and flying leap at Juan who side-stepped and lost balance. Catching himself from the fall, Juan took his hands from his pockets and grasped at whatever was available to throw at Steve. Flaying at the sticks and refuse that flew through the air, Steve did a round-house kick and caught Juan's boot as he struck out to protect himself. Reaching in his pocket, he fumbled for the pistol and brought it up to fire at Steve. Missing the safety, he could not compress the trigger and lost his concentration. Steve swung around blindly not noticing the gun that flew off into the bushes and out of reach. Juan confused, lashed out at Steve and pushed him off balance into the slippery, wet underbrush. Feeling a shot of pain in his ankle as it bounced off an outcrop of a moss-covered boulder, Steve watched as Juan bolted out of sight into the dense underbrush and foliage that surrounded the trail.

"Ouch!"

Staying close to the periphery, Edmundo eased

himself through the trees and brush to the boundary of the courtyard; not so much for covertness, but assurance of a least several minutes of unimpeded scrutiny of the ruins to the south. As before, when Brian and Steve had visited, there was a dance troop and several musicians that wandered and staged themselves in preparation for some event.

Through a pocket-size telescope, Mundie peered at the proceedings and handed the piece to Brian, "Look off to the left and rear of the front left corner."

Brian gazed through the little, glass piece, "Is that the American from the resort?"

"Yep," returned Mundie.

"What do you think he's doing here," Brian asked, handing the piece back to Edmundo.

"I dunno," he replied, looking through the glass again. "We still don't know where Shawna is, but she can't be far away."

"Yeah," sighed Brian, leaning back against a tree. "I'm counting on it."

# ELEVEN

## Diaz cinqo (day five)

Crouched low beneath the trees, Brian and Edmundo waited patiently and could see the group that had gathered at the far end of the large court. The two were hidden high on the foliage laden, unexcavated ruins of a lesser temple and could watch the captors and wait for the opportune time to snatch Shawna away. If it had not been for the politics involved, and the noticeably familiar, government heavyweights, Oz and Ocho could have taken care of this in moments; a high-powered rifle at the opportune time could produce outstanding results, but with this many civilians involved, the possible collateral damage would be unacceptable.

Near the apex of the temple Castillo, farthest from where they were perched, a man busied himself with a crate and several flag standards. A number of vehicles had clawed their way through the dense jungle to the rear of the Castillo. One, a large, black 4X4 stood ominous near the rear, a crumpled figure of a man hobbled back and forth as if anxious for the proceedings to begin. After several moments, a woman as limp as a ragdoll was dragged from behind the lower terrace that jutted out from one side of the ruin.

"Shawna," eased from Brian's lips as he recognized her wiry frame. He had not seen her for several months but his heart leaped as if they had parted just moments before. Anxious, his body tensed, readying itself for the fight ahead.

A firm hand gripped Brian's arm as he prepared to leap from undercover.

"Waite, Brian," Edmundo calmly spoke. "The time is not right yet. We will have a chance, soon." Pointing with his free hand, "See that line of trees on the far side of the court; that is where we need to be. We have back-up. They will not act unless absolutely necessary."

Grabbing his field glasses, Edmundo looked briefly to the spot tucked inconspicuously behind the banks of the ball court that was positioned parallel to the courtyard, and then handed them to his companero, Brian.

"I'm quite sure there will be only two men that will lead Shawna up the walkway to where the priest will be waiting in the alcove at the top. He will be the only one that will be in the chamber so we will have our chance then. If the memory of the sequence of the ceremonial events serves me well, we will need to be out of sight while they prepare Shawna for the procedure." Edmundo took a deep breath and thought for a moment. "Since two other individuals, as far as I know, are the only others who will be allowed to approach the sacred area, there will be lots of chances to steal her away as we hide in one of the alcoves near the summit of the temple," pointing to the apex of the temple. "The trick will be getting out alive once we have her. That is where Ocho and Oz will do their thing."

"We will cross that bridge when we get there," Brian interjected. "As long as Steve stays put and your friends do their part, I am sure we will make it. Are you ready for a fight?"

"Of course!"

Luckily, the defoliating of these ruins was very rarely ever completed and grew back even thicker after a few short months. The rear side of most temples never became clean, or the structures rebuilt to allow normal passage to the summit; this would be the advantage that hopefully would not be considered by the guards.

Receiving the binocular from Edmundo, Brian once again looked toward the small gathering that had slowly proceeded to the front of the temple. Scanning their faces through the lenses, he was surprised to see several familiar faces among the mostly native Mayans he recognized from the previous night, save one.

"That snake!"

There, tucked behind several military men was the sunglass-clad face of Magnus. What was he doing here? Just to his right was another woman of familiarity, "Amalia!"

"Be quiet, Brian! I know we are well hidden, but if you listen closely, there is no noise, only the rustling of the leaves in the wind, very strange."

"Sorry."

"We must make our way now," Edmundo suggested, motioning with his hand to go slow and backtracked down the rear face of the hill. They slowly continued on to the west side of the site.

Ignorant of Brian and Edmundo, two others had inconspicuously crawled through the trees to the dense, fern laden, north side of the Castillo; both wanted to take some shots, one with a camera, the other, a gun.

Juan had somehow gotten through the perimeter of guards unnoticed, with one purpose in mind, to be rid of the cancer that had seemed to invade every aspect of his life. Since he had agreed to the compromise with Doug for Amalia, all those years earlier, he had yearned to have him dead, her as well, but for another reason. Amalia's death would appease the continual pain he harbored for killing his father for her sake all those years before, and many others. Seeing her, resting at the front of the temple with the group, only strengthened his desire to end the life of the man that had continually belittled him, even to this day. There was another young woman just in front of him by the side of the temple. She looked drugged, swaying back and forth as if trying to stay awake. Juan watched as several men undressed her and rubbed her body with oil. It excited him to watch them caress her body and stirred an even stronger desire to act fearlessly. He would have to be patient. He recognized several of the plain-clothed guards that accompanied Doug, and they would recognize him. Behind them was another cadre standing almost as if at attention by several large, black vehicles at the tree line behind the temple El Castillo. One vehicle had its rear door open exposing a crumpled figure of a man seated; he peered from beneath a wide, brimmed fedora toward the men as they played with the naked woman. Juan had one shot left in the pistol he had carried from the city. He had wanted to kill the Canadian gringo before, but he had enough sense to let it go, till now. He could escape into the jungle with Amalia and start anew.

Owen, the journalist, ignorant of the severity of the situation, followed Juan just beyond his peripheral vision. Camera in hand, he was able to digitally record Juan's every move. The army vehicles and the shackled men at the parking lot only fuelled his curiosity. Zooming in on the temple, he was able to document the identities of the individuals as they rested before the wide, stone-carved stairs at the base of the Castillo; several of these he had vague recollections of the previous day in Belmopan; they had been with the British contingency.

Unaware of the proclivity to mayhem, the custodian, in the rear of the black, Tahoe SUV, displayed a certain level of pleasure at watching the men prepare the girl for the ceremony. In one-way, the ceremony seemed so overdone and unnecessary, but for over millennia of unimpeded execution, the more smoke and mirrors that could be added to the milieu, the less likelihood of exposure. He had in the past always been able to insure his anonymity by eliminating, over time, all those who had remotely come in contact with him and the festivity; this time would be no different. The process to him had become almost tedious, but with the return to the ancient site of his centuries old indignation, recompense would be savored sweetly. To once again have the opportunity to enlist such a fine specimen to his heartfelt cause was at the least melodramatic, rather exciting, and the princess's offspring, how ironic.

Not a quarter mile away, Steve sat in the driver's seat of the Rover, door wide open, his foot cocked up through the open window letting the wind blow up his shorts. His ankle ached and the skinned knuckle on his right hand was badly swollen. He had made a good choice in not going up to the ruins. It was better he stay in the parking area and wait for the others to return. He could only imagine what could and would be happening not half a mile up the hill, but someone needed to stay and mind the equipment and liaise between the two groups of patrols. Steve waited patiently for any word on the radios, but dare not try to contact the two. He became bored, but was content to stay to ensure the lookout guards captured earlier by Juan, stayed immobile.

From their vantage point, Edmundo and Brian could see quite clearly what was happening. The circumstances started to become clear with Amalia, Magnus and a few others being kept in the foreground out of the way and sight of the preparations that were going on just on the other side of the temple. It was not apparent whether they were being held against their will or not .The path that led up to the concourse of the temple, was well worn and accessible to the third tier, then, the way higher became more difficult and steep with cut stones strewn across the narrow, slick pathway. Brian could see Magnus looking worn, while Amalia looked uneasy and messy, not her usual demeanor. Within moments, a Teague-clad, military guard, and a well-dressed man came from around the far side of the temple. They came to within yards of where they were and in front of the small group. He looked vaguely familiar as he approached and came to stand in front of Amalia.

"Well my dear, what do you think? Are you going to do as I say and keep quiet, or will you be encouraged to silence in other ways, like these?" Doug directed his hand toward the others in the group.

She looked up with hate in her eyes and spat, "You bastard! You will not get away with this."

The back of his hand fell hard against her face bringing her to her knees. Magnus forced his way forward to shield her from another assault. The man just cursed and backed away. It was then that I realized that this was Amalia's boyfriend, the Americano businessman that had also flew in to the Ministry at Belmopan.

Edmundo's hand grabbed me once again, "Not yet, we need a plan."

"We have to get up there, right?" Brian quarried.

"Yes!"

Brian quietly slid from his hiding spot, a huge, limestone block that made up the embankment to the ball-court and gave a gentle whistle just enough to get Magnus' attention. Startled at his appearance not thirty feet away, he stood up then quickly looked around and crouched down again as not to draw attention. Amalia, noticing his attentiveness looked Brian's way as well. Backing up slightly to give himself greater cover, he signed with his hands the fact that he and Mundie needed to go up the pathway to the upper portion of the temple. A little bewildered, Magnus began to understand the intent and whispered to Amalia that they would need to make a diversion to allow the two of them to span the open area, about sixty feet to the base of the pyramid-shaped temple. Amalia, getting to her feet slowly, walked to where Doug had been standing farther across the front of the temple. Without hesitation, she bolted passed Doug and started into a run for the thick underbrush at the edge of the court. All eyes turned that way as Doug and his guards took off after her towards the edge of the clearing, oddly enough right in the direction of Juan.

Taking the opportune moment of the diversion, Edmundo and Brian took off in a mad dash for the pathway that led to the higher tiers of the temple and much cover from the audience. Magnus occasionally glanced as the two disappeared from sight. Taking a path slightly more to the rear of the temple, they scrambled as fast and as carefully as they could. Half way up the temple, they heard an almost simultaneous, double shot that echoed throughout the plaza; it stopped them in their tracks. Glancing at each other, they realized this could have only meant that Amalia had given her life for the two of them. Shattered and breathless, they stopped in the cool shelter of an overhang in the crumpled ruins.

With little choice and not much more hope, "We will have to split up," Edmundo suggested.

"I know," Brian resounded. "The only way we have a chance is if we can somehow separate the guards as they bring Shawna up."

"Well, once they get this far, they are not going to turn back if one of them ends up alone with Shawna, right!"

"I guess so."

"I'll stay back here," Edmundo continued, "and try to take care of at least one of them."

"But what if you fail? They could kill you."

"If I fail, all three of us are dead, and Amalia's death will also be in vain. We can't fail."

With that, Brian reached out his hand to Edmundo's and pulled into a firm embrace.

"We will do this amigo!"

"I'll see you soon," and with that, the Canadian cleared the edge of the wall and struggled up to the next tier of the temple.

Following the worn path that meandered through the ruins, Brian soon became disoriented and faltered at the near stone maze. Fallen walls and semi rebuilt pathways, crisscrossed and seemingly led to nowhere. Backtracking, he came across a small archway that led inside the ruin and up a set of narrow, steep steps. Knowing he had to get further up into the ruins, he considered the possibility of exposure and chose to backtrack to the far side of the tier. As he was about to leave, a shadow came to block the bright archway at the top of the stairs. Startled, he watched in fear expecting an alarm to be sounded and a fight to ensue. Trepidation was replaced with apprehension as the silhouette of a young, native boy stood to block the brilliance from beyond. Considering the situation, and the compromise a young child may cause in the present circumstance, Brian headed up the steep stairs, careful not to slip from the narrow, slippery, stone steps. Looking beyond the threshold of the arch, the near, naked boy with black, shoulder length hair disappeared around a distant corner, up the steep incline toward the front of the temple. Cautiously climbing the slope, not wishing to be noticed, he crouched low and followed in the direction the boy had led.

At the edge of the wooded area, the demented Juan could not believe his eyes. Amalia was running directly to him, and better still, Doug was following close behind. Crouching low in the shadows just beyond sight, Juan pulled the revolver, he had retrieved from the forest floor, from his pocket. He had one shot and it had to be a good one. He had patience for this sort of thing, but his heart began to race and he became anxious. Doug had grabbed Amalia from behind and was shaking her. The guards were close behind; he didn't notice them. 'Why was he shaking her; Amalia was coming back to him and Doug stopped her once again; why won't he let her go?'

Standing up from his hiding place, Juan walked from the cover of the trees, pistol pointed directly at Doug's head. Startled, but with fast reflexes, one of the guards directly behind the two fired a shot hitting Juan directly in the forehead just below the bluish bruise at his hairline. Juan's gun fired. The bullet slightly dipped to the right taking off Doug's left, lower ear. Screaming in agony, Doug fell to the grass clasping the side of his head. Juan lie dead, face-up; his anger still deep within his dimming eyes.

Owen, from his sheltered vantage point, was shocked and unprepared for the violent exchange. Camera ready, he was able to capture the episode on camera, but fumbled at the aggression and cowered low. Taking a moment to gather courage and realizing the gravity of the situation, he gently lifted his camera and continued documenting.

High above as Brian neared the apex of the incline, near the front of the temple, the paths converged into one. Looking about to find the boy, he gave a sigh of exasperation at not finding him and lifted his face to the dimming sky as if to gather strength from the ethereal. The clouds drifted in from the south-west.

Around the next turn was the platform where they had seen the fellow organizing his paraphernalia for the ceremonial display. Taking a deep breath, he peered out to the treetops that resembled a lush, emerald carpet covering the entire periphery of the complex. The mist that had lazily hung between the treetops earlier drifted away to a milky haze that spanned into the far distance; the cool, encroaching wind betrayed the inclement rain. The damp air smelled sweet, enriched by the scent of orchid and plant blossoms that emanated from the jungle below. The surroundings were deafly quiet as Brian prepared to run the course and surprise the priest in his lair. Taking another deep breath, and pumping himself with adrenaline, he took flight and raced to the front of the temple. Completely stricken with fear at what he saw, Brian stopped dead in his tracks. There, before him stood a tall, dark-skinned man with a facemask that resembled a Toucan bird. Long, colorful feathers stuck out the top of his head-dress adding an extra foot to his already imposing height. Equally as startled as Brian, the priest backed up, tripped, and stumbled over an outcropping of flagstone and fell over the edge. To Brian's delight, he remained in a crumpled heap on the stones twelve feet below, motionless. Unsure and confused at the next course of action, he looked down to the milling people at the base of the pyramid. Quickly considering the options, the most important being the guns in the hands of the guards below, Brian eased himself over the edge and jumped the remaining distance to the fallen fellow. Giving him a nudge and then a kick, insurance to his unconscious state, Brian dragged the body to a shallow niche, and then proceeded to take off the priest's sparse clothing. Not all that certain his ruse would work; Brian sheepishly climbed back to the perch on the next level and continued in the fictitious preparations for the ceremony. Stumbling around in a loincloth that kept falling to his knees, and a headdress with feathers that continually dropped down over his eyes, Brian entertained himself as best I could. The guards below noticed no abnormalities.

Within the small cave barely high enough to stand in, behind the makeshift stone altar, Brian was surprised to find, not the rudimentary knives and chisels of the ancients, but the precision surgical tools of a doctor. Scalpels, knives and saws of various sizes were laid in array on a short table and covered with sterile cloths, that he promptly put back. Two coolers filled with ice were off to one side, one already holding a plastic bag enclosed an organ of some sort, to whom or what he had no desire to know and quickly slammed the lid shut. Sitting on the second cooler and taking stock of his emotions, Brian wondered at the proceedings and if the young lad was a part of it. Why would they want a second organ if they already had one? Perplexed, he decided that it was probably best not known. They were not going to get Shawna's heart at any rate; it belonged to him. Brian tucked his loincloth between his legs and sat on the cooler.

Within moments, the closeness of the cave and the miasmic dampness emanating from the hole in the floor began to have a nauseating effect on him. Light headed and dizzy, he stepped forward out into the open. Taking a breath of fresh air, he sat down upon a large cut stone. Looking around the periphery of the landing, he took notice of the weathered stone carvings and the deterioration of the distinct etchings that had become worn with the assaults of wind and rain. Above the threshold of the alcove, just out of reach in near shade and dampness, a lone, black orchid grew from amid moss and other fragile foliage; a statement of the purity of nature's intent. Undaunted, but fragile, it spoke of the intricacies and desire for natures dominance in man's structured and finite domain. Wishing to capture its fragility, Brian rose to grasp at it when he noticed a man through the sparse raindrops, below, waving up at him. Simultaneously, screams and cries of the women, bellowed up from the small crowd. The first act had begun.

With scantily, clad warriors painted blue on either side of her, Shawna staggered across the front of the temple grounds. Some of the woman wept while others remained silent. Magnus stood erect ready to act on whatever circumstance from above arose that needed his attention. He had no idea what would transpire, but he knew he could not stand by and be witness to such a gruesome event.

Shawna was in a daze. She had no idea where she was or the fact she was dressed in white cotton. The two paraded her up the narrow path, and then disappeared for a while behind the line of limestone blocks that made up the promenade; they reappeared after several minutes at another corner of a higher tier. Most of the temples had a wide, central staircase that ran up the face, but this did not. Whether it is lack of proper excavation, or slightly different design influences from earlier dynasties, this configuration would allow for greater opportunity to whisk Shawna away. There was a maze of passageways and alcoves, great staging points for an ambush.

Edmundo waited patiently, but knew his time was coming close. If he could separate the three of them and perhaps eliminate, or at best occupy one of them, then Brian would have a better chance at the other one. There had been a section, if his memory served him well, that had a narrow opening and hallway with stairs that opened up onto the top tier. If he could position himself out of sight, this would be an ideal spot at which to act. Perched on a short shelf at the rear of the temple, he watched as the first priest leading Shawna disappeared into the crevasse of the rocks. Stopping, while the first ducked and struggled to get his tipsy headdress through the opening, Shawna half collapsed at the opening. Reaching from the opening to pull Shawna through, the first priest was out of sight and the second, with his back to Edmundo, was aiding Shawna through the narrow opening.

'Whomp!' and a light sound echoed as a ten pound rock came crashing down through the priest's headdress. Crumpled and heaped at the entrance to the oblong entrance, Edmundo struggled to drag the body out of the way. Sneaking through the opening to the hall and narrow stone stairway, he waited while his eyes adjusted to the dim light. Within moments, the silhouette shape of Shawna in her Mayan, maiden regalia disappeared into the blinding light above and beyond; it was now up to Brian. Unaware that his priestly-partner was not taking up the rear, the first plodded methodically around to the front and his fateful demise. With a swift swing of Brian's ceremonial spear, the butt end came crashing into the unsuspecting priest's temple above his ear. Like a rag doll, he collapsed with Shawna following immediately after.

With the unwilling audience below watching through the increasing raindrops, Brian raised the spear above his head and gave the signal for Ocho, Oz and Knobby to begin their assault. Collapsing to Shawna's side, he tried to waken her from the drug-induced stupor. Unable, Brian lifted her into his arms and started the long, timeless trek down the descending pathway. In the background, a barrage of gunfire began to echo through the surrounding courtyard. Retracing the steps and coming to the rear face of the temple, he could hear return fire and the revving of vehicle engines. Resting from the weight of Shawna, Brian watched as Edmundo bounced and slid from tier to tier, anxious to reach his fellow commandos, the stony pathways had become slick with the rain and mud.

From behind a stone outcropping of a temple across the courtyard, Ocho took slow aim with his Beretta, 50 caliber-with scope, at the driver of the lead car; it would take a man's arm off, so he was very careful with his sights. The outburst of gun-fire from Oz and Knobby were to disorientate and get the crowd to disperse; heading for cover, the area would be devoid of erect individuals and less chance for collateral damage. Edmundo had been quite explicit with his request for targets only, no innocents would be sacrificed today even at the expense of allowing the guilty to temporarily escape. The assault team would individually strategize from their vantage points who would be the vital targets. Unimpeded, they could sight the key personnel and immobilize the vehicles before they proceeded out under the cover of the jungle trees and foliage.

Ready to take the shot, Ocho had to abort when blurs of motion blocked his view and people at the rear of the temple ran helter-skelter. Doors slammed in the large, black vehicles as the entourage realized the compromising situation they had found themselves in. He aimed instead for the grill of the vehicle that was most in the clear. With a puff of smoke emanating from under the hood, the last vehicle limped along behind the first two vehicles that had managed to escape through the density. Oz and Knobby, who were to concentrate on assuring that the hostages would not be hurt or compromised, worked their way up the sides of the courtyard from their intermediary location, through the underbrush and outcroppings of ruins that scattered the periphery of the courtyard, to the base of the great Castillo.

Owen amazed at the flurry of activity, tucked himself as flat as he could to the boulder that had hid him safely from the unfolding, passion-play. Still obscured by deep foliage, he panned his camera toward the now hazy drama as he tried to capture the scenes as they unfolded.

Spurts of AK 47 rifle-fire, began to echo throughout the open area from all directions. The prone spectators in front of the temple were unwilling to move while bullets embedded themselves with a pop and a puff of dust into the large, carved stones behind. The few in ceremonial dress sprinted to the back of the temple and hid. The man with his ear blown off ran to a waiting vehicle and drove off in a cloud of unspent fuel, followed by several others. Some of the guards had returned fire but were ineffectual against the phantom assaults from hidden locations. The lone figure of Edmundo bent low, jumped from the lowest tier of the temple and on to the stone steps that rose empirically from the grass courtyard. He raced to where the small group of people had been held and embraced the old man.

Thunder turning into whirling radials shattered through the drizzling rain as two Gazelle helicopters hovered and swayed to gentle landings in the midst of the field. Spilling a handful of camouflaged soldiers onto the wet grass below, they returned to the misty skies with clamorous fortitude. Four more figures emerged from behind some of the lesser temples and underbrush, quickly surveyed the scene and disappeared as mystically as they had appeared. The round-up began; the recovery in the courtyard was over.

As Brian rested on the steps of the last tier before the grass-covered courtyard with Shawna balanced on his lap, her eyes began to flutter, opening and closing trying to focus on his face. A fragile palm came to rest on his right cheek as her lips parted and eased, "Brian?" Lifting her close, Brian pressed his face to hers and held her firmly.

Steve, unable to react quickly to the crackle of breaking trees and underbrush, watched powerlessly as three, black SUVs emerged from the corner of the parking lot at accelerated speed. Loosely navigating from the gravel to the paved road, they skidded sideways and squealed sharply as rubber contacted moist pavement. They disappeared down the hill and out of sight in a cloud of smoke and disruption; a Gazelle hounded them relentlessly from the sky.

Unable to land in the narrow roadway to block them, the one helicopter could only watch as the lead

vehicle drove onto the small ferry. At gun point, the
operator was encouraged to pull them to the other side.
Attempting to cross the shallows a short distance from
the ferry, the second of the vehicles became mired in
the light gravel and remained motionless, the muddy
water slowly inching up its sides to the windows; the
last, on the paved road, remained static, its hood paint
smoldering and blistering from the intense heat
emanating from below. From the bowels of the
chopper, two crewmen jumped with lines and
harnesses to the ground and stood firm ready to assault
on command, the remaining vehicle whose occupants
started to spill onto the roadway. Moments later, on the
opposite side of the shallow river, a motorcade of
military vehicles, along with some local police arrived
from San Jose Succotz. As the vehicle, laden ferry tied
up to the far side of the shallow river, the assailant's
gun was put away. The blockade was in place. For
several moments, no movement was apparent on either
side. Soldiers behind the line of blockade vehicles were
'at-arms' along with others that had surrounded the
aquacade truck. Slowly, the rear window of the Tahoe
lowered and papers were handed to one of the guarding
men and transferred to the waiting military commander
by the jeep blocking the disembarking SUV. Returning
to the jeep and scrutinizing the papers, he was seen
talking on the radio. After a fifteen minute standoff, the
commander slowly walked onto the ferry with his hand
hovering over his sidearm. After gazing at the open
window momentarily, he handed the papers back
through the window. Slow to retreat, he removed
himself from the ferry, head down-turned as if to
search for answers in the worn planks of the decking.
After communicating with the surrounding forces, he

pulled from in front of the ferried SUV allowing it passage to the Highway. Unimpeded, it headed north along the Western Highway toward San Ignacio, the second Gazelle helicopter followed at a distance. The other two vehicles were impounded, their occupants incarcerated, for now.

As the black, Tahoe SUV entered San Ignacio, the Gazelle was rerouted. "That is why we have diplomatic status," Doug stated, as he patted blood from the remaining half of his ear, watching as the helicopter headed south back toward Xunantunich.

The custodian sat motionless, emotionless, carefree to the ill-fated ceremony. "I will need your help when we get back to Belmopan to ensure anonymity."

"Yes sir," Doug replied, watching the sun filter through the clouds.

The foothills of the mountains morphed into rolling, emerald mounds that adorned the retreating countryside of Santa Elena. Trepidation crept in as Doug considered the ramifications of this failure and how he would replenish this lack condition as quickly as possible. He would need Amalia.

# TWELVE

Henry watched from his second floor office window as a lone, black SUV skirted the perimeter of the Government Compound. He felt a twinge of nervousness as he reflected on the previous days' ruse, or meeting, he had arranged for Magnus with the American. Mag was a good friend and a refusal for the request was not a consideration, even if it put his reputation in question or even his life at risk.

As the black vehicle disappeared down the sloped drive that entered the bowels of the parking area of the compound, Henry reached for the phone and tried without success to the number Mag had left for him. Placing the phone back in his upper pocket, he pondered the ramifications of his actions of setting the meeting up with Doug, and pulled the roll-chair from its resting place. Sitting behind his desk, the musty smell of the manila folders reminded him of the extent of time with which they had remained. Stacks twelve high denoted the backlog of unprocessed data of a dozen digs throughout Belize and Guatemala; he ran his fingers through his thinning hair and pushed his spectacles up the long bridge of his nose.

The Military attachment had retreated from their standoff position at the ferry crossing to Xunantunich, and the local police had started in the recovery and impoundment of the vehicles that had barred the entranceway to the site. Ocho, and his band of men, had discreetly retreated into the surrounding jungle and regrouped at an unknown location, spirited away in the belly of a Gazelle.

Below the façade of the Castillo Temple, police and emergency personnel wandered the area taking statements from the group of individuals that had gathered around the emergency vehicles. A stretcher lay empty beside the lifeless body of Juan as the coroner inspected the wound that has caused his death. Amalia, close by with Edmundo, rested on her knees and watched as they loaded Juan's body onto the stretcher and covered him with a sheet. Tears trickled down her cheeks, and her body gently raked with each sob. Confused, she was not sure whether she cried from grief, regret or release. A long and sordid relationship had finally come to a close. Her heart remembered a time when she was young, naive and in love; her tears washed away the memories of a wasted life and the lost years she yearned to retrieve. Edmundo remained close.

As detectives guided the two ceremonial priests from the steps of the Temple, another lifted the cooler that held the organ and a box of evidence, from step to descending step.

"Did you find the young boy who was up there as well," Brian asked, holding Shawna steady by his side.

"Non, Senor. No little boy."

Beneath a propped up canvas that protected them from a light rain that fell in the late afternoon, they watched as the chaotic scene that surrounded them slowly deflated to a tolerable level. The temperature had not yet cooled into the evening, and the breeze that would carry the heat of the day out to the coast had not stirred. It was very humid and Shawna was slow in the recovery from her drowsiness; she sipped on a bottle of water and continued to gather her wits.

"How did you find me," she asked, brushing a lock of hair from her face.

"It wasn't that hard, only months of study and researching all the sites in Central America." He played with the edge of the loincloth that hung between his legs. "It was a bit of luck actually. Steve and I ran into Edmundo, and his crew, at a hotel in Santa Elena."

"Who's Steve?"

"He's my brother-in-law, remember, from the boat ride in Victoria?" He eased his assertion, sensing her struggle to recollect. "You'll meet him later."

Shawna squeezed his arm and dipped her head shyly. She cuddled close, "It's nice to see you again."

Not too far distant, Magnus was close at hand beside Owen, listening as the interrogator questioned him as to his involvement. "We will have to confiscate your camera and its contents for evidence," the man demanded in a monotone as he scribbled notes down on his pad.

"You can't. This is private property and a valued asset," Owen retorted with distain.

"It will be all right," encouraged Magnus. "I'll see to it that it gets returned to you."

"And who in the bloody hell are you," returned Owen in a thick Cockney drawl. Pulling a white hanky from his shirt pocket, he wiped the sweat from his brow?

"I'm one of the archaeological directors, and someone who will decide if and when this will be returned to you."

Owen nodded sheepishly while Magnus gave the interrogator a nod.

"Can I borrow you're phone to make one call," Magnus asked of the officer?

Handing the phone to Mag, he returned to asking Owen more questions and how he happened to be at the site.

Slowly approaching Brian and Shawna, Magnus gave him a big smile. "You Canadians show up in the darndest places, and in the cutest outfits." He looked down to the breastplate and oversized cloth dangling freely between his legs.

"And you Dr. Magnus, know how to through the wildest parties." They gave each other's hands a firm squeeze and shake. "This is Shawna, Magnus. She is the reason I am here."

"Yes, I know. We just spent some quality time together," Magnus stated with an air of admiration. "You, are one-hell-of-a young lady. 'Pillars of the Moon", back to its home." He swayed his head from side to side. "I am so pleased this has turned out the way it has. When they took you this morning and left me in the van, I was sure I would never see you again." A fatherly smile broke across his face. "The heavens were at war this day."

Shawna blushed and shrank from his assertion, still overwhelmed by the circumstances and her physical condition.

"Forgive me, my dear. I have you at a

disadvantage. I have been able to learn more of the circumstances surrounding your abduction and the conditions prior. Even though we could not talk much at the time of our incarceration, I was aware of the Pillars, and also the true purpose of your kidnapping."

"Nothing surprises me anymore, and I think I know a little more of you now, Doctor, than you give me credit for," she said teasingly with a smile. "I could not have lasted through all of this without your help, and for this, I must thank you."

"Perhaps, we can talk more a little later. I am about to phone Henry, an old friend in Belmopan, to reassure him of my condition. We will all be heading to Belmopan shortly to help the police determine what just happened and what to release to the papers. Owen," Magnus looked in his direction, "will have to come to terms with the reality of the idiom, 'freedom-of-the-press."

"I hope they allow us the luxury of a change of clothes," Brian retorted, flapping the cloth vigorously.

They all started to laugh, more out of nervous reaction to the extreme emotion of the last hours than the immediate spectacle.

"From what I gather, we will all be accompanied by a constable for the time-being, until we are debriefed at the Police Headquarters, or the Ministry; I'm not sure which."

"Joy!"

"It won't be all that bad Brian. You and Steve should be absolved of all charges, if any, in regard to your conduct here. The Department of Defense will take care of the rest." Magnus looked a Shawna, and wondered at her native beauty and the resemblance to his daughter and wife. "Where will you be taking her," he asked of Brian, looking warmly to Shawna.

"We have rooms at the Aguada, in Santa Elena."

"I know it well. I will see you there."

Steve rested in the yellow, rental car in the parking lot, with his swollen ankle elevated up on the dash. The flurry of activity had passed him by as the police retrieved the incarcerated goons from the van. Assurances over the radio had left him relatively at ease amid the gunfire and flurry of events up through the jungle beyond his sights. He watched intently as the ambulance and Police cars came and went along the access road to the rear of the Castillo. It was only when Brian, arm in arm with a visibly shaken Shawna, appeared, did he attempt to arouse from his position in the car. Slipping out of the seat with several bottles of water in his hand, he limped to the couple as they entered the periphery of the parking lot.

"I'm happy to see you Shawna," Steve asserted, as they all met just beyond the hood of the car.

"I'm very pleased to see you as well Steve. It has been some time and distance from Port Angeles," she sighed, leaning close into Brian.

He smiled and nodded gently as Magnus, Amalia and Edmundo sauntered up to the car from the pathway beyond the parking lots edge. Several police officers slowed and paused at a short distance to light cigarettes.

As Edmundo approached, Shawna broke her grip from Brian and came to stand in front of Edmundo. With near tears in his eyes, "We have yet again thwarted the gods of a tasty morsel. They will not be pleased."

With a smile and tears welling in her eyes, she embraced him hard, "Thanks Mundie." After several moments, she released him and motioned for Brian to take her side. "This is Brian, the fellow I told you about from Canada."

"Yeah, I know. We have been hanging close these last few hours." Mundie reached forward and gave Brian a light punch in the shoulder. "It has been a pleasure to get to know him."

Noticing Amalia standing to the rear and somewhat out of place, Brian called her forward and introduced her to Shawna; Edmundo slipped his arm around Amalia for support. Magnus puffed on a cigarette and motioned to Steve to come over and made comment about his leg, and the bluish color of his ankle. He took a bottle from Steve.

Within minutes, the chief investigative officer came to the group and announced they could leave. "Do you all have rides?"

"You can ride with us Mag, since you're heading back to the Aguada," Brian offered.

"I'll go back to the San Ignacio with Amalia, if we can get a ride." Edmundo stated, looking to some of the abandoned vehicles left in the parking lot, and throwing Steve the keys to his pickup.

"Follow me," the officer suggested and motioned with his hand.

"These officers will accompany you into town and wait till we head back to Belmopan tomorrow. I must ask you not to leave the area, and you must inform the officer assigned to you if you need to communicate outside the area. We will meet at the Police Station in San Ignacio, in several hours; approximately 7:00 pm."

Amalia and Edmundo followed the Chief to a waiting Land Rover and disappeared into the back seat. Nearby, the musicians, and the entourage that had accompanied the celebratory events, were being loaded, under guard, into the back of a military truck. They did not look too festive. Magnus crammed into the back of the compact, yellow Fiesta, while Brian helped Shawna into the passenger's seat and proceeded to the drivers. As they retreated from the lot, a Howler monkey began his call to dominance and proclaimed his territory once again. A brightly colored, Keel-billed, Toucan dipped and fluttered to perch in the boughs of a Cohune Palm; the sun began to dip beneath the forest's canopy of the temple's plateau.

The Aguada Hotel was well lit and festive when they arrived at the parking lot forty minutes later. Laughter and music boomed from under the thatch of the out-door lounge. The tin-pan ponged and reggae music spilled out into the night air like a fresh breeze off the cayo on a moon-lit night. Exhausted from the ordeal of the previous days, Magnus and Shawna headed through the screen door to the restaurant. Brian and Steve gathered some things and went to talk to the constables assigned to the group, who had pulled up to beside Mundy's blue pick-up. Shawna, now more like herself, sat in the cool of the corner and waited for one of the waitresses to accommodate the two of them.

"Coke, with lots of ice," escaped from Shawna's mouth with a determination that left no doubt.

"Ice tea, with a little ice," Magnus iterated with resolve as if to mock Shawna. She questionably looked at him. "I'll have a drink a little later," he replied, knowing that tea would seem an oddity for him.

She placed her elbows on the table and slowly ran her fingers through her matted hair. She looked down at her soiled and worn clothes that had been supplied by one of the female attendants at the Castillo. "I smell terrible."

"No matter how bad you smell, you will never smell as bad as I do."

They both were laughing as Brian and Steve entered through the screen door from the lot. "Do we look that funny," Steve asked?

'Yep," blurted from Shawna's mouth without hesitation. Brian came along side and plunked himself down in the chair. "Boy, what a treat we must be. Look at us."

They all looked at one-another and burst out laughing. Patrons around the room became aware of the oddity of the four and gave side glances and smiles till Jackson came along side.

"Well, what a sorry bunch of hoodlums you four look like." He had a tray with a couple of cervasa perched in the center. Plunking them down he asked, "Can I make a suggestion for you? Why don't you go upstairs and get cleaned up before my restaurant vacates. In the meantime, I'll get the kitchen to make up some primo enchiladas, some guacamole dip and salad; a spread that will be fit for kings, and queens." Jackson looked down at them as if no was not an option.

"Thanks," Magnus replied with a smile that spoke reams of understanding.

They drank heartily for several minutes till Steve and Magnus left respectfully to their rooms. Shawna and Brian were left at the table.

"I have a suite upstairs with a shower," Brian stated with a shy, but willing smile.

"Is there room for two?"

The San Ignacio Resort was well lit up from the

outside as Amalia and Edmundo were let off at the entrance. A constable exited from the opposite side of the vehicle and entered the foyer to place himself in a chair close to the front desk.

From his and Brian's earlier presence in the hotel, Edmundo knew the layout and did not need direction in escorting Amalia to her room upstairs. Visibly shaken and worn from the day's activity, she stood trembling, uncertain as what to do.

"Would you like me to come in for a bit while you shower and get ready?"

She took his hand and guided him to the door. Swiping the card before the photo-sensitive eye of the passage set, a green LED light illuminated ushering them to open passage.

"Make your-self comfortable on the balcony while I sort out the mess that Doug left this morning," Amalia started to gather up garments that were strewn over beds and chairs alike. "If you'd like a drink, there may be some beer in the fridge."

He scanned the wall unit for a cabinet door big enough to hide the unit. Amalia, in the alcove that housed the dresser, began to stuff crumpled clothes in the drawers while simultaneously removing the ones that she wore. Edmundo, not wishing to invade her privacy, twisted the cap off and began to proceed to the balcony.

"Could you bring me one?"

Nearly choking on a half swallowed swig of beer, he managed, "Now?"

Placing his beer on the coffee table, he crept back to the fridge and popped another cap from a bottle; he could feel his heart starting to race. Amalia, with her back to him, slipped herself out of her under garments and walked from behind the bed to face him. Not knowing how to react and where to put his eyes, he stared directly into the ebony darkness of hers, and wondered at their sparkle. In his peripheral vision, his mind was making mental note of her flawless, firm swimmers body. She took the bottle from his near trembling hand, kissed him on the cheek, and disappeared through a door that must have been the bathroom. Edmundo stood motionless for what must have been a full minute before retracing his steps to the coffee table, his beer, and ultimately the balcony. The last vision he saw of Amalia, was her beautiful back, discolored and bruised from a beating she must have taken in the immediate past. Anger began to build in him for this man called, Doug.

**Belmopan Catacombs**

As Doug patted the blood from the side of his jaw below the missing piece of his ear, anger began to replace the confusion he had felt for the disruption and abortion of the ceremony. His contempt for the whole situation with the custodian was beginning to fray his already raw nerves. Juan and Amalia had done their last to aggravate an already crumbling relationship that should have ended years before.

The door slamming on the other side of the vehicle, and the shuffle of feet, announced the retreat of the custodian through the automated security doors; the bespectacled assistant waited patiently on the far side of the glaciated portico. The barely audible click of his cane on the cement, garage floor echoed, and then ceased as he entered. The custodian slowly turned to face the beleaguered Doug. His face was drawn and pale as words, "Go get her," slipped from his chapped and bleeding lips.

Disdain for the order was hard to hide, but the need to rectify an injustice to his male psyche was necessary. It was what was required to sustain his own predilection for control and power. Climbing back inside the rear of the waiting 4X4, "Take me to the estate," pierced the dull silence, directed to the driver. He would make some calls and find where his own driver, and friend, was being held and set bail, if needed.

### Aguada

It had been months since Shawna and Brian had been together. Still weak from her ordeal, Brian carried Shawna into the shower area and ran the water to a tepid flow. Easing themselves into the small stall, they embraced and kissed; their bodies responding to the each other's touch and the pulsing water that flowed over their skin. Almost faint from excitement, he carried her to the bed and embraced her gently, like a butterfly in the palms of his hand. Kissing the length of her body, she responded in passion and deed. With their bodies entwined, they rolled, sweated and convulsed; they were lost in intense passion.

Steve had chosen to take a dip in the pool. Changing his clothes, to his bathing trunks in his room, he had considered the passion and the need for privacy of the two in the adjoining room. Showering in the pool area, he had taken a Bud from the passing waitress and proceeded to cool himself in the water. Looking over to the swampy, irrigation pond that lay off to the far side of the garden, he noticed the resident iguana, approximately three feet long, sunning himself in like manner. They both were content, listening to the music that floated on the air as easily as Steve's air-mattress on the water.

Magnus, showered and shaved, stood and gazed from the balcony of the second floor overlooking the pool. He looked content, at least for now, over the outcome of the last days. He would need to be clear on his pronouncements to the police, whom they would meet within the hour. Explaining the custodian and his true intent, would be difficult and not at all prudent considering the possible ramifications. He would need to explain something though; murder, if he could prove it, to the Police Chief in San Ignacio. Divulging the custodian's true nature and purpose for the ceremony, would bring unnecessary attention and perhaps his escape. The doctor would lay out a more detailed and direct course of action when he met with Henry the following evening. With all things considered, it would be difficult to explain the near supernatural nature of this being, or thing, and its penchant for source DNA and genetic alteration. Magnus speculated, it had survived and existed in near obscurity around the world for centuries, within the confines of a timeless institution. Coming to Central America centuries ago, was its only way to remain concealed and private to continue with experimentation and its political meddling, till now. Magnus still needed time to set up the means to restrict, confine, incarcerate, and ultimately bring about the demise of this horrific, senseless, careless being.

Looking down at his watch, he shouted down to Steve, "It is time my friend, to get that foot out of the water."

Steve lazily looked up and gave him a wave while taking another sip of beer. Back-paddling the blow-up bed, he reached for the side and hoisted himself onto the concrete patio stones that surrounded the periphery of the pool.

"I'll be right there," he yelled back.

Steve sat for several moments at the edge, watching the sunlight reflect off the gentle waves as they lapped the side of the pool. The bright, turquoise blue bottom shimmered through to the broken sparkling surface. He was cognizant of the day's events and wondered whether he had done the right thing in not pursuing Juan into the jungle when he'd had the chance. Perhaps, Juan would still be alive. Feeling drained and emotionless, he watched as the remaining rays of light winked out from between the trees at the far side of the garden; he wanted to see Rose and the kids. The iguana was no-where to be seen.

A half-hour later, clean shaven and wearing fresh clothes, Steve gently put his ear to the door of the next room and heard nothing. The exterior, balcony walkway was open to the pool area below and he could see Magnus sitting by its edge in a reclining chair, smoking a cigarette.

"Leave them," Magnus suggested. "Shawna needs all the rest she can get. I'll have a word with the guard to remain here and wait for them to awake, as if that will be any time soon," he said whimsically.

Steve sauntered down to the restaurant area after Magnus and nodded to Jackson as he wiped glasses from the inventory on the shelf. After gulping down a tasty enchilada, the screen door slammed shut with a bounce that almost kept rhythm to the music from the bar. Magnus spoke with the officer waiting near his car close to the festivities about Brian and Shawna, and climbed into the Fiesta. With a groan of discomfort,

Steve attempted to press the clutch pedal with his sore foot. A forced grin came to his face, "You ready doc?"

They bounced away from the parking lot in a cloud of dust, off toward their meeting with the Chief in San Ignacio.

The San Ignacio Police Station was cramped and hot. The overhead fan did little to move the air around the waiting room that felt no larger than a lavatory cubicle, and smelled little better. Several drunks slept on a corner bench, snorting at every disturbance that affected them. Owen was perched on the next seat beside them covering his nose with the hanky he had used previous to wipe his brow. Edmundo and Amalia were opposite, waiting patiently for the proceedings to begin. The Chief was in an adjoining room with a boisterous crowd of individuals still dressed in costume from the day's ritual. Mayhem ruled supreme.

Exasperated, the Chief, a balding, heavy set man, entered the waiting area and nodded to Magnus. His attempt at neatness of appearance was obvious, but the stains of sweat beneath his arms and the disheveled hair that rimmed his skull at ear level gave a true account of his demeanor. Turning, he gather some pens and several clip boards and looked to the five with metered disdain at the condition of his overcrowded offices.

"Would you all come forward," he stated, putting the clip boards in order on the counter before him. Looking up again, he asked, "Where are the other two; the young lady and the other fellow?"

Magnus cleared his throat and began, "They will be along shortly. They were held up for medical reasons and are with the officer you left at the

220

Aguada."

"Oh," he replied and looked down to the forms on the clipboard. "You need to give me your names and addresses while in Belize; a contact number where you can be reached over the next twenty-four hours, a cell number perhaps; a detailed account of what you were doing at the Xunantunich site; what you saw; what you think you saw, and, if any, your relationship to the deceased." He looked over to Owen, "and what you were doing filming the whole thing?" Owen looked down to his feet and wondered at his predicament. Magnus giggled.

Leaving the waiting area, the chief re-entered the room next door and began another round of questions and assumptions. Gathering close, they all looked at one another with the same bewildered look.

"Where do we begin," Edmundo asked, looking to Magnus for direction?

"Start at Caracol, the night Shawna was abducted. Just leave out the important parts as to why you believe she was taken. If you feel you need to, just say, 'a ransom for the 'Pillars of the Moon'." He peered reflectively at them all, "We need to be similar in our accounts as to why we were at Xunantunich." Magnus looked directly at Amalia in sympathy," Some of us had no choice," then continued. "All of us have our personal reasons for wanting to see Doug and the custodian put away, but they are connected to some powerful politicians. At this point, we have only clues as to who they may be; they have remained protected and active for many years for a reason; we just don't know how, yet!"

They all nodded in agreement and went back to sit in their respective areas and started to write. Twenty minutes later, all but Owen were finished and eager to leave the fetid confines of the waiting area.

Waiting for the Chief to return, Steve began to wonder at Edmundo's condition and asked in concern, "Can I get you anything from the Aguada? I know your friends have all left, but if there's anything I can do for you, let me know."

"I'll be heading back to the resort with Amalia," Edmundo stated, looking up from the paperwork. "If you could bring my duffel bag and truck, I'd appreciate it." He reached in his pocket and threw the keys back to Steve in one quick motion.

"I'll see you in an hour."

Within moments, the front door opened, and Brian and Shawna slipped into the vacancy on the bench made available by Steve, Amalia and Edmundo. Squeezing by the couple, they retreated from the cramped office to remain outside the front door.

Reaching for several papers that remained on the front desk, Magnus motioned for Brian to collect the loose leaf. "Fill out these as indiscriminately as you can. I'll do my best to have it cleared up by Henry at the ministry."

Refreshed from the shower at the Aguada, and relieved from the intimacy experienced earlier, the two sat quietly together and started to pen the impressions the last few days had conjured.

The door from the adjoining room swung open and spewed the Police Captain and a young, female assistant. "What in the heck that bunch was up to, I'll never be able to figure," he belched. "The court system will have to sort it all out!" He shuffled some papers and looked over to Magnus, "And what do you have to say for yourself. How did you get mixed up in all of this, as if I need to ask?"

Magnus just smiled and shrugged his shoulders.

The chief noticed Shawna and Brian penning their forms and made no effort to arouse them.

"I suppose the Ministry will have a lot to say and do through all of this." The Chief gave a forced chuckle and slapped his hand down hard, startling everyone, including the prone drunks that gave slight motion and extruded grunts again. "And how is Henry," he asked, as he peered down over the counter to where the doctor sat, as if a switch of melancholia had been flicked in the room.

"Fine," was all that Magnus offered.

"As soon as everyone has finished," the chief brandished, "put your reports on the counter, sign the log with the assistant here, leave the pens, and get out!"

### Aguada
The moon was full and illuminated the parking lot as Steve threw Edmundo's army green duffel bag in the back of his truck. With a cough and a chug, the engine sprang to life and jerked profusely as Steve unevenly popped the clutch to get the vehicle in motion. The din of crickets and bull-frogs, by the river's edge, almost drowned out the low cough and sputter as he proceeded along the Western Highway, through the town toward the bridge that crossed over to San Ignacio. The water below sparkled and rippled in the moonlight as he crossed unimpeded to the upper reaches of the town and the cathedral that stood bold, reminiscent of better times in the past.

As the Police vehicle pulled away from the entrance to the San Ignacio Resort, Edmundo and

Amalia stopped just outside the front doors and turned to look at the sky and the stars that twinkled above the tree's canopy across the road.

"Would you like to sit by the pool and have a drink," he asked Amalia, who was visibly more relaxed now that time had passed from the ordeal of earlier.

"I'd love to," she replied, looking up to him and taking his arm.

Both receded through the doors, oblivious to the van and the occupants that sat several yards away. Doug, and his driver Carlos, waited patiently and watched for an opportunity, and location, to snatch Amalia away. Getting from their vehicle, they observed through the doors as the two walked past the stairs and through to the patio and down to the pool area beyond. Doug paused for several moments to think of the alternatives and the lack of police at the time.

"You go around the side to the rear and stay undercover," he suggested. "I'll see if I can separate them and get her alone to talk to her." Doug grabbed him by the arm after some thought, "If you see me walk with her back to the front of the hotel, make your way to the truck. I'll get her there somehow. If worse-comes-to-worst,  shoot the bastard."

Edmundo had just given the waitress their drink order when Doug waltz up to beside the table, ducked the umbrella, and stared down to Amalia without a word. Edmundo rose to his feet, the hair on the back of his neck stood to attention. He automatically poised himself in a protective, offensive stance that was barely noticeable but for the few who sat in reclining chairs and at tables close by.

Doug looking to the patrons that sat either side of their table and back to Edmundo, "I only want a private word with her."

Edmundo, sensing the tension rise within Amalia, and the flash vision of the bruises and markings on her back, "I don't think so!" Standing his ground and watching the reaction in Doug's eyes, Edmundo didn't move a muscle.

Reaching down to grab Amalia by the arm, Doug was shocked at the lightning quick reaction of Edmundo's foot stretching out toward his forearm, kicking it from the advance. Surprised, Doug stood motionless considering the attack, and looked back to the patron that sat just off to the side. Edmundo, in like, looked to the reaction; his considerations becoming soft, from his years away from the military, and forfeited his defensive posture. Doug taking advantage, placed a precise kick to Edmundo's upper thigh and punched out with lightning speed toward his face. Both hit their mark before Edmundo could block and counter-punch. Startled, and correcting himself before he fell into the bystanders table, Doug kicked out with a firm foot to his chest, Edmundo stumbled back winded, and into the pool. Female patrons screamed while the males stood unable to determine a course of action, apart from subdue, should the altercation continue. Reaching down, Doug pulled Amalia to her feet, "Come with me, and don't make a scene, or more will get hurt."

Edmundo, barely able to catch his breath, grabbed the edge of the pool-side and watched helplessly as the two disappeared through the rear-entrance doors to the patio and back through the lobby. From behind the pool's waterfall, and the thick foliage that surrounded the outside perimeter of the pool area, Carlos watched, replaced his handgun in its shoulder holster, and the eased himself from his hiding spot to continue around to the front of the resort.

As Steve pulled up in front of the resort, he could not help but notice a couple arguing in the shadows of huge, black vehicle just down from the front doors. He sat for a moment not wishing to interfere and allow them privacy when he heard a slight scream and a whimper. Thinking it over for a split second, he decided to take a closer look, but not to conspicuous. To his surprise, there was Amalia in the forceful clutches of Doug. Bandage over his ear, Doug turned to view the intrusion expecting to see Carlos. Equally surprised, Steve looked at a tearful Amalia and lashed out with a hard punch that crumpled Doug's nose and sent him flat through the open door of the truck. Not moving from the sprawling position over the seat, he remained quiet. Amalia, unable to comprehend the quickness of the actions and reactions, hugged Steve around the belly.

"Are you alright," Steve asked.

"Uh huh." was all she replied.

"I don't think so," came a disembodied, heavily accented voice from beyond the truck door. The door slowly closed on the dangling legs of Doug, and remained ajar. "I suggest, senor, you back away and leave the girl here." A black revolver protruded from the fingers of a closed fist. Carlos reopened the door to recognize, a prone Doug in the shadows of the interior. Steve reacting very slowly, backed out from between the parked vehicles, pushing Amalia clear behind him. "Not all that wise Senor," Carlos stated, a slight smile on his lips.

"For who!" came a familiar voice from behind the

open door.

Kicking the door as hard as he could, Edmundo tried to debilitate Carlos, but only pushed him further between the parked cars toward Steve and Amalia. Not knowing what to do, Steve stepped forward and swung down as hard as he could, dislodging the gun from Carlo's grip. Edmundo, from behind, struck out with his fist, hitting Carlo in the temple. A semiconscious Carlo crumpled to the ground.

"Let's go," yelled Steve, running toward the Edmundo's pickup. "You'd better drive," he suggested to Mundie. "I think I broke something."

"That's if I can sit down," Edmundo replied easing himself behind the driver's seat.

In a puff of smoke from the tail-pipe, the three, squished together on the small, bench seat, bounced their way down the hill toward the downtown area of San Ignacio and further on to Santa Elena, and the Aguada.

The moon became dull as a cloud slid before its brilliant hue, signaling yet again, that the gods were thwarted of a tasty morsel this fine, balmy evening.

Jackson looked up from behind the bar counter, amid the empty cervasa bottles and rum, to the slamming of the screen door. The motley three laughed as they entered, arm-in-arm, the crowded restaurant. He shook his head and continued wiping the water spots from glasses with a white cloth. Magnus approached to greet them from a table in the shadows of the far corner. "You guys OK?"

# THIRTEEN

It was early morning when the chime rang for the gate to be opened. Even though the limo, from the government facility, was a regular occurrence, Doug did not want his privacy, and security compromised by anyone, or anything. The house maid and grounds keeper, were responsible for every day household functions and deliveries, while Carlos, his bodyguard and driver, was responsible for security.

This morning was slightly different, while both master and servant were recovering from their failed exploits of the night before. Doug wanted to remain in his cave, while Carlos had no alternative but to respond to the intrusion. Opening the entrance door from the marbled foyer, he was not surprised to see one of the familiar drivers from the Catacombs Branch, a ghost department of Internal Affairs, standing at near attention before him.

"Good morning," the driver announced cordially. "A request for Mr. Baldwin, to attend a meeting this morning at the offices, has been given. I have been ordered to wait for Mr. Baldwin. You are to follow at a later time. You will be notified and given instructions for a specific time, and place for pick up."

"Carlos, a little uncertain as to how to handle the request, gently closed the door and proceeded up the large, central staircase to the upper floors and private quarters of Doug.

The Baldwin Estate was more than just grounds, but a conglomerate of real-estate holdings, shipping companies and shares in some of the most predominate, pharmaceutical companies in the world; most were acquired during the last twenty years in association with the custodian. The estate grounds which overlooked a small valley close to Belmopan, in the foothills of the Mayan Mountains, bordered a small river called Roaring Creek. It emptied into pristine freshwater lake that was encompassed by a conservation area that ended closer to Belize City. Birds, crocodiles, tapirs, and the occasional jaguar were all home to this near native habitat. Grounds acquired from native farmers, through a variety of means, were kept in order by the very people who were forced to give up their lands a hundred years previous.

A gentle knock on the ornate, paneled door, brought a grunt as a response from the interior of the room. "What is it," rang loud and clear.

"A meeting sir," Carlos replied from the mahogany, paneled hall outside the door.

The door slowly opened revealing a near broken man with black, near closed eyes, accented by a swollen and red nose. Doug tilted his head to get a better view of the abrasion, and bruise to the side of Carlos' head, where Edmundo had struck him. "Nice."

"But not as pretty as yours," Carlos vehemently returned.

"We will return the favor in due time," Doug retorted.

"You are requested at the office shortly. What would you like me to tell him?"

Doug thought for a moment and finally said, "Let them wait. I have a few things to clear up." He turned to re-enter the room, but stopped short, "I have a plan for you when you come later." He gently closed the door and retreated to his private locker that housed a private collection of firearms.

The drive to the Government Compound seemed slow, near timeless to Doug as scenarios ran through his mind of the purpose of this meeting. He had an inkling, it would be his last. But, if all went well, it would be he who re-surfaced to the land above the catacombs, not the custodian who had become so enigmatic to him these last few years. It would be dangerous, his plan, but if executed properly, would rid him, and the rest of the world, of a cancer that had plagued the world for too long. The polymer pistol, he cared in his pocket, was undetectable by conventional security systems, and carried deadly, needle-like projectiles that could penetrate all but the newest of armament and protective alloys. From what he knew, of the last few years, nothing had been done, or added to, the already outdated system that protected the catacombs. He was anxious, but remained calm to the outside; besides no-one would be able to recognize any changes to his eyes or skin tone due to extent of damage to his face. All would go as planned.

The blue sky was dotted with thick, fluffy clouds that seemed to stretch from horizon to horizon, as the 4X4, that delivered Doug, disappeared into the bowels beneath the freshly mowed, grass common that covered the catacombs. He began to feel strangely odd. Sad that the life he had been accustomed to, these last thirty-odd years, would soon be coming to change. He watched as the security gates opened and closed, allowing the vehicle that housed him, to continue down, further into the bowels of the earth and concrete.

Lifting his hand to adjust the tape that crossed his nose, he found that the itch had persisted and tried again to relieve the annoyance. Shocked at the slowness of the response to move his hand, he tried with the other to support the endeavor. Doug's mind raced at his inability to lift his hand. Reaching for the pistol that hung lifeless within his inner jacket pocket, he realized the gravity of his situation. The custodian had long prepared for this day by charging the interior of the rear seating area of the vehicle with a paralyzing, odorless gas to accommodate, with ease, the incarceration of whomever he pleased. The driver occasionally checked in his rearview mirror to witness the reactive time and thoroughness of the procedure.

By the time they had reached the glass doors to the inner sanctum of the catacombs, Doug was paralyzed and unable to move a muscle. Two orderlies, with a sheeted gurney, exited the doors and pulled alongside the truck and waited for the driver to unlock the rear door, allowing them to extract a near panicked Doug.

Laying him down, they started to ventilate him with oxygen, not to help bring him around, but to oxygenate the tissue, and cells, that would be necessary for the operation about to take place. Helpless, he watched the ceiling flash by and listened to the gentle hiss of the escaping oxygen from the tank that lay close to his ear. They quickly wheeled him down the maze of corridors and ultimately to a preparation room.

The room had been kept cold while the orderlies stripped him of his clothes and shaved the hair from his chest and lower abdomen, A prick in his arm and a face came to block the light that had blinded him from all the equipment that surrounded the room. His eyes came to focus on a pair of glasses and the piercing eyes of the custodian's assistant that he had continuously loathed and treated with disdain. The buzz of the overhead light became more dominant as warmth started to spread through his body. His mind wandered to the past and to the many things that he would be accountable for. A scene of his drunken father, as he lay bleeding from his ears, had entered his mind. Another, of his mother, beside him, as they knelt in the pews of the Cathedral they had attended when he was young, and his father not present. His mind began to drift more, and unable to focus, he softly spoke the words of reconciliation, "forgive me Father, for I have sinned."

His body began to glow and pulse, as flashes of light began to strobe before his eyes. The custodian had entered the operatory.

Later that day, Carlos' phone rang. Surprised, at the long wait outside the obscure, service door in the tunnel of the drainage aqueduct, he expectantly waited to hear the direction that he was to take. Doubtful, at hearing an unfamiliar voice, he was given directions as to where to pick Doug up. Uncertain of the location, he followed the direction of the GPS co-ordinates along a dirt road, close to the Baldwin Estate, almost obscured by jungle foliage. Stopping his vehicle close to the edge of the Macal River, more of a creek at this tributary, he exited and called for Doug. Walking down to the river's edge, he called once more. Wondering at the absent response, he headed up a path that led to a clearing just up from a bend in the river. A Cardinal chirped, and flew off at the intrusion, while a Macal flew off to a perch not far distant. Almost stumbling over a green garbage bag, he called once more and scouted his surroundings. Carlos began to realize something was amiss. Beside the green bag, the toe of his shoe had hit something solid, but moveable. Looking down to the plastic bag, it was belled out at the bottom as if filled with liquid and solids. Reaching over, he picked up the item his toe had touched. He pulled forth the polymer pistol that Doug had taken with him to the catacombs. Looking back to the bag, and several others in close proximity, a sickness began to fill his being. Carlos threw-up.

# FOURTEEN

It was late in the afternoon as Brian and Shawna pulled along the edge of the boulevard to the grass covered shoulder that fronted Henry's house. Several other cars, as well as Magnus's dusty Land Rover, sat perched at an angle off to the side. The sun was beginning to set beyond the mountains in the near distance that cradled Belmopan. A light breeze blew the sheer fabric of Shawna's cotton, knee-length skirt, cooling her legs from the heat of the short car ride from Santa Elena. Brian wore a crumpled, light-colored, cotton shirt that had obviously been pulled from a duffle bag; his jeans were no better and frayed at the rear just above his worn sandals, his sneakers had been discarded.

The door to the quaint bungalow, opened to a ceramic tiled foyer, and the smile of a short, brown lady of native decent. Slipping their shoes from their feet, the two crossed the cool tile to a sunken, living room that housed several couches and a vista to the valley and the mountains. Magnus rose to his feet and crossed the expanse of living space to give the greeting of a kiss to Shawna. Reaching across, he took Brian's hand for a firm shake and pulled him close for a hug.

"Where's Steve," he enquired, looking toward the door?

"He'll be following shortly," Brian replied. "He needed some more patching after the little tussle with Doug and his driver last night."

"I think the Chief in San Ignacio will be happy to see the end of us," Magnus returned smiling.

"Yeah, he has had more attention and paperwork in the last twenty-four hours than he has seen all year. There is a lot to explain, and a few missing pieces that will need to be filled in."

"Yes," Magnus returned. "Caution is of the essence. We will have to be careful how much we divulge regarding the nature of the Custodian. It will only further entrench the resolve of those involved in his anonymity to sweep the scenario under the rug," Magnus motioned in the direction of the sitting area, following after Shawna and Brian. "There are some, who have been embarrassed by their inaction in the past, knowing the implications to his clandestine research, while others have chosen to turn a literal blind-eye."

The short woman, who had straightened the shoes, skirted the periphery of the foyer, and disappeared through an arch to the kitchen area. Henry's head popped up from behind the counter, decanter of ice in hand, and cleared the opposite archway in long strides.

"Well, hello my dear," came the warm salutation from Henry as he noticed Shawna now sitting on the couch. "It is a pleasure to meet you at last." He placed the ice down on the side-board and reached forward to greet her outstretched hand. "I have been somewhat aware of your work prior to now, but have never been able to put a face to your name," he squeezed her hand lightly. "And now, with the repatriation of the 'Pillars of the Moon' that came through my department several months ago, you will not go unnoticed." He looked to Brian, now standing tall beside Shawna, "You Mr. Alexander," he said with a sigh, "we owe you much more than we could ever repay. The Department of Archaeology is much in your debt."

"Perhaps, we could make a deal for Steve's medical bills," Brian suggested with a laugh.

"We can discuss it over a drink."

The three sat down and watched as Henry scurried about, intent on making them their drinks. With smiles and much conversation, and relief from the tension of the last few days, the atmosphere lightened. Brian started to go into embellished detail of his dealings with Magnus in Mexico; laughter abounded whilst Henry retreated to the kitchen to help with preparation of the meal and the laying of the dining table. Littered with cutlery and empty crystal wine glasses, the heavy, mahogany table became congested with the pre-feast accoutrements. The aroma of roasted lamb, and the faint scent of mint, began to drift into the living room area to tease the appetites of the waiting guests and send tummies rumbling. All had eaten sparingly over that last eventful days due to the circumstances. The many visits to officials and dignitaries had left them all rather undone. Henry popped a bottle of red wine and poured it into a decanter to breath just as a knock came to the door.

"Come in," he shouted in the direction of the door, without lifting his head from the preparatory work of the meal.

The wooden door swung open to reveal a stunning Amalia. Dressed in a satin, mid-thigh dress that clung to her form like a spray of turquoise paint, she stood motionless and waited. Magnus and Brian rose to their feet as Edmundo came to her side and they entered together. Clean and shaven, Edmundo still sported the bruises and walking gate that alluded to the previous night's encounter. Down the walkway behind, Steve struggled with a bound foot, and now a cast on his hand where he had fractured a meta-carpal in his wrist. He would need to hold his glass in his left hand.

After several moments of greeting, and cordialities, Henry yelled to Mag to make sure all had drinks and continued on with the preparation.

After several hours, several bottles of wine, and multiple courses of a delicious meal, they all retired back to the living room where aperitifs were served and all settled down into comfort. With windows wide open, and a gentle breeze that blew away the concerns and fears of the coming months, they relaxed.

Shawna cuddled close to Brian's side. He considered the men in the room and asked his host, "Henry, how are you and Mag professionally related?"

"As far away as possible," he retorted with a hearty laugh that melted into a concerted frown. "Mag and I have known each other since we were young men, new to Belize. We had coordinated personnel, and pooled our skills on a number of digs in the field; we have been through a lot together." He took a slow look to an aging and frail Magnus and returned a smile. "We've done lots of things we should have, and far more things we shouldn't have - a paradox of life for sure." He sat pensive for several moments before looking up again.

Edmundo, not at all familiar with the inner workings of the ministry due to his military and tourist involvement, asked of Henry, "What about this fellow, 'the Custodian', the name that everyone refers him to?" He gave Amalia's hand a gentle squeeze. "Who is he? How is he able to be involved with this subversion and yet go unimpeded? The guy was let go at the Macal River, and continued on to wherever he goes."

Henry's eyes gave a quick flick in Magnus direction as if in concern. Magnus gave him a nod and looked in Emundo's direction.

"Many years ago, before most of you were born," Magnus started, "Henry and I travelled around a bit, visiting archaeological sites, putting together a timeline involving certain events that were reoccurring throughout ancient history. We had found things, the remains of surgical instruments and tools of a quality far beyond the supposed technological skills of the allotted dig's timelines. The ones we had chosen to investigate, had certain semblance, or blueprint to them. Some of these findings had occurred in one area of the world at one time, and re-occurred again in another, in a different time, perhaps even different century. We were trying to find correlation and evidence that would show how these events may have been connected. There was congruency. These events were the ones we pursued. As we dug deeper, somewhere, feathers were ruffled; perhaps the 'feathered serpent', mind the pun" he smiled and stopped.

Henry sensed his pause to gather his emotion and thoughts.

"It was at that time that death threats were made to Mag and me, in regard to our research," Henry continued. "I took heed and backed off, while Mag persisted, unabated in his quest for the truth." Henry stopped to pause. "Unrelenting, he continued till it cost him the dearest possession he had."

"Your wife," eased from Shawna's lips as she looked toward him. She thought for several moments, "While we were bound in the shed together, you mentioned your wife occasionally. When you hesitated in your recollection of your life together, you became sad." She paused again, and then continued, "It was difficult for us to communicate with the guards' right there, but I did sense a change in your mood whenever you talked of her. You never mentioned, or alluded to her death, till now."

With a certain ease while looking back to her, Magnus replied, "You remind me so much of Angelina, and especially then. I felt so powerless to get you from there; I was feeling a double whammy of guilt, and fear. There was nothing I could do for you, as I could not all those years ago. I felt useless, and helpless." He stopped for several moments to gather his thoughts, "I had a chance to kill the man that abducted her all those years ago, and I failed. He was much younger then, barely out of his teens." Magnus looked over to Amalia who was held captive by his story. "I recognized the voice more than I did his looks. Men change over the years, with age and weight, but the voice never changes. His cadence and words are burned in my mind these near thirty-some-odd years, never to be erased." Without mentioning his name, Magnus lowered his eyes to his drink and took a long sip.

"Are you saying Doug had something to do with the murder of your wife," Amalia questioned with reserve in her voice? "He had done a lot of business with a pharmaceutical company and met occasionally with someone running it, or at least I thought so."

"It was more than likely this fellow," returned Magnus pensively.

"Now that you mention it, the old van, in the parking area at Xunantunich, had some faded RX letters on its side," declared Steve, shifting to get himself comfortable on the couch.

"Doug has worked alongside the Custodian for many years." Henry took another sip of his drink and continued. "I am a little familiar with him due to the reports of artifacts crossing my desk and about an export company that Doug is a director of. If memory serves me well, in the beginning, Doug's father ran supplies and goods down from the eastern seaboard of the United States, and returned with a hold full of rum and other substances. Doug just took over his father's business and contacts when he died. He had an apprenticeship in the shipping business that very few individuals have ever had. I believe he and the Custodian met over some incident regarding a shipment of medical equipment, destined for Cuba, that was high jacked. Lucrative for both parties, but swept away in the red tape of bureaucracy; the two found an alliance, of sorts, mutually beneficial." Henry shook his head in recollection and glanced toward the kitchen and his wife cleaning the kitchen while he entertained the guests. He rose and left to give her a hand.

"Can you tell us any more of this 'Custodian', Magnus? I remember you teaching some of this in class, about trans-Atlantic crossings, and migrations of early native tribes- huge demons with glowing, red eyes; the stuff that kept us interested in this boring field-of-archaeology."

Magnus gave a chuckle and thought for several moments, "If we look to the ancient scriptures, they tell us of a battle in the heavens. One third of the heavenly hosts were cast from above, to this earth; whether, we deem this true or not, there are incredible stories of Greek gods and oracles that spoke prophesy; also, Nordic tales of great wonders and wisdom. In the archaeological sites around the world, there are amazing designs and structures, some built with outstanding enginerial calculation of which we are still analyzing to this day. If these structures were built by the intellect of man alone, then we have lost the gift." He reached over to grasp the small, stemmed crystal glass and took a sip of his aperitif.

"Apart from very few gifted individuals, we have been unable to break beyond the constraints of our limited thought-processes. Technologically and spiritually, we are still struggling to find our identities and place in the universe. Some academia would have us right dead-center at the apex of intelligence. We know for a fact, that the earth occupies one billionth of a billionth of space, if there is such a thing. I have come to believe that all animal life, up till man's introduction to earth, was to form a 'prototype being' of systematic, bodily functions. This body-vehicle allows us, a 'spirit based being', to live within the density of the earth's environment, and yet not be affected, for the most part, by the gravity, electronic fields, and the bombardment of cosmic rays from the sun. You may ask, why so isolated spiritually from this collective genius; the creator wishes to share and cohabit with us, His creation."

Magnus took another sip and thought for several

more seconds. All sat quietly, listening and digested his words along with much mutton and desert. "But, we cannot do it alone, without example," he continued. "The Gods of Greece and the pantheon, were meant to inspire us, but did quite the opposite. This being, the Custodian, has manipulated us into his own domain for his own purpose and survival."

"Come on Mag, lighten up," Henry chimed from the kitchen.

"The human race has become like a rich man's son, who has no desire to go out and work to make a place for himself in society. Instead, he wishes to stay at home and laze, and on occasion go out and party with his friends. In so doing, he visualizes only one aspect of his existence. His father begins to realize that his son can never be like him, because there is no way for him to absorb the valuable lessons needed to be learned to make him a treasured participant in the world. He needs to go out and experience, first hand, those involvements that will help him develop an understanding, empathy for the entire physical world around him. Once the son begins to see the potential for his existence, the son begins to grow."

Steve sat wide eyed in quiet dismay, moving every few moments to ease the ache of bruised bones and stretched muscles. "So you think this guy has been around for thousands of years?"

"Really," Edmundo suggested, looking toward Amalia who seemed intent on hearing the story.

"More wine," asked Henry adorned with wash apron, bubbling out from behind the kitchen counter, wine decanter in hand.

"I'll have some more," reacted Brian, reaching out his empty glass. "This is interesting stuff. Alchemy has been around for centuries and has slowly developed into what we have today."

Shawna sat quietly by his side.

"There have been some very brilliant men throughout the ages, with some very out-there stuff." Edmundo interjected. "Are you suggesting that, this Custodian, may have been there all along, influencing the science of the time?"

"It would have needed to be in isolation," Shawna eased in. ' The Crusades and the Reformation of the church, would have made, and did make, a very dangerous, intellectual climate for those forward thinking individuals – definitely for some, a life of isolation and hiding."

"Consider Galileo," Brian interjected. "He was a brilliant mathematician and astronomer, yet found to be in opposition to the Pope and luckily not put to death, but instead spent the rest of his days in isolation under house arrest. I'm beginning to see a paradox forming in the attitudes of the science community at that time. If what you say is true, the need to adhere to known, and accepted, evidential theories of the church and governing bodies, would be paramount. Yet, still have the requisite to reach out to new concepts and possibilities impelled by commodities and products from new and uncharted lands. The Custodian, even though aloof, would be catalyst to this change through his research and experiments. He could not do this alone and would have had assistance, and that would be in secret."

"Yes! The Custodian," Magnus continued, "would need secrecy, and anonymity to continue hiding his intent and existence in the time of inquisition."

Henry walked over to where Mag sat and refilled

his glass, then returned to the kitchen.

"So you believe, this creature was in Central America a thousand years ago, maybe more, and then was present in Europe during the great transition, and then back to Central America?"

"Well, yes! The key is isolation; especially for the Custodian." Magnus thought again and grabbed his knees to give them a rub. "He has travelled around the world for centuries, stirring things up to a state of near anarchy with unresolved murders and mutilations, then quietly hopped on a boat and disappeared to a new country to proceed with his sordid ways. It has only been recently, that events like these once isolated and unnoticed by the rest of the world, have become more visible with the advent of modern communication and the web. He could have been, to quote the old axiom, 'foiled-by-his-own-petard', by instigating the basis for these new technologies. "But," he stated with a firmness in his voice, "I believe the biggest conundrum that vexes him still is, he can't figure out how we tick."

Magnus got up to remove himself from languidity of the couch to the window and its fresh breeze that blew in from the paddock.

"This is why the Custodian wishes to experiment with us," Magnus stated as he turned to face them all. "He is unable to realize his potential as a spiritual being, because he cannot. In the 'Popul Vah', it talks of the four sons of the creator, and how they have lived on earth, and those sons' birthed nations. Whether the text speaks metaphorically, or these be angels of the bible, Arch-angels, or just stories, we may never know, but this one, I believe to be the Custodian, was different. The story tells us, he chose not to procreate. Why, because, he could not? Instead, I believe, he chose to experiment with us genetically, to find a way to morph, as we do, and evolve, as we will, and as the ancient scriptures tell us happened two thousand years ago, to one individual."

Magnus cheeks became moist as he tried to explain, "He needed the purest genetic material he could find, and he killed my wife for it. He searches far and wide using blood banks, like the one in Belize and others in Central America, to get DNA samples for scrutiny. He found yours Shawna, and others." He took a deep breath keeping his emotions at bay, "His bride to be, a thousand years ago, at the temple at Xunantunich, I believe, is a direct ancestor of yours, as well as my wife's. The 'Pillars of the Moon', a wedding gift, he has finally acquired once again. I am happy I was able to help save you."

Shawna, who had until now remained seated, eased herself from where she sat and came to stand beside Magnus. With arms around him, she kissed him on the cheek and said, "Thank you." They wept tears of anguish at his loss, and relief at her liberation.

All was quiet until Amalia got up from her place on the opposite couch. "Come look at this," she notioned to the others as she peered out of the large bay-window that overlooked the valley.

Edmundo and Brian eased themselves from their sitting spots and responded to her desire for them look. The distant hills were alive with little specks of light that danced and twinkled, and then disappeared only to reappear at another reserved spot. Fireflies danced their whimsical way to proclamation, then procreation, and finally, annihilation, all on this warm, late, spring evening.

"Come," Amalia motioned to Edmundo, and

taking his hand. "Let's walk down to the meadow and feel the grass beneath our feet."

Feeling stuffy and full, Brian motioned to Steve to get up and take a look, "Let's go for a smoke."

"You don't smoke," Steve asserted.

Brian bent over to lend him a hand up off the low couch. "I know, but you do." Then looking over to Shawna, still talking with Magnus, "Come on Mag, time for a smoke and a walk."

Henry, watching from behind the kitchen counter, as two, and then four, retreated out of his front door, thought it had been a good day. He shuffled over, in his Mohawk-Indian slippers, to his wife and gave her a gentle hug in appreciation, "The dinner was delicious."

# FIFTEEN

The Aero México plane stood idle on the tarmac in the baking sun. A light breeze blew through the open door just off to the right past the curtains of the galley and cockpit vestibule. The young, boarding stewardesses stood patiently by and chatted while the Brian watched out the window, waiting for Shawna. Steve, across the aisle and stretched out in a first-class lounge seat, leafed through a day old US Today paper.

A young boy, with a face somewhat familiar, passed by being dragged by his mother and swatted at Steve's paper in mischief. Steve, without motion apart from a quick swing of his lose slipper which hit the boy's butt, continue reading unfazed.

The immigration, clearance paper-work for the clay figurine Shawna had found in the dig at Caracol, was taking a little longer than expected. He could see Henry through the glass windows of the office, signing papers and chatting profusely with an officer. The Archaeological Department, which was more or less Henry, had allowed the release and courier-ship, of the little pregnant lady, to Shawna, to be delivered to the

University of Washington State. It was to be put on display in the Natural Sciences Department. Very much a favor for Shawna and the head of the department there, much notoriety and fanfare would be forth-coming for the find. The up-and-coming archaeological student writing her thesis, who found it, would be the toast of Seattle.

It had been a week since dinner at Henry's, and much had transpired in relation to the inquiry into the Xunantunich escapade. 'Pillars of the Moon' had been brought out of the archives and put on display with a number of other jade artifacts in the Museum of Belize. There had already been inquiries, according to Maria, requesting its presence on a world tour with a number of other Mayan and Olmec artifacts to circle the globe for several years. Due to its recent arrival, all requests, to date, had been turned down.

The archive catacombs had been under lock-down for a number of days, while investigations continued in the gruesome discovery of an American business man's remains in a secluded area close to Belmopan. He was last seen leaving his premises for a meeting with officials of the archives and not seen alive again. Amalia had gone into seclusion in the mansion, awarded her temporarily by the Attorney General, under recommendation of several ministry officials and witnesses of her nuptial arrangement with Doug Baldwin. She was being consoled daily by a young, fledgling, archaeological student, who doubled as a Department of Tourism Agent.

Magnus had chosen to stay aloof, and steer clear of the proceedings surrounding the Xunantunich affair, deferring all inquiries to Henry and his office. After Henry's dinner, he drove late to Belize City, and called upon his daughter, who was happy to see him. She doted on him for several hours with tea and cakes while they talked, sat and walked through the secluded gardens of her condominium compound. As the sliver of a moon tried to lift itself into the night sky, he left and retreated to his private quarters and continued with his clay figurines and artwork. The two had talked briefly, weeks before, about the blood samples that had been securitarily compromised, and the names of the donors having been released. The integrity of the blood, screening department of the Health Services Department was shaken, but little was done, and little could be done to rectify the breach. The investigation alluded to the impropriety of two, fledgling lab-technicians, with evidence pointing to funds being released by a local pharmacy to them, but nothing could connect the infraction to the Custodian. A large, pharmaceutical conglomerate in Europe, footed the lawyer's bill.

Doctor Magnus would continue with his endeavors to expose the custodian for who he was and the illegal practices he conducted in genetics and stem-cell research; it would take more time, but he was not alone.

Henry waited and waved to Shawna as she entered the doorway at the top of the mobile staircase. She turned gave him a smile, waved and retreated into the shadows of the interior of the plane. The small, almost square, brown, imitation- leather suitcase remained by her side as she passed the stewardesses. The exterior door was quickly secured shut. She proceeded to her seat beside Brian, across from Steve.

"Glad you could join us," Brian teased, as he

gently squeezed her hand.

"The acquisition had to be faxed through from Washington State with a different signature. I managed to talk to my friend Julie, and she was able to get the documents signed and faxed," Shawna sighed, with a puff of air that blew several strands of loose bangs from her forehead. "Man, what a hassle."

As she settled down and fastened her seatbelt, she couldn't help but wonder about the feeling of great relief that overwhelmed her. With tears welling her eyes, Shawna glanced at the man beside her, thankful that he had loved her enough to pursue her down to Belize. Without his involvement and inquiries to Dr. Magnus, and Maria at the museum, things would be very different; in fact she owed her life to him. Could she ever repay him? With the roar of the jet engines drowning her thoughts, she figured she could try.

The seat belt sign blinked off allowing Brian to switch seats and talk to Steve across the aisle. The dense jungles of Belize, and then Mexico, grew less defined as the plane ascended to greater altitudes. The lush greenery reminded her of her home near Neah Bay, and the emerald carpet of trees that would melt into the aquamarine hues of the coastal seas. Shawna became homesick for the ruggedness of the coast, and the gentle hugs from her aunt and grandma. Her mind wandered to the little wood cabin and the smells of cooking that would greet her as she rushed through the gnarled, wood door that protected the presence within. Fond memories of her childhood flooded her thoughts as she recalled the years she had spent in the custody of her grandparents. She squeezed Brian's knee as she relived in her mind, the passionate, first night the two of them had spent together by the hearth of the cabin's huge, stone fireplace; the smell of the wood burning-the blanket of fur caressing her sensitive skin-the smell of his sweet perspiration as their bodies entwined. Trying to get her thoughts under control, she blushed, crossed her legs and grabbed a magazine from the seat pocket in front.

The tourist magazine Shawna opened was encouraging travelers to come and visit the lush Belizean jungles and the Mayan heritage that lay within. Her mind drifted back to the ubiquitous foliage and her incarceration. She thought of the Mayan woman who had so selflessly given her life so Shawn's might be spared. Her emotions began to well; she began to tear and tried to control the lump that was growing in her throat: she leafed through the pages without regard.

"Rose is going to meet us in Seattle, with a car to take us back to B.C.," Steve stated, looking up from his paper.

Steve had been pensive, and excited to get back home with the kids. Several quotes for building projects, needed to be completed, so his presence north was necessary. The last week had been arduous with all the meetings, seeming interrogations and medical appointments. His ankle had shrunk from its swollen state of a week earlier, and could now walk without the aid of a cane. His knuckles had now reverted back to their normal size and color, and did not hinder him at all. All expenses had been taken care of by Henry, through the ministry, and even a little extra on the side to compensate him for his suffering. Magnus had also given him several relief rubbings of stone stelae, which he hid in his luggage, to take home and consider the possibilities of retail in the north.

"That'll be great," Brian said, "but I will be spending a few days in Seattle with Shawna while she gets things settled with the university. Plus, I haven't touched my camera in weeks," looking down to the leather back-pack tucked beneath the forward seat. "I've got to go through a lot of pics and videos." He rubbed the arms of his seat and thought for several moments, "There's also Victoria I have to deal with, my cars being repaired."

Brian had left Victoria Harbor, with his relationship with Marese very much up in the air. The month he had spent in research at Vincent's study, the University of Victoria, and travelling back and forth to Vancouver, had not left much time for socializing, not to mention the uncertainty of furthering their relationship. He had felt drawn, determined with the near obsession of finding Shawna and the where-abouts of the little, jade bowl. Guilt had sprung up from time-to-time, but not strong enough to pull him away from his resolve. His heart was drawn to another. He would have to make an effort with Marese to alleviate any animosity and ill-feeling that may have resulted from his seeming selfish actions, but not for his sake, but for hers.

"What do you think you'll do after?" Steve asked, just loud enough to be heard over the drone of the engines.

Brian looked back to Shawna, slightly glowing while she read her magazine. "No expectations," he sighed, leaning back in the direction of the aisle. "She has a tremendous career ahead of her; much more important and lucrative than mine."

"A budding archaeologist could always use a good

photographer," Steve returned with a twinkle in his eye.

Brian just smiled, "We'll see."

The two hour stopover and change of planes in Mexico City was tiring with crowds, humidity and little air-conditioning. The remaining flight to Seattle was uneventful, and after a steak dinner, and several small bottles of red wine, Steve was difficult to get motivated. He was near the last individual off the plane and only followed by the attendants and pilots. Getting through customs was always a concern, and with the special paperwork and designation of the Bill of Lading, for the Museums artifact, Customs supervisors were a necessity.

An hour later, Rose welcomed them. She was glowing with her radiant, red hair cascading down over her shoulders, a smile from ear to ear that exposed her near perfect teeth. With open arms and a suggestion for a night cap and snacks at 'Lolita's South of the Border Cantina', a favorite of theirs in Vancouver, they all headed down by the waterfront. Enchiladas and quesadillas were the best you could get anywhere.

After several beers and tummies full, they all rolled out of the restaurant into the night, feeling no pain. A fresh, cool spray of mist, so absent in tropical Belize, caressed their upturned faces. Heading out from One-Post-Alley, they turned on to Pike Street and down the incline to the market. Trying to see the lights of the Space Needle, not visible from there, and obscured by low cloud cover, they wandered arm-in-arm to the car. Across the Alaskan Way to the pier beyond, they found a parking space and clambered out, giggling and joking into the light bustle of the waterfront walkway. A seagull circled, and then

squawked in anticipation of a snack that was
nonexistent and disappeared into the night's anonymity
along the jetty. All that was left was the hollow sound
of traffic that resounded along the wet pavement
beneath the overpass and bestir along the freeway. The
evening was brisk, such a contrast to the humid, sticky
nights of the previous weeks. The four strolled down
passed the Aquarium to the Water Front Arcade and
down the boardwalk to the open bay.

"It's good to be home." Shawna whispered, as she
slipped her hands around Brian's waist and pulled him
close. She rested her head against the black tea shirt
that was exposed between the open flaps of his damp,
leather jacket, her back against the wooden hand rail.
Snuggling close, they absorbed each other's warmth.

Rose and Steve continued to the end of the pier
and gazed out into a fledgling mist that caressed the
timid moon light. As romantic as the setting was, Rose
sensed the need for Steve to get home. After a cuddle
and kisses, they talked briefly about Steve favoring his
leg and the circumstance that led to its condition, and
decided it was time to go. Returning up the damp
boardwalk, they settled in close to Shawna and Brian,
said their goodbyes, made the arrangements to off-load
the luggage, and disappeared from sight across the
boulevard and down to Pier 69, to get their car.

Brian and Shawna slowly edged their way along
the dock and remained to watch the moon continue its
allusive pantomime amid the low cover of cloud; its
fractured reflection sparkling in the pools of water that
lay in the cupped recesses of the wharf's planking.

"Ixchel has still not caught yet her lover," Brian
whispered in Shawna's ear, watching the mystical,
little fishes trying to lift her body to the moon. She

returned a smile and said nothing in response.

"We'd better go," he suggested and bent to give her a kiss. "We still haven't confirmed our reservations at the hotel."

They slowly walked the boardwalk, back to Alaskan Way, that ran the length of the shore. Flagging a taxi near Broad Street, they nestled in the back seat as they drove to Westlake Blvd. and the Seattle Marriot. From a short distance up the terraced, waterfront buildings, a large, black, SUV rested, seeming vacant till it pulled in behind them. Through the tinted, glass windows, two, grey suited, well groomed individuals, a man and a woman, remained alert and determined. They had sat recording, with a high resolution camera, the four unsuspecting lovers. Now, the two remaining lovers were being scrutinized, oblivious to all except the emotions that welled within them.

### Belmopan

The lockdown of the catacombs in Belmopan, was of little consequence to the Custodian. He had needed weeks of rest to allow the recent marrow transplant and the injection of stem cells into his spinal column to take effect. His skin was beginning to clear and the tear ducts in his eyes were now able to flush the stinging poisons from his system as his kidneys began to function again.

Andreas, his male secretary and assistant, had taken care of the sordid business of Doug and instituted the necessary precautions to ensure no backlash would result from the accusations and circumstances that alluded to the Archival Ministries involvement in his death. All security cameras had undergone a temporary reboot at approximately the same time as his arrival, for a systems update; no evidence could be culminated. He too would undergo a session to revitalize his immune system. He was a centenarian, but would have to wait. The sources of fetal-cell extracts had been temporarily halted from their source, due to chance association with the catacombs. It would not go well for the research that had been so successfully conducted in private, completely isolated with autonomy for decades, to end.

From before Andreas' association with the custodian, the lab had functioned well and in obscurity. Andreas became a necessary addition to the operation with the advent of computers and synchronized surveillance that could be conducted from anywhere in the world. His adeptness with emerging, electronic systems and his penchant for calculation, enabled him to run the worldwide conglomerate of pharmaceutical and real-estate holdings from Belize, while its head office appeared to be in New York, leaving the custodian to meddle in his medical procedures and play at world politics. It had only been recently, that any threat had arisen to impede the stability of the catacombs, and they would be taken care of in due time. There was also the gene pool of the Native American girl that still intrigued him.

From inside the plushley, decorated, sitting room of the Custodian's private quarters, the creature contemplated the release of his treasured, jade bowl. As a precautionary measure, to ease the heat of inquiry, it was a slight inconvenience for him to have it sit in a glass case not an hour's drive from where he sat. This situation could easily be altered if the treasure was to make an unscheduled stop on its way to an ulterior destination not of his liking.

"Have you taken necessary steps to find and follow our two love birds?" the custodian asked of his assistant sitting close by at an oversized, leather trimmed, antique, mahogany desk.

"They were located at the Seattle airport and are now being followed to their private residences."

"Don't forget, we do not require the girl as of yet, so let her wander free for the time being. Collect all the intelligence and people associated with her and upload it to the data base." He considered for a moment, "The Canadian, I want dead."

Andreas nodded as acknowledgement without saying a word. He would contact one of the board members of the Northwestern Region, and have it done.

**Seattle**

Inside the foyer of the Seattle Marriott, the woman in the crumpled, grey suit sat patiently in a high-back chair, waiting for a sighting of Brian or Shawna. The morning sun shining through the overhead skylights bothered her. Having spent a restless night, taking shifts with her male counter-part, she was tired and wondered at her manager's insistence of her accompanying the floor's security guard on this excursion and stakeout. A chance sighting of the targets with the convenience check-out in place, and the fact they could rent a car right from their hotel room, made the likelihood of seeing them fifty-fifty. A small, ear piece and microphone on her lapel were the only contact she had with Delbert, her partner, who was lord-knows-where.

Nodding off peacefully behind the wheel of the SUV tucked inconspicuously behind a cement pillar, her partner, by chance happened to notice a couple climb into a late model sedan in the car rental section of the garage. Perking up, he got sight of the almost black hair, and dark complexion, of the female passenger.

"Hop to it Sandy, they're on their way."

"Way, where," she replied, gathering her magazine and papers from the table before her.

Loosely grabbing them up, she stuffed them under her arm and plodded to the glass, front doors. Legs scissoring rapidly back and forth, impeded by her tight, knee-length skirt, she burst from the entranceway. Pausing, Sandy looked left and then right to determine the direction of Delbert's pick-me-up, she also caught a glimpse of Brian, their target, behind the wheel of the grey-silver, compact sedan. Waving a hand full of papers at her driver, who finally caught glimpse of her, Delbert skidded to a stop, picked her up and squealed after Brian and Shawna. Almost a block behind, and now with a red light stopping them, they began to tense, more from lack of sleep than the need to be effectual. Impatient with the length of the wait-time, Delbert jumped the light and started in after the sedan. Within a block, the red and blue flashing lights of a police cruiser followed them with unrelenting persistence.

"Come on Delbert," Sandy cautioned, slapping her thighs, "we have no choice but to stop."

Delbert pulled over with the persona of a kid caught with his hand in the cookie jar. With the resolve of a deflated balloon, he watched as several blocks away, the sedan disappeared behind a coffee bar. As he handed his license to the officer through his opened window, to his astonishment, the couple parked and exited their car and sauntered to the fenced-in area of the café'. After ten minutes, the officer brought back the license and a ticket and waited patiently for Delbert to acknowledge him.

"Delbert," Sandy whispered, giving him a nudge.

"What!" oblivious to all except the couple getting back inside their vehicle two blocks ahead.

Sandy tipped her head in the direction of the officer, whose face now filled the entire driver's window.

"Oh, sorry," he offered, taking the ticket and papers offered with it.

Nearly running over the constable's toes, Delbert pulled away, careful not to squeal the tires. The officer just stood with hands on his hips, as he watched the black truck pull into the early, morning traffic, without an indicator light flashing.

Following at a safe distance, the two crisscrossed their way through the streets of the downtown area to the freeway on-ramp. Losing sight of the car, they quickly headed up the north ramp to the I-5. Dodging heavy, rush hour traffic, with squealing tires and rocky maneuvers, they eventually caught up to the silver-grey sedan. Elated they had not lost their mark, Delbert and Sandy yelled a "Yahoo!" and backed off to stay hidden behind a transport truck.

Within several minutes of a steady drive, Sandy's cell chimed and she answered with a "Yes, sir." After listening intently, she replied with another, "Yes, sir," and hung up.

"What are you doin Delbert!" Sandy screamed.

"Whatchin you," he replied.

"You're supposed to be watchin them!"

In the third lane over, the two of them observed Brian and Shawna driving the off-ramp west to Hwy.

520.

"Ok. Ok," Delbert screamed, "hang on!"

With no warning or indicators, Delbert weaved and swerved over to the cement guardrail on the western side of the freeway and began to reverse along the shoulder to the exit of 520, half-a-mile back. With horns honking, and Sandy screaming, they eventually made it to the turn off and squealed forward down the ramp and onto the highway. At ninety miles an hour, they sped in wild pursuit. The truck listed frantically and rocked back to stabilization as they entered each lane with breaking action. They eventually got the advantage.

"What was the phone call about?"

"That was my boss, Mr. Katz" Sandy replied." He wants us to meet up with some more people who will take over from us."

"And how are we to do that if we have no idea where our targets are or where they're going."

"I don't know Delbert. Just drive."

He gave a side glance and a childish huff as if to mock her demeanor and continued with the sporadic drive.

"There they are," Sandy screeched. "They're turning off on 513. Looks like they're heading to the university.

"Ok. Gotcha," Delbert replied, as he slowed and pulled off onto the ramp.

"Ok. I'll phone my boss back and tell him we're heading along Montlake Blvd. and onto the university grounds.

As Brian and Shawna crossed over the grated, Montlake Bridge, they were unaware they were being followed. They harbored such relief at being home, and a thousand miles from the incidents of Xunantunich, that they were as carefree as the harbor seals that splashed and coursed through the waters of Union Bay. Turning left on N. E. Pacific Street, they continued passed the science buildings on the left and then turned north on 15th Avenue.

"Don't lose them Delbert, "came Sandy's caution as he fell back several car lengths. "They're turning right."

"I got it," Delbert returned with an air of misguided confidence.

They followed patiently passed the Henry Art Gallery, and then on to the Burke Museum of Natural History, without saying a word.

Reminiscing about her previous associations with the Department of Anthropology at the University of Washington, Shawna became filled with anticipation and squeezed Brian's knee. As they turned into the gates of the University from N E 45th Street, she could feel the excitement of meeting her old friend, Julie.

Shawna, and Julie now the head of the department, had originally met at the dig in Ossette, on a miserable rainy day and had shared a flask of hot tea together. Studying local strains of mollusks, in and around the Puget Sound tidal areas, Julie had been asked by the Anthropological Department, to lend a hand and expertise in the scrutiny of Ossette mollusk shells to help in determining the exact date of the landslide that obliterated the village hundreds of years previous. With no lack of wit and intelligence, the two became good friends, bantering back and forth as they dug, sometimes perilously, amid the muck and refuse that was once a prideful, and prosperous village. Somber moments arose during their professional time together when the remains of Shawna's ancestor's bones, and personal artifacts, were uncovered. Prayers were granted by the few remaining Makah elders able to make the trek from Neah Bay and the surrounding area. Very emotional times were spent during the few weeks they worked together at the dig, which only deepened their relationship. Many artifacts were sent back to the University for cataloging, stabilization, and preservation. An approximate time frame of A.D. 1520, was attributed to the devastating slide. Shawna was much comforted by the strong and respectful, mentorial Julie.

"There is a parking lot just to the left if you turn at the next corner passed Gate 2." Rummaging through her purse for some cash, she handed Brian a twenty.

"Place the ticket on the dash-board," the attendant smiled, as she handed the ticket to Brian. "You may receive change on your way out;" she continued jokingly, "so don't lose it."

Ensuring the car was locked tight, with the small, brown suitcase in-hand, they continued down some steps to a tarmac pathway that led in the direction of Paccar Hall. Approaching the rear of the building, they skipped down a flight of concrete steps, out into the open and Klickitat Lane. Approaching Denny Hall from the west, Brian could see the time-worn, metal grills and lead, sash windows that adorned the lower floors of the timeless institution. Built first of many buildings on the Lake Washington Campus, in 1894, the grandeur of the original architecture was apparent, but needed refreshing. Approaching the three, frontal arches above the wide steps that graced its frontal elevation, Denny Hall's facade was as striking as the day it was dedicated.

Dialing her cell, Shawna sat at the base of the stairs with Brian, waiting for her companion to answer. After several short minutes, a muted scream of delight came tumbling down the stairs and embraced the ecstatic Shawna.

After giggles and tears, Shawna looked toward Brian who stood off to one side watching in quiet amazement while the two embraced and exchanged cordialities. "This is my close friend Brian, Julie," Shawna sighed, pulling Julie into close proximity to him, far too close for his liking.

"It is a pleasure to meet you," he replied, stretching his hand toward her in greeting.

"It is also my pleasure to meet you; from what I understand, the man that brought my friend back from the brink of death." Brian blushed slightly at the inference to his exploits with Steve and the many others.

"Thank you. But I assure you, it is Shawna's wit and stamina that has us all in a state of awe."

Julie smiled at his statement and brought her arm back around Shawna's shoulder pulling her close. Julie was tall enough that her arm fit perfectly above Shawna's shoulder, which gave the two of them a comfortable look of comradely. She was nearly a head taller than Shawna, and at least ten years her senior. Her sandy-brown hair was tucked up into a loose bun at the back of her head. Solidly built, but not fat, and a face that shone of vitality, her body wiggled in excitement beneath her loose clothes that alluded to her readiness for a hike. Julie gave an heir of ease, and intelligence with no pretention.

Shawna looking down to the hand-held suitcase, gave Julie a nod, "We need to get this upstairs." Looking back to Brian, she stammered thinking of the protocol that barred all but faculty into the reaches of the Archaeological Department.

Sensing her dilemma, "It's OK, I'll head over for coffee at Orin's and wait till I hear from you." He glanced toward Paccar Hall and continued, "I have to charge my phone for a while anyway, so don't hurry. I won't wander too far."

"I won't keep Shawna too long, but we are not sure whether to take the 'little lady' to one of the Natural Science museums for submission or not. There has been a bit of a furor as to where she will be displayed, and it seems everyone wants her."

"I'll be waiting," Brian replied, as the two of them climbed the steps and disappeared into the confines of the foyer without looking back. "Bye," he sighed in moped farewell and turned to walk away.

Begrudgingly paying the toll at the gate, Sandy and Delbert waited patiently from a short distance while Shawna and Brian exited their car and started off down a path on the opposite side of the lot.

"Hurry, Delbert! Find a parking spot."

"Alright! Alright! Don't get your knickers in a twist," Delbert replied, still in a bit of a snit at having to pay the parking, even though Sandy had.

"Excuse me!" was Sandy's reply, getting upset over the reference to her knickers, which she so desperately wanted to change. As a matter of fact she wanted to take a bath so dreadfully; she was considering a dip in the Drumheller Fountain, near the entrance to the University.

"Come on!" Sandy continued, as they circled the parking lot looking for a vacancy. Then they circled again, and yet again. "Let me out here," she sparked, jumping out of the car as he slowed near the pathway the two had retreated.

Within seconds, she could see them passing the Cedar trees and foliage that lined the path to the clearing at the head of the stairs that descended to the grounds beyond Paccar Hall. Several moments passed and Delbert came on her cell, "Your friends are here? They spotted the truck and flagged me down." He paused for a moment, "Sandy, they don't look so friendly."

"What do you mean?"

"They're pretty big, and I think one of them has a gun in a case," Delbert replied, a slight breaking in his voice.

"Are you sure?"

"Yep," he continued. "I've seen those cases before at the gun club. They are compact, high velocity, telescopic thirty-five caliber hand guns, with attachments to turn them into a sniper rifle."

"Are those legal?" Sandy inquired.

"Dah! No!"

"That can't be good," she replied thoughtfully. "What are they doing now?"

"Apart from watching me and scouting the area, they are waiting for me to get back to them about location," Delbert replied, nervously.

"Stall them for a minute or two. I'll get back to you."

"OK."

Within moments of their conversation, one of the nasty's came over and stuck his massive head in the window of Delbert's SUV. "Get your partner on that thing."

"Yeah, no problem," Delbert replied, careful not to show the intimidation that was welling up inside. "Umm, Sandy, someone wants to talk to you."

"Not now Delbert, I told you give me a couple of minutes. They've just split up, and the woman joined with someone and has gone into a building."

Not liking the response, the goon grabbed the cell from Delbert, "Listen bitch, give me your location, now!"

'Bitch', Sandy repeated under her breath at the request. Slowly angering at the unnecessary response, she mumbled 'bitch' again. Pushing the 'end' button on her phone, "I'll show you bitch," she cursed in enraged response. "Waite till I shove my dirty knickers down your throat, 'bastard'!"

Responding slowly to the request, she watched from behind the retaining wall alongside the cement landing as Brian leapt up the stairs and proceeded to the coffee bar inside. "The male target has just entered Paccar Hall from the front entrance," she reported over her cell, figuring it was best to relinquish the surveillance to the new comers.

"Thank you," came the condescending response to the call. "Retreat back to the parking lot and we will take over from here."

Walking back up the stairs to the rear of the building, she noticed a stout, and lumbering hulk, with an oblong, musical, instrument case in hand, proceeding along the path she had previously navigated. Ducking out of sight, she watched from behind a blooming, Hydrangea bush as he continued along to the open, grassy expanse that languished before Paccar and Denny Halls. As she withdrew to the parking lot, from across the lane, she caught a glimpse of a black SUV, similar to Delbert's, turning left on Memorial Way. She was not liking this at all.

As Brian followed King Lane through the grassy common, he was struck by the architecture and design of Savery and Raite Halls. Retreating from Paccar Hall, the Tenino sandstone, building's façade stretched up before him. Above the foundations, ornate, arched windows reached majestically to the underside of the baroquely, decorated soffit and mansard. Benefactors and philanthropists peered down from a finely, chiseled façade, fixed in time with repose to scrutinize the many students as they scurried to ongoing classes. Entering the Quad Courtyard, adorned with blossomed trees and flower gardens, he dodged a Frisbee that was thrown haphazardly by a young female student. Apologizing profusely, she smiled with bright, young eyes and returned to the game amid jeers and laughter from her companions.

The familiarity of the vein took him back to his College years at Simon Frazer, when he too experienced the strange, symbiotic relationship between carefree abandonment and the unrelenting conviction to study. The tall cedars that guarded the entranceways to some of the buildings were bold and resonant of the campus at UBC. They were some of the best years of his life.

The university grounds here were the stateliest and colorful he had ever seen. Originally instituted in 1861, on ten acres of land previously named Denny's Knoll, in the downtown area, the fledgling University of Washington, struggled through hard times. Attendance was sporadic, and in later times, with finances difficult, they moved to the greater area just north of Union Bay. Its first new building, Denny Hall, was as splendid as any previously built, and was the foundation of the modern new campus. The years that followed were more kind, reflective of the years of prosperity throughout the Seattle area. World War 1, and then II, brought growth in the way of utilizing unused university buildings and lands that were key to the war effort. The rise in available raw commodities, minerals and forest products, and foreign markets to sell them in, were all key in the rising economic tide of this northern shipping port. Today, Seattle can boast of a university that is world class, and rated amongst the highest.

Settling down on a bench in Grieg's Gardening, Brian couldn't help but admire the manicured coppice of lush grass amid a perimeter of cedar trees and ferns. An aged, cement pathway circumvented the grassy patch with several radials of pathways emanating outward towards the surrounding buildings and lanes. Beds of Periwinkle dotted with Northern Maiden Hair, and Lady Fern, over-shadowed the walkways and added sweet scent to the air already fragrant with the damp humus that reinforced the lush undergrowth.

Secluded and alone, apart from the stolid statue of the composer Grieg, staring off into the distant eithers, Brian closed his eyes and napped, breathing in the freshness that revitalized him. Startled, only minutes later by the clatter of a bag-lady skirting the perimeter pathways beyond the garden, pushing her cart, he remained oblivious to all and dozed.

Sandy and Delbert, sat in their vehicle contemplating the circumstances that vexed them sorely.

"How do you feel about this Delbert," Sandy inquired, thinking about the instrument case and its purpose. "Are you sure of what's in that case Delbert, because if your wrong?"

"I'm sure of it," Delbert sighed. "These guys were on their phones to someone, confirming the identity and purpose. The one didn't say it out-right, but I think they intend on killing the guy."

"What do you think we should do," Sandy asked, running her fingers through her tangled hair?

"We could call the police," he replied.

"And say what. We think there's about to be a murder." Sandy paused for a moment and thought. "Plus, you and I were ordered here by our Mr. Katz."

"That would mean he's a part of this."

They were both silent and watched as several people entered the car beside them and drove away.

"What if he doesn't know? These people we're following arrived from Mexico on a plane from who knows where. He may know no more than us and just obeying orders."

"Yeah, right!" Delbert agreed, feeling slightly more at ease at the possibility of getting involved in something that was not completely sanctioned by their boss.

"Do you think we should go after these guys?"

"Now wait a minute Sandy. You're a woman, and if these guys are going to beat someone, it will probably be me."

"No Delbert. This is the land of human rights and opportunity," she returned, a glint of sarcasm in her voice. "They'll beat me as much as you."

Delbert was not at all assured by her candid disposition; but he did give it some thought.

"Look," Sandy continued. "I'll follow the big guy with the case and you follow the truck. Stay in touch by phone, and we should be OK."

"Yeah, alright. I can't stand by and watch someone get hurt. I gave an oath to protect and serve when I became a security guard." He slammed his open hands down hard on the steering wheel, startling Sandy. "And this is what it's all about!"

Sandy gave a comical side-glance at Delbert's enthusiasm and eased herself from the truck, her shoulder purse swinging profusely, "Remember Delbert; keep your phone on intercom."

Sandy watched as the black SUV disappeared around the corner on Memorial Drive, and then headed off in the direction of the common languishing before Denny Hall. Moving cautiously from retaining wall to tree, and then following a line of bushes, she was troubled to find no sign of her mark. He was a professional, she knew, but he was not expecting to be hunted. Entering the Quad, she scouted in either direction. Satisfied he was not in the area, she continued down King's Lane to Thompson Hall, and sat on the retaining wall across from the entrance to Grieg's Gardens. She sat wondering where he could be and caught sight of Brian lounging on the bench below Grieg's tall, cast-bronze statue. Panning the area to each side and sighting nothing, she was about to rise when she saw the hulk down the incline to the left. Cautiously, she leaned closer into the foliage and watched as he flanked the garden by the Husky Union Building. A thousand possibilities flooded her mind; the most vivid was the hulk's size and how much it would hurt should she try and stop him. There had to be a way; an opportunity would present itself.

Oblivious to all, and concentrating on the bumps in the pavement that would hinder the smooth rolling of her shopping cart, a bag lady stopped at the recycle bin close by, to forage for whatever might be deemed worthwhile. Sandy, watching from her short distance, felt a pang of remorse at her condition. Scenarios flashed through her mind as to the reasons, or circumstance, that had brought her to this condition. She sat pensive, watching this spectacle of human fortitude. As she sat and considered, a light went off in her head.

Sandy strolled over to the animated lady and waited till she was done her task.

"Excuse me," Sandy sheepishly addressed the woman. "I am working with a security agency patrolling the grounds," flashing her Insurance Security Card photo I.D., "and I was wondering how often you did your rounds to collect these items. You know, the university has a recycle program that relies on a certain amount of volume to make it…"

The woman backed away with a bewildered and frightened look on her face. Her wispy, grey hair floated from beneath the edges of a grimy, wool-knitted toque. "I don't understand." Confusion quickly turned to anger, "I have been at this university for twelve years and have never been asked to share my work. Carl, my friend at the Custodial Services Building, said that I can help him as much as I like." Her eyes were ablaze and piercing with consternation.

Realizing she may have indeed been in the wrong, and causing undue stress to the woman, Sandy backed off. "I'm sorry. I had no idea you knew Carl." She smiled and timidly backed away realizing she had been insensitive and confrontational. Sandy returned to her seat and scanned the area once again for the hulk. A cluster of Shamrock spilling out over the boarders of the walk opposite from where she sat, called out for 'better luck next time'.

"Are you a friend of Carl's too?" the woman asked as she followed Sandy slowly to her resting place on the wall. Her cart clacked and clambered as it bounced over the cracks and uneven areas of the concrete. Brimming with cans and bottles layered on the top, she was careful not to lose any from the rocky motion. Below in the cart, surrounded by cardboard and plastic, appeared to be her whole life's possessions.

"I only met Carl briefly a few days ago," Sandy replied, trying to play along with the deception. Thinking of it better, she continued, "Well, not really. I only saw him in his truck." She resigned herself to the willful intercourse by motioning her to sit down. "Sandy's my name, what's yours?"

"Carolyn," she offered, side-glancing Sandy with uncertainty. "Oh, it is a big truck isn't it," she cooed. "He always waves to me from it while he empties all the bins."

Realizing this was going sideways and compromising the few short moments she had to spare; Sandy tried to focus on gaining her trust. If her idea was to work, it would have to take shape immediately. Fidgeting and uncomfortable at being in such close proximity with this unwashed woman, Sandy began to rise, "I think I need to go for a coffee."

"Oh, I'll get you one," she offered excitedly. "I have another friend who gives me coffee and buns for free. She likes me."

Sandy returned, "I don't think so. I…" considering the generosity of a person so ill-affording of the gesture. Reaching for her purse, she motioned to offer money.

Cutting her short, "It's just over there and around the corner. You look after my stuff, and I will be right back." Looking back as she ventured off, "But be careful!"

"Are you sure?"

"Oh, yeah! You're my friend too."

Racing off in her tattered, knee-high stockings that ended above the knee and below her grubby skirt, Carolyn looked droll as her worn boots flapped profusely with each stride.

Relieved she had finally left, Sandy began to concentrate on the task at hand. Losing sight of the hulk that had disappeared through Hub Park, caused her to panic. Looking over to where Brian rested, she was relieved to see that nothing, for the time-being, had changed. Reaching for the cart to help her up, she toppled one of the cardboard sides exposing shoes and clothing of various colors and states of repair, or decay, whichever you chose to consider. She had no time to waste in implementing her plan; but would it work??

Delbert could barely see the tailgate of the truck as he followed along behind through the pedestrian packed George Washington Lane, that was designed more for cycling and walking than a truck of his size. Passing the Henry Art Museum, he watched as the lead truck turned left at Gate Five, and approached Red

Square. Presumably, it would continue to Grant Lane, and then from there, the occupant would need to proceed on foot. Unable to stay back out of conspicuous sight, Delbert parked in Johnson's Loop. Facing the parked SUV, he got out without regard and walked to the entrance to Gerberding Hall.

"Sandy, are you there," he asked, as he found an inconspicuous spot behind a bookshelf close to the front doors.

"Hang-on Delbert. I'm having trouble getting into...there! OK, I'm done."

"Yeah, I followed the truck over to near Allen Library," Delbert stated, from behind the tinted glass. He looked over to the waiting vehicle and could barely make out a face in sunglasses behind its steering wheel. "Where are you and what's that racket?"

"I think I am just on the other side of the library, pushing a shopping cart." She struggled with the uneven concrete and the floppy shoes she had adorned. "Stay put for now. I am working on something. Are you near the truck?"

"Which one?"

"Ours, you idiot!"

"Be nice. You may need me before you're done. I'll go back to it." He grabbed a Varsity paper and headed back to the truck. Sitting askew behind the wheel again, he watched in the reflection of the side window his unaware prey.

Methodically plodding along the path beside Hub Yard, Sandy, adorned with an assortment of multicolored clothes and a broad-brimmed, cloth hat, worked her way around the rear of Grieg's Garden. Along one of the periphery trails, she could see the shadow of the colossus tucked within the bushes and miniature trees. Unable to stay inconspicuous with all the noise, she continued along to one of the benches and plopped herself down within ten meters and started to rummage through the paraphernalia in the cart. Motionless for some time, the near giant began to move within her peripheral vision. Careful not to take note of the action, she pulled a tattered, wool blanket across her legs and settled in for a nap. Eyeing previously a short length of steel pipe in the cart, she was careful to have it at the ready should he recognize her or sense the infringement.

Watching intently from beneath the low brim of the hat, Sandy could tell he was readying to take a shot at the mark lounging peacefully below the statue in the garden. Along the path that head back to Hub Yard, she could see Carolyn looking from side to side with two cups in her hands. Turning to a large, garbage truck making its way along the narrow paths, Carolyn was screaming at the driver who Sandy assumed was Carl. Turning away from the truck that was continuing through the small maze of paths, she could only conclude that within moments, Carolyn would be screaming at her. It was now-or-never.

The hulk, concentrating on his target and talking on his phone, was oblivious to the stealth that was being enacted beyond the shadow of the tree. Sandy had grabbed the pipe quietly from the cart. Amid the ambient noise of bester about them, and now the drone of the engine from the garbage truck, she was able to creep unnoticed to just beyond the tree's edge. With her heart beating wildly in her chest and fear grabbing her, she was careful not to cast a shadow within the periphery of his vision. She stepped forward just as he was sighting and unlocking the safety of his gun.

Wishing only to hit the gun from his hands as he lay prone on the ground, she slipped on a moist, moss-covered root and the pipe came crashing down on the base of his skull. A hallow bonk resounded in the immediate area, and with a grunt and a gasp, the behemoth toppled to one side with Sandy almost spread-eagle over his languid body. Rolling him slightly to attempt arousal, he lay limp and unresponsive.

Panicked, Sandy slapped his face, then slapped it gain. "Wake up you oaf." Yet unresponsive, he laid, his mouth open with drool oozing from one side.

"Oops," she groaned, looking about her to see if anyone had noticed the incident. The only person she observed in the immediate vicinity was Brian, unfazed, and Carolyn aimlessly wandering the pathways surrounding the garden.

Sandy rose to return to the cart and remove the clothes that were key in implementing the ruse. Leaving the sheltered area, she looked back to see how noticeable the brute was from the path. Unless someone followed the exact route, there was no way he would be noticed. Somewhat concerned for his wellbeing, as misguided as it appeared to be, Sandy returned to the prone man lying unconscious in the cool, isolated spot and checked to see whether he was still alive. His breathing was steady and deep. Scanning the immediate area, a sly smile rose to her face. She lifted the loose, grubby dress to expose the tightfitting, grey skirt of her uniform. Shimmying it up over her thighs, she gently slid her panties down and gingerly stepped out of them. Looking about once more, she leaned over and shoved the black, lace fabric into his open, rictus mouth, "Here, choke on these."

Sandy, back at the cart, began packing the used articles to where they belonged. Brushing the face of her phone, "Delbert, what is the driver doing?"

"Uhh," he sighed, looking over his paper to the opposite truck. "He appears to be talking on his cell."

The driver unable to get a response on the phone to his partner, opened the door a crack, ready to make a move if need be.

Alerted to his action, Delbert placed his hand on the knob of the door ready to close it and spring into action.

"Delbert, don't allow him to come this way under any circumstances!"

With possible situations racing through his mind, Delbert started the truck immediately. As the driver of the other vehicle slipped from his seat, Delbert's SUV shot across the expanse in seconds and slammed into the door. Trapped, panicked, and pinned, he spat with bulging eyes, "What in the hell do you think you're doing."

Delbert easing himself from the seat and around to face the confined driver, "Stay where you are." Reaching for what Delbert presumed was a gun he yelled, "Don't move."

With people starting to surround the vehicles, Delbert flashed his security badge and screamed at the crowd to stay back.

"You son-of-a-bitch! You back that truck up, or so help me."

"Or so help me what," Delbert replied?

Squirming like a stuck pig, the driver dropped his phone by accident on the pavement by his feet. Wriggling more, he was able to reach his arm around the door-support to grab the steel, front edge of the window brace by the wind-shield. Slowly, Delbert re-entered the driver's seat in his truck, and with one foot on the gas and the other on the brake, he was able to apply a few more pounds of calculated pressure on the drivers sternum. He watched as the assailant's eyes began to bulge, and his face turn red. Eventually succumbing to the pressure, and banging the door with great force to reflect submission, he waved his hand. Delbert eased a fraction off on the pressure. The people, milling around the two vehicles, watched in bewildered amazement. Delbert waited to hear from Sandy.

Pleased with herself, Sandy quickly replaced the used clothes and hat back into the approximate location they were in before she borrowed them and chased after Carolyn who was still wandering the pathways.

"There you are Carolyn. I must have missed as you walked around the other way."

Angered, and unable to control her emotions, Carolyn threw her coffee in the direction of Sandy. "Here's your coffee. I don't like you anymore." With those words, she grabbed her cart from Sandy and shuffled off, dejected, trying to avoid the cracks and uneven portions of the cement walkway.

Sitting back where she had originally been on the wall, across from the Shamrock, Sandy felt remorse at what she had had to do, but knew there was no choice. She had possibly saved a man's life, and Carolyn had been a part of it. Observing the man she had protected, answering his phone, Sandy got up and entered the serene, little park. Brian, paying no attention to her, sat back for a few minutes and ran his fingers through his thick, dark hair. Bending forward, he then rested his elbows to his knees and stared at the weathered, concrete path before him. Taking the opportunity at hand, she casually strode to the open space beside him on the bench and sat down.

Peaceful, isn't it," Sandy stated without looking at him.

He lifted himself straight and looked at the pixie, cute face beneath a shock of ruffled, mouse-colored hair. Noticing the small, security pin and insurance logo, on the upper portion of her jacket lapel, he replied, "Yes, it is."

Taking a breath so deep that it appeared to tickle the bottoms of her lungs, she then exhaled with such force he looked sideways at her.

"It sounds as if you've had an exasperating day?"

"Not really," Sandy replied, but returned thoughtfully, "well, parts of it."

"It must be difficult dealing with people sometimes. I saw the lady throw her coffee at you."

"Well," Sandy replied, with guarded cynicism, "It was my coffee." She bowed her head as she considered the last fifteen minutes of orchestration, "It was my own fault. I had been insensitive to her situation, and well, I deserved it."

Just then Sandy's phone rang, "Delbert! Is all well?" She made no motion and listened intently to the voice on the other end, "I'll be right there."

Looking at Brian and considering what might have been, "I gotta go," she uttered, tears of elation welling in the corners of her eyes.

"Well, nice to meet you, uh," he sighed, questioningly.

"Sandy! My name is Sandy," she replied.

"Nice to meet you Sandy. My name is Brian Alexander."

Their eyes met, and he, noticing the sparkle of a tear at the outer corner of her eye, took her hand in a cordial shake.

"Take care of yourself Mr. Alexander," she answered with a degree of consternation and got up to leave. His eyes followed her around the remaining arc of the path that led to the exit, opposite to where she had entered.

Several students had gathered on the other side of the adjacent pathway, making advances into the dense bushes. Allowed only fleeting shadows and muffled conversation, he became inquisitive and got up to see what the fuss was about. Strolling to where he could see through the flowering Hydrangeas and lush ferns, the first object to come into view was the muzzle of a pistol. Kneeling down and reaching in to spread the radials of the Northern Fern, he was shocked to see the groaning mass of a man lying prone. Realizing the intent of his action, with the rest of the makeshift rifle pointing in direct line with the bench on which he had sat; Brian cautiously rose to retreat out of the garden. Warily looking form side to side, he scanned for any sign of another assailant. Confident all was well and back on King's Lane amid the student traffic, Brian felt more at ease.

Heading up the incline, he was confronted by the mournful, bag lady trying to navigate the few steps leading up between Smith and Miller Halls. Greeting her with trepidation, he grabbed the front end of the overloaded cart and helped her to the top. Leaving her with a nod, he continued up the lane and on to Denny Hall; his phone chimed, it was Shawna.

Delbert had watched the driver of the truck,

jammed in the door, squirm for several minutes then slowly relax and resign to the fact he would be going no-where. Picking up the phone from the ground and redialing the number, he waited while the phone rang to its taped message and hung up. Scanning through the last several numbers, Delbert came to the unfamiliar area code 501. Slipping the phone in his pocket, he skirted the rear of the truck and eased into the passenger seat, careful not to get within reach of the trapped masher. Rifling through the vehicles papers, he could find no identifying documents except for the rental agreement.

"Let me go, asshole," came the belligerent grunt of the ensnared gorilla.

"Do you have a license for this," Delbert snidely asked, poking the Smith and Wesson revolver with the rubber end of his pencil. Heavy and awkward, he slid it to the edge of the seat and into his gloved hand.

"What do you think, jerk," he scowled.

Easing himself from the truck, Delbert looked in the direction of the Allen Library and could see Sandy briskly walking in his direction. Both entering their truck from either side, they sat watching the squirming goon from beyond the hood; he was sweating profusely.

"What do you think we should do," Delbert asked placing the revolver down on the consul between the seats.

"Well," Sandy considered thoughtfully. "The other fellow is unconscious in the bushes the other side of the library, at least I hope so. This guy is trapped for now. If the police don't come and we let these guys go, they'll beat us to a pulp, or kill us, and still go after Brian."

"We could squish this guy and fane insanity!"

"Right, Delbert," she sighed, and then considered. "But you might be on to something; if we could somehow get them to back off." She sat pensive looking at the driver who glared back at her. "They are certainly not afraid of us, or anything we could threaten them with; but what about failure. What if they didn't do the job, or lied about it?"

They both sat watching from their seats as the small crowd standing off to the side of the circle talked and pointed. "We'd better do something soon. I wish I had of grabbed the guy's phone, we could have…."

Delbert reached into his pocket and pulled out a black cellular, "Will this do?"

"His," Sandy nodded bewilderingly toward the driver.

"Yep," he smiled from ear to ear! "I think I have a number, and an idea."

Getting out of the truck, Sandy walked over to the driver with the phone in one hand and a pair of cuffs in the other. Delbert put the truck in gear and placed his foot on the gas and brake, and started to put more pressure on the trapped driver.

Swearing and screaming, he turned a bright red and yelled, "Stop!"

Easing his foot off the gas, Delbert released the pressure just enough for him to breath.

"I think you have a phone call to make," Sandy stated.

"OK! OK!" he gasped, trying to move air into his lungs. "What do you want me to say?"

"This 501 number, where is it?"

"Belize."

"Stretch out your arm." Clamping the cuff on his

wrist, with renewed courage, Sandy pulled the remaining stainless-steel cuff to the window style, and clamped down. "Is this the contact that ordered the hit?"

He nodded gingerly.

"All you have to do is say the job is done, and you go free."

He thought for a moment looking at Delbert behind the wheel, and then back to Sandy, phone in hand. The driver nodded; Sandy pushed the dial button. A short and near wordless conversation alluding to the mark's termination ensued. With a nod, the driver acknowledged the confirmation, and looked to the cuffs.

Accommodating the driver, Sandy returned to passenger seat, pointed in the direction of the library, and yelled, "He's that way. And enjoy the money; no-one needs to know."

Delbert, with the Smith and Wesson resting on the dash pointing in the driver's direction, slowly eased the vehicle into reverse and back away.

Clamping his chest and falling temporarily to the ground, the driver watched as the black SUV gradually pulled away out of Johnson's Circle, back down passed the Molecular Engineering building, and on to Gate 5. Delbert watched in the side-view mirror as a running figure dashed down the lane and disappeared behind the library.

# SIXTEEN

The little, pregnant lady, barely four inches tall, looked stunning within the confines of the display cabinet. Still, and expectant in travail, the small figurine knelt elevated on a black, velvet throw. She was radiant beneath the halogen light that pointed directly at her from above. Her large breasts were an earth-tone color of golden-ochre, and below across her protruding belly, raw-umber bleeding into burnt as it flowed between her parted thighs; these colors were accented only by a thick layer of madder-colored hair wrapped loosely on the top of her head. The display was only a temporary fix within the staff office area, to appease the inquisitive anticipation that surrounded her coming; a permanent site would be forth coming.

Julie gave a hug to Shawna as she prepared to leave the confines of the museum. Riding down the escalator, Shawna turned and gave her a parting wave before she exited. Out through the large, glassed, front entry doors and into the warm and late-spring air, she rummaged through her purse to find her phone and pushed the touch-tone face to dial Brian. Amid the blossoms of the surrounding Dogwood trees, she plodded along the cement walkway, talking intently. She zigzagged the pathways passed Number Two Gate and back to the parking lot.

The staff had thinned in the early afternoon at the office when Delbert and Sandy finally arrived. The office director and liaise between North American subsidiaries, had been calling every ten minutes since the mystery call had been made to Area Code 501. Not able to get to proper facilities to clean up, let alone home for a shower, the two dragged themselves into the empty board-room. A large, shiny, mahogany table, with burgundy, leather-backed chairs lined its perimeter; a panoramic view of the wharf and bay was all that greeted them.

After several, timeless minutes, they were startled by the door quickly being opened by the director

"Well, how'd it go," Mr. Katz asked, as he seated himself at the head? Seeming oblivious to any of the situations that had gone on, he motioned them to sit.

"Well," they both slowly replied in unison, looking toward each other for support.

"OK," Sandy finally stated with reserve. Delbert nodded his head in affirmation.

They both again nodded and did not offer anything else in reply. The director looked at them both and tried to formulate the words to milk a report out of them.

"I've recently had a call from Belize for an update on your surveillance of the couple that landed from Mexico; and told them I would phone back as soon as I had something to give them."

Sandy and Delbert sat idle, not offering any explanations.

"Well!" Katz half blurted. "I don't need to know all the details, just how it ended up!"

"Umm," Sandy started. "A couple of other guys took over when we got to the university, and we were not all that sure what all happened after that." She stopped and looked at him bewildered.

Then Delbert started in, "I followed the one in the truck after we had been asked to leave the surveillance." He rubbed the side of his leg, "I know I wasn't supposed to, but I wasn't sure what they were up to, and uh…" he stammered.

Sandy picking up the pace, "After they left us, I followed the other guy, but couldn't find him. Eventually, I saw a group of students huddling around a bunch of bushes deep in the interior of the grounds. There was a fellow lying there on his side, not moving. I thought about getting closer, but thought twice about it considering the fact I have a security uniform with our company logo on it. They would have expected me to do something. I would have then become involved."

"That was probably wise," Katz replied. "So you think it was the fellow from Mexico lying in the bushes?" Sandy said nothing. Rubbing his hand along his face in concern, "Did an ambulance come? Or anybody," he asked, with apprehension reflected on his face?

"I saw the driver of their vehicle run off in the direction where I suppose," he shrugged, "the body was."

"Did you follow him?" the director asked of Delbert, who shook his head no. "It went beyond surveillance, didn't it," the director suggested with a knowing grin?

"We think so, sir," Sandy returned without

emotion.

"Alright then," Katz stated, without looking at their faces. "Do me a favor; don't mention this to anyone, please. Until I have all the details, it is best left unspoken." He went to leave the room and turned back, "And go clean up. You look terrible, both of you."

The director entered his office and closed the door. Approaching his desk, he lifted the phone and pushed the key to a preprogramed number and spoke, "Extension 421." He listened intently to the voice on the other end waiting for confirmation, "There is a body, and an ID," Katz whispered into the phone and was silent. "Yes, sir," he replied, "As far as we know, the girl has been unharmed." Hesitation again, "No sir, not at present, but we will sir."

A south westerly was whipping the surf into frenzy as Brian and Shawna passed Oak Harbor on their way to the ferry terminal at Coupeville. The terminal was the farthest western point of Puget Sound, on Admiralty Bay, and allowed the shortest travel time over to Port Townshend; the alternative was a lengthy drive west from Olympia and up the eastern coast of the Olympic Peninsula along a winding, scenic, but time-consuming road.

Turning into the ferry lanes from S. Engle Rd, Brian pulled over to the drop-off area and waited for Shawna to return with her ticket. There would only be a half hour wait as the ferry was docking and the stop-over was just an hour. One of her cousins would meet Shawna at Port Townshend to take her to Neah Bay, and on to her grandparent's house, by the coast further along.

"Will you be alright," Shawna inquired, as she

fingered through her purse to find an accessible spot for the ticket within its confines?

"We've spent a lot of time together these last weeks. It will be hard to get out of bed in the morning; even harder to get in without you there enticing me," he returned jokingly. She slapped him hard on the arm and looked at him longingly. "Oh, I'll be alright. There is a lot to do in Vancouver, closing down my apartment in Kits. I hate to do it, but with those guys after me, it is best I disappear from there for a while." He looked to the shafts of sunlight that were streaking down between the clouds over the Strait.

"When do you think you'll make it back to Neah Bay?"

"Not too long. Perhaps a couple of weeks," he returned, leaning close to give her a kiss. He could feel the emotion welling up inside him and fought it.

"That's OK," she replied. "Julie has asked me to spend some time with her over the next few weeks, taking samples of mussel shells in some of the isolated bays in the region. It will keep me busy until you're finished with what you need to do."

Brian could tell she was as uncomfortable as he. "I still have to make it back to Victoria and check in on June, to see how she is doing."

"Give her my regards," Shawna encouraged, giving him a firm hug and letting go.

The announcement for foot passengers to embark came over the loud-speaker. Exiting the car together, they walked hand-in-hand across to the gate where Brian could go no further. Taking her in his arms, he gave her a long, passionate kiss. He could feel her melt in his arms and knew he could not live without her.

With the sound of its setting-sail horn, the ferry's

alert echoed throughout the bay. Within moments, it slowly eased from its moorings. Watching the silhouetted face behind the glass, nearly obscured by the reflection of the clouds above, Brian teared as a lone hand was pressed against the window's interior. He waited till the ferry was almost at the far side of the channel before he returned to his car and headed back up the highway to Oak Bay, and beyond. He was remorseful, yet optimistic that all would work out the way it should, and Shawna would be safe from that monster in Belmopan.

Emptying the apartment in Vancouver, and boxing most of his prized artwork and possessions, was very difficult. Kitsilano had been his home for the last five years and Brian had come to love the interaction with his neighbors and the weekly forays to the local pub for long drinks and tall tales. Rose and Steve were more than welcome to store his furniture and belongings for a time until more permanent accommodations were found.

Back in Victoria, as always, June and Lilly, her Lhasa Apsua, had welcomed him back to study in the confines of Vincent's office. Afternoon tea and endless homemade cookies, of the canine assortment as well, were brought daily for refreshment and comfort. The study had brought back some closure to Vincent's intent on art reclamation to the surrounding nations, but also opened up the chasm, left unsutured by the circumstances still torrid in Belize. The custodian of the catacombs - Dr. Magnus, and his accusations toward him, were still troubling to Brian. The proof of the doctor's relationship with the creature in regard to his deceased wife, confirmed by Henry, and now with the near abduction and thwarted murder of Shawna, were all foremost in his mind. It boggled Brian as to the ramifications this genetically altered creature's actions had had on the innocent, unknowing populations on which he had preyed. If Magnus was indeed right in his accusations of the entities migrations from various parts of the world throughout the centuries, it would only fuel the contempt he felt for this being. Brian began to feel furry at the ongoing autonomy the custodian was apparently entitled, and now with the percolating resolve to team with Dr. Magnus, Brian was determined to be rid of this plight on mankind. The incident in Seattle was evidence enough that the issue would not go away by itself. He resigned himself to the task of exposing this fiend at whatever the cost. He now had the resources, with Vincent's bursary and library, to pursue the endeavor, but not just yet. He had a career in photography and film-making to nurture with a fledgling star-bound archaeologist. One thing had become certain over the last few months, where-ever 'Pillars of the Moon' was to be shown or received; the custodian would not be far distant. That was his weakness; that would be his demise - a little jade bowl in the likeness of the Maya.

As Brian sat back in the leather-bound chair, he scanned the books shelves laden with paraphernalia and photographs of Vincent's life's work. Black and white photographs of colleagues and associates, posing meritoriously at various universities and archaeological sites, were numerous. Paintings and scenic photographs in Technicolor splashed the walls in an otherwise austere but stately raised-panel study. A few portraits of notable, Victorian high society individuals dotted its perimeter, some famous, some infamous, but all respected in their due. Papers and manila folders, stacked high in corners and the flat surfaces of side tables and shelves, some of which Brian had gleaned, most still untouched, lay beckoning him.

All the while a slight, clicking nose, barely audible, was constant in the ambient noise, as if a cockroach was skittering across the ceramic, tiled floor. An innocuous, little snickering, amid the audition of birds outside the window, was barely noticeable amongst the buzz of insects in their late, spring orchestrations to maternal instinct. A gentle breeze laden with the scent of early, blossoming roses blew in through the culprit, open window. Barely visible, in the reflection of one of the glass-encased pictures adorning the huge desk was the image of the small shaggy, half-naked doll in a loincloth. Qweti (Kuwatsi) had come to visit once again.

"Well, little fella," Brian asked, as he swung in his chair to stare up at the little doll perched atop the book-shelf, "is it time for me to pack and come back to visit you?" He waited for several moments as if to absorb what the apparition had done for him in the past. "I guess so!"

## Ossette

The inside of the cabin was warm and humid when Brian slowly lifted his lids from tired, bloodshot eyes. Particles of smoke exposed the shafts of light that pierced the room like the number of hunting spears that hung laterally along the walls by the door. The cot was empty on the other side of the hearth. Shawna had risen early and left to help with the morning duties and necessities that kept a life by the sea prosperous.

Placing his feet firmly on the ground, Brian contemplated the trip of the night before and the help of the braves from the local band. When he had got to shore in Port Angeles at that late hour, he had to be certain there would be no-one unsuspecting in the shadows. The cousins were familiar enough with the locals, and the feel of their surroundings to know they were not being followed. Brian had learned to trust their instincts, besides they were not going to let anything happen to their cousin's favorite person - now would they? There had been no sign of the pursuers from Seattle and further from the south, but he knew they would appear one day. He had not become paranoid, but thought it prudent to be cautionary.

Slowly getting up and stretching the tightness from the muscles in his shoulders, he opened the door to the freshness of sweet, yet unique scent of the sea. The gentle shushing of the pebbles along the beach, rolling to-and-fro in the surf, was borne up on the wind from the shore. Shawna's laughter, as she prepared and unloaded the morning's catch of fish from the skiff, close to the dock, blew up as easily and more whimsical. Watching her gave him great pleasure, and welled within him the desire for permanence and stability. Closing the door, he retreated to the cot by the fire and once again buried himself in the cotton sheets and blankets of skins to sleep.

Shawna had packed a picnic lunch and water for their hike to Cape Flattery. They had considered a visit to Ossette, but the walk alone, with an overnight stay, would be more than either of them wanted to endure. Plus, Brian had only visited the cape in his dreams and had an interest to see the beauty and ferocity of the cliffs and its tidal surges, first hand.

"Come on, Mister Alexander," she joked as she threw a light, lumber jack's jacket at him. The glass and wood beads, her grandma had weaved into her hair, swung loosely in an arch about her shoulders as she turned back to lift the tote bag that housed their lunch. Her face shone in anticipation of their excursion, she looked half her age.

Brian could not help but wonder what he had ever done to deserve such happiness that he felt at this moment. The day was warm and animated with the sounds of the sea and the forest that abounded with life of every kind. The west-coast rainforest, although unforgiving at times, was a cornucopia for the senses. He felt more alive and refreshed than he had for months. His little friend, the waif in the woods, Qweti, had not returned to date, and he supposed that was a good sign.

Gathering some light, rain gear, camera and a rifle, they headed west along the trail that would lead them to the higher ground and shores of the north-western most point of Washington State. The trails were long and slippery with moss and humus that deteriorated beneath the packed earth that made up the illusive trail. Birds chattered and flew to higher roosts in the upper canopy, while small, earthbound creatures took to motion to allude or confront; the larger ones were not to be seen.

Once they arrived within the confines of the National Park, the trails were much more worn and easier to navigate. A board-walk meandering through the marshy lowlands along with a wooden bridge over the severe crevasse, made for a delightful hike.

Stopping briefly for a drink, atop a bridge along the lush, hard-packed, earthen trail, they cuddled and breathed deep the fresh scent of the trees and flora that scattered itself ubiquitously about them.

By late afternoon they could hear the faint crashing of the waves and felt the wind-borne mist that blew in from the shore. Heavy with salt, it dampened their hair that trailed in wisps beyond the confines of their hoodies. Excited at the prospects of finally seeing the cliffs, Brian raced off ahead of Shawna who trailed behind. Taking in the majesty and tranquility of the surroundings, he became oblivious to the damp and slick conditions. His feet beat the hard packed earth resounding in a hollow, thumping sound; his camera swung loosely over his shoulder. Mesmerized by the beat, he looked down at his feet as they scissored back and forth. Brian was reminded of the small feet, and naked legs of the boy and those of his companion from his dream. He raced incautiously to the cliff's edge to experience the pounding, crashing waves. Unaware of the closeness of the cliffs and the slipperiness of the soil, Brian continued running, feeling the wind in his face and the beating of his heart.

A scream echoed in his ears, "Brii-aan!"

Hearing the scream, he turned his head to see a young girl barely twelve years old. She held her head between her hands; her young face distorted in terror, her mouth in gaping rictus. Trying to stop in mid stride with unsure footing, he slipped down onto his side and sailed to the edge of the steep precipice. His camera now loose, careened over the edge and shattered into pieces as it dropped to the rocks and surf below. Just able to save himself, he grabbed the branches of a shrub and held tight. He hung there trying to catch his thoughts and breathe.

A small pair of hands came to grab his arm. The dark flesh was young and near perfect except for the dark band of earth rimmed beneath the nails. Pulling with great strength, the hands heaved at his sleeve trying to lift him from the vision that had become too familiar. Below, in the depths of water, he watched, once again, as a young boy screamed for his mother and slowly succumbed to the warmth and numbness that was enshrouding him. The smiling face of the waif came back and watched the tragedy in wonderment and dismay.

Feeling the tug once more, Brian awoke to the hands of Shawna holding him tight. He looked up to her shocked and frightened face, "Are you OK?"

"Wow! That was close."

He steadied himself and looked once again to the depths below. The undulating, turquoise water crashed and upheaved in great plumes, sending spray half way back up the grey and craggy cliffs. The sound was deafening and yet exhilarating as the ground seamed to shake with every assault on its rugged buttress'. The great pools below swirled and eddied with such force and torrent that they would twist a man in two.

"I'll need a new camera."

Shawna smiled, gave him a kiss on his forehead and helped him to his feet.

Arm in arm, they continued on and came to rest on the platform that extended itself out over the cliff face. Gnarled and stunted Arbutus trees reached out with weathered branches, from their perches about them on rocky cliffs. The view was enormous and almost too magnificent to describe. They held each other close and looked out to the great expanse of endless ocean.

As the sun began to set, the wind began to die down and the clouds disperse. They sat and watched for hours as the puffins fluttered and eddied with the air currents that rose with the gentle breeze off the ocean. Seagulls squawked and pranced in the tidal zone, scrounging the abundance and bounty the sea would grant. Cuddled close on the wooden rails of the lookout, they talked about their dreams and aspirations of the coming months and years. The warmth their bodies shared was a small token of the intimacy that they would share throughout their time together.

As the sun began to set, its reflection ignited the ocean on fire with one great, golden pillar that laid itself before them. And as before, in the Mayan tale of several thousand years ago, a million little fishes tried to collect the pieces of Ixchel, reflected in the waves, and lift her to her lover the sun. And as the pillar slowly shrank into the waiting arms of the sun, they both disappeared behind a ribbon of crimson and vermillion to continue in the never ending story of love and renewal. Ixchel was finally with her lover.

Made in the USA
Charleston, SC
17 March 2013